I KILL ALWAYS LOVE YOU

A RIGHT ROYAL COZY INVESTIGATION MYSTERY

HELEN GOLDEN

DREW BRADLEY PRESS

ALSO BY HELEN GOLDEN

ISBN (P) 978-1-915747-30-3

Edited by Marina Grout at Writing Evolution

Published by Drew Bradley Press

Cover design by Helen Drew-Bradley

First edition March 2025

Dedication

To my BS16 girls: Katie, Janie, Ruthie, Ju, Karen, Rach, Deb H, Deb V-S, Lisa, Ange, George, Em, and Chrissy

Behind every successful woman is a group chat full of encouragement, terrible advice, and excessive use of emojis.

You always show up, cheer the loudest and remind me that I can. I love you all x

NOTE FROM THE AUTHOR

I am a British author and this book has been written using British English. So if you are from somewhere other than the UK, you may find some words spelt differently to how you would spell them. In most cases this is British English, not a spelling mistake. We also have different punctuation rules in the UK.

However if you find any other errors, I would be grateful if you would please contact me helen@helengoldenauthor.co.uk and let me know so I can correct them. Thank you.

For your reference I have included a list of characters in the order they appear, and you can find this at the back of the book.

A NOTE ABOUT THE SETTING...

I Kill Always Love You takes place in Portugal in a luxury gated compound called The Marisol Estates, referred to locally simply as Marisol. Marisol sits on a peninsula in The Algarve in Portugal and consists of three large villas — **Villa Mer** which sits on the east side of the peninsula, next to it is **Villa Sol**, which is on the end of the peninsula and next to that is **Villa Luz**, which is on west side of the peninsula. Staying in each villa are:

• **Villa Mer**: Lady Beatrice; her partner, Superintendent Richard Fitzwilliam; her son Sam Wiltshire; Sam's best friend, Archie Tellis; her best friend and business partner, Perry Juke; Perry's husband, Simon Lattimore; and Simon's daughter, Isla Scott.

• **Villa Sol**: American actress, Ariella 'Ella' St Gerome; her husband and film producer, Jason 'JT' Kenda; her sister Pearl Mitchell; and Pearl's husband Peter Mitchell.

- **Villa Luz**: Film producer, Derek Stone; his wife Vanessa 'Nessa' Stone; and his daughter Chloe Stone.

1

9:47PM, THURSDAY 5 AUGUST

He knew he'd probably had too much bourbon tonight. But he loved the warm and smoky feeling as it slipped down his throat. *Am I drunk?* No, it felt different somehow. Jason 'JT' Kenda swayed as he made his way along the edge of the pool, his vision shifting in and out of focus. The pool lights rippled in the water, shimmering like a mirage, but his head felt disconnected, like it wasn't entirely his own. He blinked hard, but the haze only thickened.

Why do I feel like this? "I need to get to the pool house," he muttered under his breath, the words slurring as they left his lips. This was his routine. The nightly swim—his way to sober up, clear his mind, and wash away the evening's excess. His body, though sluggish, was determined to follow the plan. He stumbled. He stopped. *Try again. One foot in front of the other*, he told himself. The pool house wasn't far.

A voice cut through the fog in his brain, startling him. "JT!"

He turned towards it unsteadily, his brow furrowing as he tried to make sense of the figure coming at him. It was too dark to clearly make out the person against the glowing water, but they looked… familiar. He shook his head slightly, the movement sending him off balance. He threw his arms out on either side in an attempt to steady himself. "Who is it?" His voice came out weaker than he'd expected, lost in the nightly hum of cicadas coming from the surrounding trees.

He blinked again, squinting, trying to focus, but the face before him seemed to blur and shift. The words—stern, pointed, were a meaningless jumble in JT's ears. His head lolled slightly, and he shook it again, trying to clear the feeling that it was stuffed full of cottonwool. But the movement only made the spinning worse.

The shape got closer. "Forget your swim, JT. Go to bed. You're drunk." There was frustration in their tone, but he barely registered it. His limbs felt too heavy. His thoughts slipped away before they fully formed. The warmth of the bourbon had turned into a strange, sluggish heat coursing through his veins.

Something is wrong.

He felt it deep in his chest. He wanted to ask for help. But the words wouldn't form in his muffled brain.

The person muttered something that made no sense to him before they faded into the darkness.

What's happening to me?

JT exhaled slowly. "The pool house," he whispered again. His mind latched onto the idea like it was the only thing tethering him to reality. The pool house. Get changed. Swim. Routine. It would make everything better. It always did.

He stumbled forward, his legs buckling slightly. His body felt foreign, like it belonged to someone else, but he willed it on. The path curved ahead, but something shifted beside him —a heavy presence, cold against his skin. He turned, unsteady, his sluggish brain struggling to catch up as he noticed the statue beside him. It teetered dangerously on its plinth. For a moment, he thought he might have brushed it— or had it moved on its own? The thought flickered and faded as gravity took hold.

The statue still wobbled on its base. A slow, ominous sway.

"No…" The word came out as a whisper. His hands shot out instinctively, but his movements were too slow, too clumsy. The statue tilted, teetered, and then crashed forward with a deafening thud. Pain exploded in his forehead as it struck him.

The impact sent him reeling. His feet slipped on the tiles, and the world spun violently. A brief, dizzying moment of weightlessness overtook him before the cold shock of water enveloped his body. He gasped as it rushed into his lungs, burning his chest.

Then there was an eerie calm. Dreamlike, he felt himself sink, his limbs heavy as if encased in lead. It was a comforting feeling, like the one he normally got the second before he fell asleep.

Darkness crept in from the edges of his vision as the shimmering pool lights blurred above him.

Within minutes, the world faded into silence.

2

10:10PM, THE SAME NIGHT, THURSDAY 5 AUGUST

The night sky was a deep, inky blue, dotted with stars that twinkled like distant diamonds. Lady Beatrice, the Countess of Rossex, gazed out at the moonlit garden from her cosy vantage point inside Villa Mer. She sat in a comfy armchair in the open living area, with one leg tucked underneath her. The leather was cool against her skin. The open bifold doors allowed the gentle evening breeze to drift in and mingle with the scent of fragrant flowers outside. It was a blessed relief after another scorching hot day. Not that she was complaining. Three days in the sun, and she could feel the tension from the last few months leaving her body. Melted away by the heat…

As the laughter from her companions floated through the air, her attention was far from the film she was supposed to be watching with them on the giant TV screen; instead, she found herself captivated by the illuminated swimming pool through the open doors, its surface glimmering like liquid silver from the soft glow of underwater lights. The water rippled with each gust of wind, creating mesmerising patterns that danced before her eyes. In the distance, the low hum of cicadas serenaded the night. *This is the life...*

"Come on, Rich. Do you really think he's the killer?" Sam's voice drew Bea's gaze back into the living area. Her sixteen-year-old son, Samuel, was talking to Detective Superintendent Richard Fitzwilliam, her boyfriend (*Boyfriend? What am I? Sixteen?*), who was sitting on a small sofa facing the screen, while Sam and his best friend, Archie Tellis, were on a larger couch at a right angle to him. Her West Highland terrier, Daisy, was snuggled between the two boys, her small furry body rising and falling gently as she slept through the noise.

"Have you seen those shifty eyes? He's definitely hiding something," Rich replied, pointing at a man on the screen.

"Maybe they're just how his eyes are," Archie chimed in, grinning as he popped a piece of popcorn into his mouth. He pushed his unruly mop of brown curly hair off his face. "My eyes are close together, and Sam says it makes me look shifty."

"It does!" Sam chipped in, laughing.

Archie gave him a look and shrugged. "But it's how I look."

"Your eyes don't make you look shifty, Archie," Rich reassured the sixteen year old. Archie smiled. "It's that hair of yours that does it. Who knows what you're hiding under there?" Rich shook his head with mock concern.

Sam and Archie burst out laughing, the sound echoing through the open space, filling Bea's heart with pure joy. As the three of them continued their playful debate about who the killer was, Bea's thoughts drifted back to the garden and the pool, where everything seemed so serene. *Long may it last,* she thought, grateful that the press back home had all but forgotten about her and Rich's romance, focusing instead on

Bea's brother, Lord Frederick Astley, and his fiancée, TV presenter Summer York, and the announcement of their wedding date a few days ago. She was glad of the distraction it offered.

This holiday was what they needed after the whirlwind of events that had led up to last month's opening of SaltAir, the restaurant owned by Simon Lattimore and Ryan Hawley. The business was still thriving under the watchful eyes of Ryan and his girlfriend, Fay Mayer, with a new chef at the helm— something Simon was extremely grateful for. It had allowed him to join them here in Portugal, along with his husband, Perry Juke—Bea's best friend, and Simon's recently discovered daughter, Isla Scott.

Bea idly traced the rim of her wineglass, the faint clink of crystal barely audible above the banter bouncing between Rich, Sam, and Archie about the movie's plot twists. She gave a contented sigh.

"Are you regretting not joining Perry and Simon for drinks at Ariella St Gerome's tonight?" Rich asked, turning to look at Bea with a quizzical expression.

She smiled slowly. Ariella St Gerome ("Please call me Ella,"), the famous American actress, and her husband, Jason 'JT' Kenda, a film producer, owned Villa Sol, one of the two other villas in the Marisol Estate complex. They were very Hollywood, and, of course, Perry was hugely excited to be staying in the villa next to them. After Tuesday afternoon's pool party at theirs, Bea had been happy to give a further invitation to post-dinner cocktails this evening a miss. Perry, on the other hand, had been eager to mix with their neighbours again so soon and had dragged poor Simon and Isla along with him. Isla had returned a couple of hours ago, announcing that the party had been, "utterly boring", and had gone upstairs to watch a TV show in her room.

"Absolutely not," Bea replied, smiling. "I'd much rather be here with you three. After all, I didn't come here to spend time with a bunch of strangers, however glamorous and showbiz they may be."

"They're certainly an interesting mix of personalities." Rich grinned. He reached over and gave Bea's hand a gentle squeeze, his touch sending a familiar thrill through her. "I'm glad we didn't go either."

He dropped her hand and turned back to the film. "Oh, come on. Look at him! He's definitely the killer," he cried, reaching out and nudging Sam's shoulder.

As Sam and Archie pointed out to Rich just how wrong he was, Bea's heart brimmed with pleasure. She loved the way Rich interacted with her son.

She looked out into the starry night, smiling to herself. In the past few months, she and Rich had grown incredibly close, their connection deepening into something that felt both comfortable and yet still exciting. As they'd spent more and more time together at The Dower House, her home on her parent's estate, Francis Court, they'd seemed to balance each other perfectly, working seamlessly as a team whenever challenges arose—much like they'd done once they'd learned to solve cases *together* rather than on opposing sides. It was all perfect.

Well, almost.

Despite the undeniable bond between them, Rich had yet to say those three little words that held so much meaning. Even though he showed it in so many small ways, she still longed to hear him say, "I love you."

And, of course, she wanted to say it to him too, but *he* should be the first to say it, shouldn't he?

"Mum!" Sam called out, dragging her away from her concerns. "You're missing all the good bits."

"Sorry," she murmured, tearing her eyes away from outside and turning back to the film. She frowned, not recognising half the faces on the screen, and realised that she'd literally lost the plot while she'd been drifting along in the stream of her thoughts. "Er, what's going on?" she asked.

"Mum!" Sam rolled his eyes. "Remember—"

Her mobile buzzed on the table in front of her. A notification that there was a message from Perry flashed up on the screen.

"Sorry," she mouthed to Sam as she picked up the phone and opened the message.

Perry: *OMGA. You won't believe this! JT is at the bottom of the pool. DEAD!! It looks like an accident, but I've taken pictures in case. Will be home soon, get the wine out! xx*

THREE DAYS EARLIER. BREAKFAST, MONDAY 2 AUGUST

"Perry…" Rich gave Perry a stern look across the large glass dining table at Villa Mer.

Perry quickly dropped the piece of cheese in his fingers onto his plate.

"Daisy is on a strict diet now, remember? No unscheduled food or treats, please," Rich reminded him.

"Okay," Perry said reluctantly, looking down into the pleading brown eyes of the little terrier sitting by his side. He lowered his voice and leaned down towards her. "I'm sorry your life is being made so miserable by the mean man, Daisy."

Bea suppressed a smile. She was glad Rich was taking the vet's recent comment of Daisy being, "Still a little on the chubby side," so seriously, particularly as she'd always found it hard to say no to that little face too. Picking up her cup of coffee, she took a sip and gazed out of the open bifold doors as the morning sun cast a warm golden glow over the lush garden. The swimming pool shimmered invitingly, surrounded by plush loungers and an outdoor bar that promised lazy afternoons and laughter-filled evenings in the future. Beyond the manicured grounds, the sparkling sea stretched out towards the horizon like liquid sapphire. She couldn't wait for this holiday to begin.

"Isn't this place marvellous?" Perry exclaimed between mouthfuls. "I could get used to waking up to this view every day."

"Well, you can do that for the next few weeks," his husband, Simon, pointed out.

"I can't wait to get in the pool," Sam said, gulping down his orange juice.

"Are there any inflatables?" Archie asked, toast in hand.

"Probably in the pool house." Isla pointed to the low brick building off to the side.

"Yes, there's a shower in there too, if I remember correctly," Bea added. *How different life is now compared to the last time I was here all those years ago…*

Recently widowed, she'd been grateful for the invitation from one of her mother's closest friends, Lady Grace, to stay at Villa Mer to escape the press. Even two months after Bea's husband's death, they'd still been obsessed with the fact that there had been a female passenger in his car who had also been killed in the late-night crash.

I was so young back then. Only twenty-one *and* pregnant with Sam. *How on earth did I cope?* Certainly, being here, away from the press, had helped her heal, and she was grateful to Lady Grace for having given her that asylum. The gentle pace of life, with just Lady Grace, her daughter Sybil (a childhood friend of Bea's), and Bea's cousin, Lady Caroline Clifford, to keep her company had been what she'd needed. The other two villas within Marisol had been empty. She smiled. This time around, however, not only were there seven of them staying at Villa Mer, but the other two villas were occupied too. She stifled a sigh. *It would've been nice to have the place to ourselves.*

A few days before they'd left, Bea had asked Lady Grace about the other villas at Marisol and their residents, but her mother's friend had been vague. "It's all extremely private, Beatrice, and we all keep ourselves very much to ourselves," she'd said. "All the gardens are quite separate from each other, with their own pools. So apart from the beach, where, although we all have our own access, you can see along the coastline of the whole complex, you really won't have to have anything to do with them if you don't want to."

Bea hoped Lady Grace hadn't been deliberately hazy about the details. Perry had done a little digging around the internet before their departure and had told her excitedly that if the rumours were to be believed, then their neighbours were part of the Hollywood elite. She hadn't been so keen. Hollywood or not, they were still strangers.

The approaching sound of footsteps on the tiled floor interrupted her thoughts as Ana Rodrigues, the housekeeper and cook, appeared. Bea gave her a grateful smile as she set down a fresh plate of toast on the table. "*Obrigada*, Ana."

"*De nada*, madam," Ana replied with a warm smile as Sam and Archie eagerly helped themselves.

"Ana, I hear the people staying in the other two villas are famous Americans?" Perry asked, his eyes shimmering with interest.

"Ah, *si*," Ana replied. "That would be the actress Ariella St Gerome and her husband, JT Kenda, at Villa Sol. He's some big shot film producer." She shrugged and raised her hands.

Perry leaned back in his chair, sipping his coffee with a mischievous glint in his eye. "Oh, I know something about them!"

Bea smiled wryly. Perry always knew all the up-to-date celebrity gossip.

"So," he said, raising his eyebrows. "As you all know, she's normally the star of all the films her husband produces."

The others exchanged blank looks. "Er, do we?" Simon asked.

Perry rolled his eyes. "You must've heard of *Resonance*? It was like a huge blockbuster of a film that came out a few months ago."

Bea and Rich looked at each other and shook their heads. Simon stroked his beard. "I think I remember you going to see that while I was busy with the restaurant."

Perry let out a huff.

"I've not seen it, but I've heard of it, Perry," Isla chimed in with a smile.

"Thank *you*, Isla!" Perry said, patting her on the arm. "Okay, well the rest of you will just have to trust me on this. Anyway, I read on *CelebBuzz* that she's been offered a *supporting* role in JT's next film. Apparently, she's only playing the main character's much older sister." He paused for dramatic effect. "And she's reportedly spitting feathers about it."

"I bet that's making for an interesting holiday for them then," Rich said, taking a sip of orange juice.

"Awkward!" Perry added with a knowing look. He turned to Ana, who was transferring the remaining pastries onto one plate. "Ana, what are they like next door at Villa Sol?"

Ana's face clouded over. "My daughter, Maria, works there as a maid. She says the tension is high. JT is always unhappy and shouting at everyone—his wife; that lovely girl, Lucy, who is Ms St Gerome's assistant; his wife's sister; and his brother-in-law. Even my poor Maria."

Bea shot a worried glance at Rich. An angry, shouty next-door neighbour wouldn't be conducive to the relaxing holiday she was looking forward to. Rich gave her a reassuring smile.

"Do you know he accused her of stealing one of Ms St Gerome's necklaces? As if my girl would do anything like that!" Spots of red showed through Ana's olive skin as her hands flapped by her sides. "Even Ms St Gerome herself believes she's misplaced it." Ana shook her head, mumbling, "*Não é um homem legal*. Not a nice man."

Oh my goodness. He sounds like someone to avoid.

There was a slightly awkward pause, then Simon asked, "Er, what about the other villa?"

Ana dipped her head. "You know Enzo, my son? He picked you up from the airport yesterday." They acknowledged her words with a soft murmur. Enzo worked for Lady Grace and her husband, TV's favourite entrepreneur Sir Hewitt, as their driver and handyman at Villa Mer. "His best friend, Miquel Gomes, is the head gardener for Marisol. Miquel has told him there's been lots of arguing over at Villa Luz, where Mr Stone and his wife are staying."

"Vanessa Stone, the model?" Perry asked, his eyes dancing.

Ana dipped her chin. "*Si.* She's beautiful."

Bea looked at Perry quizzically. "Is that Nessa Stone, the interior designer?"

Perry grinned. "Interior stylist to the stars!" he said with a flourish. "Yes, that's her. She was a model before she turned her hand to design."

A pinch of excitement ran through Bea's body. Nessa Stone was an icon in the interior design business, and although her aesthetic was more contemporary than Bea's, she could still imagine the ex-model would be interesting to talk to.

Ana gathered up a handful of used plates. "They have

their daughter here with them too. Always about the place on that phone of hers." With that, she excused herself to fetch more coffee.

"Chloe Stone!" Sam exclaimed as he stared wide-eyed at Archie.

"*The* Chloe Stone?" Isla asked.

"Yes!" Archie turned to Bea. "She's a huge social media star with millions of followers, Lady B." He was barely able to contain his elation. "Sam and I follow her religiously."

Bea looked over at her son, whose cheeks were turning a little pink. *Do you now?*

"Er…yeah, she posts every day," he said a little sheepishly.

Archie and Isla pulled out their phones at the same time.

"Ah, so she's posting all those beach and pool photos from here…" Isla said to the boys as she scrolled on her phone. "That's pretty cool."

Bea swallowed, her mouth feeling dry. *Not if she posts pictures of us here too. It won't take the press five minutes to work out where we are.* Her stomach dropped. They would descend on this place like a pack of wolves. She spun around to look at Rich.

He seemed to have already guessed where her mind had gone. "Don't worry, Bea. Simon and I will check out the security arrangements for Marisol this morning." He turned to Sam, Archie, and Isla. "I hope it goes without saying that we want to keep our presence here off the radar. So no posting pictures on social media while we're here, okay?"

The teenage trio nodded.

"Shall we go to the beach and check it out?" Isla suggested to the boys. Sam nodded, his eyes still glued to Chloe's social media page. Archie agreed enthusiastically.

"Alright, but don't venture outside the estate on your

own," Bea told them. She and Rich had checked the beach out during their early morning run with Daisy, part of Rich's new exercise regimen to slim down the little terrier. "It's safe, but don't swim out beyond the yellow buoys."

"Got it, Mum," Sam replied as he and Archie rose from the table.

"And put on plenty of sunscreen!" she cried out after them as they dashed out of the room.

"Don't worry, Bea." Isla grabbed a banana from the bowl in the middle of the table as she stood. "I'll keep an eye on them and make sure they don't drool all over Chloe Stone if we see her."

Perry snorted into his mug, while Bea gave her a grateful smile. As Isla left, Ana returned with a fresh pot of coffee.

She placed it on the table, then handed Bea an envelope. "This was delivered by one of the gardeners, madam."

"*Obrigada*, Ana." Bea took it, and the housekeeper cum cook left the room.

Bea's eyes narrowed as she scrutinised the handwriting on the front, all in capital letters. *'TO LADY ROSSEX, VILLA MER.'*

"Well? Who's it from?" Perry asked, leaning forward.

Bea opened the envelope and took out an elegantly written note. She quickly scanned the few lines. "It seems we've all been invited to a pool party at Villa Sol tomorrow afternoon."

Perry nearly choked on his coffee, his eyes alight with excitement. "A pool party at Ariella St Gerome's? Oh my goodness. We simply must go!" He turned to Simon, who was finishing his toast. "Do you think she'll give me some acting tips for my upcoming role in *The Importance of Being Earnest*?"

Bea caught Rich's gaze. His eyes crinkled, and he winked

at her. Perry had recently accepted the part of Algernon in The Windstanton Players' upcoming production of Oscar Wilde's play back at home in Fenshire and was taking it *very* seriously.

Simon rested his hand on Perry's arm and said diplomatically, "She might not want to talk shop if she's on holiday, so let's play it by ear, shall we?"

Bea sighed. Mingling with strangers—especially famous ones—was hardly her idea of a relaxing holiday.

"Come on, Bea. Please, can we go?" Perry urged, sensing her hesitation. "It'll be fun!"

I doubt it! But it would be rude to refuse to go, wouldn't it? She looked over at Rich, and he gave a subtle nod.

"Alright," she conceded. "We'll go. Let's get it over with and then we can ignore them for the rest of the time we're here." She turned to Perry. "But I can't promise I'll be the life and soul of the party."

"Never fear, my dear," Perry reassured her with a wink. "That's what I'm here for."

4

10:30AM, MONDAY 2 AUGUST

The sun blazed down on the pool as Bea relaxed on a lounger in the shade of a large palm. She pulled her floppy straw hat over her face and closed her eyes. Isla, Archie, and Sam had trailed off to the beach, loaded with towels, sunshades, a bluetooth speaker, and three different factor sun creams. Simon and Rich, in sunglasses, shorts, and baseball caps, were meeting with the head of security for the villas to get the lowdown on their screening and protection procedures. Daisy was safely inside away from the heat, still recovering from her five-kilometre run earlier this morning. Bea let out a satisfied sigh. No one to disturb her. Just the warmth, the gentle breeze, and—

"Yoo-hoo, Bea!"

Perry! She peeled the hat from her face as Perry scampered across the garden.

He plonked himself on the lounger next to her, his blond hair shimmering in the light. He lowered his sunglasses. "I've been thinking."

"I'm never sure that's a good thing, Perry," Bea said, a smile tugging at the corners of her mouth.

"Oh, ha ha," he replied, wafting a piece of paper rapidly in front of his face. "As I said, I've been thinking, and rather than have Enzo deliver this note—"

She stared at his hand. *Is he using the acceptance note I wrote to Ella St Gerome as a makeshift fan?*

"I thought it would be a bit more friendly if we were to hand deliver it ourselves."

She huffed as she sat up. "Why would *we* want to do that when *we* have just got comfy by the pool?"

Perry scoffed playfully. "Where's your sense of adventure? Besides, it'll be fun to meet Ella before the party tomorrow!"

Fun? "Why can't you go on your own?" Bea asked, still reluctant to move.

"The invitation was addressed to you..." he said, placing his hands together in front of his face, his blue eyes pleading with her to go with him.

Oh, okay! "Alright, fine," she said, pushing her hat onto her head as she rose. "But we have to be quick." She glanced towards the villa where Daisy was still asleep. "I don't want to leave Daisy alone for too long."

Perry grinned, clapping his hands together. "Perfect!" he said, rising. "It'll be a pleasant break from all this relaxation."

What relaxation?

He headed across the grass towards the far right-hand corner. "Where are you going?" she asked, following him.

"There's a side gate that connects our villa to next door," he told her. "Enzo told me it's left unlocked during the day so the gardeners can move freely between each of the villa's grounds."

Bea frowned. "Are you sure about this? Wouldn't it be better to go around the front and knock on their door?" She knew she wouldn't want her neighbours walking into her garden without an invitation.

"Positive!" he replied, confidently striding through the gate. "You worry too much. It's just a friendly visit, after all."

As she and Perry strolled along the path that meandered through the palatial gardens of Villa Sol, the air was thick with the scent of blooming flowers and freshly cut grass, making Bea momentarily forget her earlier apprehension. But when they rounded the bend, the serene scene before them shifted dramatically. A couple stood by the swimming pool, immersed in what appeared to be a heated argument.

She couldn't make out exactly what they were saying, but she caught the man say, "How dare she give me an ultimatum like that!" The woman then responded in a voice too soft for Bea to hear, but she caught the words, "too old", and the phrase, "finished in this business; I'll make sure of it," in his reply.

A thrill raced through her, anxiety flooding her system. "I told you we shouldn't have come barging into their grounds unannounced," she hissed at Perry, heat rising up her neck. She grabbed his arm. "We should turn back."

But it was too late—the shouting had ceased. Her stomach dropped. They'd been spotted. The woman waved them over, leaving Bea and Perry with no choice but to join the couple by the pool.

"That's Ella St Gerome," Perry whispered from the side of his mouth as they approached the pool. Ella's dark hair framed an exquisite face, with piercing blue eyes full of intensity. There was something undeniably commanding about the actress' presence.

Next to her, the man seemed agitated, his tall, fit frame radiating tension. His handsome features were marred by a menacing smile that sent shivers down Bea's spine.

"Well, hey there!" Ella greeted them warmly, extending a hand. "I'm Ariella St Gerome, but please call me Ella. And this is my husband, JT. You're Lady Rossex. I recognise you from the papers. I'm stoked to meet y'all," she said in a soft southern drawl.

"Delighted to meet you too," Bea said, taking the woman's small tanned hand. "This is Perry Juke." Bea indicated Perry, who was now hovering by her shoulder. "He and his family are staying with us," she felt compelled to add unnecessarily. She turned to greet Ella's husband, but he'd already walked off towards a table by the side of the pool, his sulking demeanour leaving an awkward silence in his wake. He picked up a half full glass of amber liquid and downed it in one.

"Isn't this just divine?" Perry gushed to Ella in a voice that sounded a lot posher than normal. He swept his arm around in an arc that encompassed the area they were standing in.

Divine? Bea stifled a giggle as her gaze wandered around the pool area, taking in the opulent surroundings. A detailed statue stood proudly on a plinth on the grass near the pool, its stone form bright under the sun's rays. Large palm trees were scattered around the edge of the pool, providing clumps of shade, and large bushes of pink flowers broke up the enormous expanse of grass.

Bea cleared her throat, feeling the need to explain their sudden appearance. "We came by to accept your invitation for the pool party tomorrow afternoon," she said, trying to sound casual. She cleared her throat and gestured to Perry, who had the acceptance note in his pocket.

He was still staring at Ella.

"Er, Perry. Do you have the note?" Bea prompted him.

He looked at her, smiling. "Sorry, what?"

"The note I wrote accepting the invitation." She tried to keep the impatience out of her voice. *Come on, Perry. Get a grip!*

"Oh, yes. Sorry," he tittered, delving into his pocket and handing the piece of paper to Ella with a small bow.

Bea suppressed a grin. *She's not royalty!* "There will be five of us in total," Bea said to Ella. She hoped Isla would come with them but knew the boys would prefer to stay at the villa and play video games than make polite conversation with a group of adults they didn't know. *And they can look after Daisy too.* "I hope that's alright?"

"That's marvellous! The more the merrier," Ella cried, her eyes lighting up. "I'm so glad you'll be joining us. Can I offer you a drink?"

"I—" Bea began, intending to decline, but Perry jumped in before she could finish.

"Absolutely! Thank you," he said, giving her another bow.

Bea stifled a sigh. *He's got it bad!*

"Lucy!" Ella called out, and a petite woman with short blonde spiky hair, shaved at the back and sides, appeared through the open bifold doors and hurried towards them. As she got closer, she adjusted the brown round glasses that framed her blue eyes and stopped in front of Ella.

"Can you arrange some drinks for our guests, please, Lucy," Ella said, smiling. She turned back to Bea and Perry. "Is iced coffee good for you both?" They nodded. "Oh, and I suppose another bourbon for JT," she added, a weariness in her voice.

Another? At this time of day? It isn't even lunchtime yet...

"Right away," Lucy replied.

"That's Lucy Harper, my PA," Ella told them as they

watched the young woman return to the open door of the villa. "She's a treasure."

JT gave a loud huff and threw himself down into a lounger by the side of the table where his empty glass now rested.

An awkward silence settled over them as they waited for their drinks. Bea looked at Perry. Normally, he was the one who filled gaps like this, but he was staring at Ella, his mouth gaping slightly open, with a goofy look on his face. Bea pressed her lips together to stop a smile that was desperate to escape. *Oh my goodness! He's actually starstruck.*

"I absolutely adore England," Ella suddenly blurted out.

Bea turned to her and smiled. "Indeed. Have you spent much time there?"

"Er, we filmed a movie just outside London not too long ago. Oxford, was it?" She glanced at JT hopefully, but he said nothing, his look sullen and disinterested.

"Oxford's a beautiful city, isn't it, Perry?" Bea said, giving him a nudge.

"Er, oh, yes," Perry replied, his eyes still glazed over.

"Ah, here are our drinks."

Bea breathed a sigh of relief.

A young Portuguese woman appeared on the patio, carrying a tray. There was a striking resemblance between her and Lady Grace's cook cum housekeeper. *She must be Maria, Ana's daughter.*

"Thank you, Maria," Ella said, taking two iced coffees from the tray with a smile. She handed them to Bea and Perry, then took the remaining glass, with what looked like champagne in it, for herself.

Maria moved swiftly to JT as he rose. He snatched the short glass from the tray and threw the bourbon into his mouth. He swallowed, then slammed the glass back on the tray with such force that Maria had to grab it with her other hand to stop it from toppling to the ground. With a mumbled, "Excuse me," in their general direction, he stormed towards the villa.

"Please excuse my husband," Ella apologised, her eyes following JT's retreating form as he disappeared into the villa, slowly followed by Maria. "He's dealing with some, er… casting issues for his next film," she explained in the manner of someone who was used to making excuses for her husband's poor behaviour.

Bea gave a small tilt of her head as she took a gulp of her coffee, savouring its icy bitterness. *I hope his mood improves by tomorrow afternoon…*

Lucy reappeared. "I'm sorry to interrupt, Ella, but your agent is on the phone and says it's urgent."

Ella turned to Bea. "I really should take this. I won't be long."

Seizing the opportunity to leave, Bea said, "Of course. We should be going anyway." She exchanged a glance with Perry, who was standing with his empty glass in one hand, a wistful smile on his face. "Perry!" Bea barked. He looked at her. She gestured in the direction they'd come from. "We need to go." She finished her drink as Lucy came forward and took her empty glass. The assistant then turned to Perry, her arm outstretched.

"Er, yes. Thank you," Perry said as he handed her his glass.

Ella was heading towards the villa. She stopped and turned back, all poise and grace. "I'm so looking forward to seeing you both tomorrow at the party. We'll have time to talk properly."

————

"What was up with you?" Bea asked as she and Perry strolled through the rich foliage on their way back to their villa.

"Can you believe we met Ella St Gerome? Isn't she amazing!" Perry said as he opened the gate, completely ignoring her question. "Did you see the way she held herself? So authoritative." He paused, then taking a deep breath, he lifted his chest up and raised his chin, resting his hand on his stomach. "I'll try this stance when I'm on stage. What do you think?"

Bea smiled at him fondly. "Very commanding."

He let out a rush of breath as he gave a quick nod.

"It was rather awkward though, walking in on that argument between her and JT," Bea said as they continued towards the pool.

"I know! What was it about, do you think? I wonder if it's linked with what the papers said about JT not casting Ella in the lead role in his next movie?"

"Possibly. But whatever it is, I hope it's resolved soon. I don't want to get involved in any drama," Bea said with feeling. She rather wished they weren't going to go to this pool party at all.

"Come on, Bea. It'll be fun," Perry reassured her, his voice light and teasing. "Besides, we're here on holiday. A little excitement won't do us any harm, will it?"

"Excitement, yes. But not arguments and tension." She shook her head. "Let's hope things are more pleasant tomorrow afternoon."

5

THE NEXT AFTERNOON, TUESDAY 3 AUGUST

Bea stepped through the ornate wrought-iron gate and into the luscious gardens of Villa Sol, the chatter of the party guests floating on the warm breeze. Beside her, Rich looked relaxed in cargo shorts and a T-shirt. Just ahead of them, Perry was eagerly strolling towards the villa, the sunlight highlighting his spiky blond hair. He'd told Bea as they'd left that he was now over his crush on Ella and would behave like a confident fellow actor. Bea was keen to see if he could pull it off. Simon followed close behind his husband, his head bent towards his willowy daughter, Isla, as they walked and talked.

Bea and Rich chatted as they followed the stone path that cut through the trees and large bushes of white oleander. As they passed under a pergola covered in grapevines, the shade gave a brief respite from the scorching sun. Turning by a cluster of terracotta pots filled with small brightly-coloured flowering plants at an intersection, they took the path towards the back of the villa.

"What on earth is that monstrosity?" Rich said as the pool came into sight.

Bea pulled a face. She'd noted the statue depicting some Greek or Roman god holding a pronged weapon yesterday when she and Perry had been here. In fact, you couldn't miss it. At around seven feet tall, four for the statue, three for the plinth, it stood on the grass by the side of the tiles that surrounded the shimmering water. It looked weighty, the weathered stone adding a sense of age. "Yes. Ghastly, isn't it?"

"Who puts something like that right next to a pool?" he asked, a frown creasing his brow.

"Maybe it's handy for hanging your towel on to dry?" she suggested with a smile, doing an impression of the statue with her arm outstretched. Rich laughed.

Ahead of them, Perry, Simon, and Isla had arrived at poolside and were greeting Ella and her husband, JT. The film producer looked more genial than the day before. *Perhaps his wife has told him to be on his best behaviour this afternoon?* Bea thought as she and Rich approached.

Ella spotted them, her smile wide. "Ah, Lady Rossex," she said, wafting over from the others to greet them. "How swell to see you again!" She held her hands out, her beautiful maxi dress shimmering around her.

Bea introduced Ella to Rich. As Rich thanked the actress for the invitation, Bea couldn't help noticing the sudden softening in Ella's eyes as she returned Rich's smile. Bea's stomach hardened. She stepped closer to Rich and placed her hand on his arm. Ella gave a tight-lipped smile, then spun around, spotting Maria expertly balancing a tray of colourful cocktails. She waved her over. "Now let me get you both a drink."

Rich gave Bea a quizzical look as she gently manoeuvred him towards Simon, Perry, and Isla, who were talking to JT. Ella's husband, dressed in a yellow shirt with palm trees on it and green shorts, was wearing mirrored shades. *Very* Hawaii Five-O! "I was saying to Perry here that I'm sorry I was being a bit of a grouch yesterday, Lady Rossex. Work issues. But that's no excuse. I hope you can forgive me." He smiled widely, his grey eyes twinkling, and gave a deep bow.

Bea dipped her chin and smiled back. *He can clearly turn on the charm when needed.* But was he sincere?

"Ooh, there's Chloe!" Isla said excitedly, pointing to a young woman who had stepped out of the villa. She turned to Simon. "I'm just going to say hello."

Bea suppressed a grin. Isla had been unconvincingly nonchalant when she, Sam, and Archie had arrived back yesterday afternoon from the beach, having accidentally-on-purpose bumped into Chloe. The boys had been thrilled to have met and talked to the social media star too. So much so that Sam had expressed an interest in attending the pool party this afternoon when Bea had told them about it, but Archie had persuaded him it would be more fun to hang out at their own villa's pool instead. Bea appreciated the backup plan; if the party turned out to be too dull, she could always use checking on the boys as an excuse to leave.

But as Isla and Chloe greeted each other, it was clear from the way the influencer's nostrils flared that Isla's excitement to see Chloe wasn't matched by the social media star. *Poor Isla.* Bea just hoped that Chloe was kind to the younger girl.

"Here you go," Ella said as she handed out the drinks. Bea examined the hurricane glass: filled with ice, visible layers of deep-pink and golden-yellow liquids sparkling in the sunlight, and topped with a slice of passion fruit half speared on the rim. "I call it the Villa Sol Passion," Ella said with a flourish.

Bea took a sip. The bold tart tropical passion fruit that hit the back of her tongue was mixed with the subtle heat and vanilla notes of white rum, closely followed by the sweetness of Grenadine, smoothing out the sharp edges of the fruit. *Umm… delicious.* Opening her mouth to compliment Ella on her concoction, she closed it again as her gaze briefly met the red-rimmed eyes of Maria, who stood by Ella's side, holding the tray. The maid turned away quickly and lowered her head, her blotchy complexion gaining a slightly pink tinge. *Has she been crying?* Bea looked over at Perry and subtly tipped her head in Maria's direction. Perry looked, a corner of his mouth quirking up.

Simon tapped Perry's arm. "Isla's waving. I think she wants us to meet Chloe."

Bea smiled and inclined her head slightly at Perry. *Go…*

"Okay. We'd better make sure she doesn't completely fangirl out in front of her," Perry said, pulling a face. Bea stifled a grin. He seemed completely unaware of the irony after his behaviour over Ella yesterday. Simon led him over to the steps leading down from the villa to the patio where Isla stood grinning as Chloe tapped away on her phone.

Bea turned around to look for Maria, but before she could ponder any further on the cause of the maid's distress, Ella said, "You simply must meet my sister, Pearl, and her husband," while sweeping an arm towards a couple standing near the edge of the terrace. "Pearl's an author, and Peter's an… artist." Her tone hinted at disapproval when she said the word 'artist'. *Perhaps she isn't a fan of her brother-in-law's art?*

Ella guided them over to a pale, mousy-looking woman with a nervous smile and a tall, scruffy man who seemed distinctly out of place among the glamorous crowd. "Pearl, Peter, this is Lady Beatrice, the Countess of Rossex, and her partner, Richard Fitzwilliam. They're from England, and they're staying next door."

"Lovely to meet y'all," Pearl said in a quiet voice. Peter grunted, his gaze flitting around like a cornered animal. He peered between his strands of long brown hair at JT, who had wandered off to join Perry, Simon, Isla, and Chloe, carrying the tray with the remaining cocktails. A frown creased Peter's forehead, then he huffed. *He looks like he'd rather be anywhere else but here.*

Rich tried to engage with Peter. "So you're an artist? What kind of art do you create?" Peter launched into a bitter tirade about the struggles of being a misunderstood creative genius in a world that didn't appreciate true art.

Bea tuned out his whining, her attention caught by Ella, who had moved away from them and had discreetly pulled Maria aside. *Is their conversation anything to do with Maria's apparent distress?* Ella placed a reassuring hand on Maria's shoulder, her face a mix of empathy and determination. Bea attempted to lip read their exchange but only caught Ella saying, "It'll be alright." *What will?* Ella looked up as she dropped her hand from Maria's shoulder, and Bea quickly glanced away, shifting her attention to Rich, who was still trapped in conversation with Peter. Nodding politely at the seemingly never-ending tales of artistic woes he was being forced to listen to, Rich sipped his drink as his brown eyes glazed over. Poor Rich. She really should rescue him. He looked at her pleadingly. She suppressed a grin. *In a little while...*

"Tell me about your books, Pearl," she said, turning to Ella's sister and offering her an encouraging smile. Beside her, she thought she heard Rich groan into his glass.

"Oh, I write women's fiction," Pearl replied, her southern voice soft and hesitant.

"Anything I might know?"

"One of my books, *Whispers in the Wind*, was made into a TV series last year."

"I've heard of that," Bea said. She vaguely remembered seeing adverts for the show. "That's quite an accomplishment. You must be delighted."

Pearl ducked her head, a modest blush colouring her cheeks. "JT and Derek are also hopefully making my latest book, *The Secrets We Keep*, into a film next year. I feel very fortunate."

"Our friend Simon over there is also a novelist," Bea told her, tipping her hand towards where Simon, Perry, Isla, and Chloe had joined another couple over by the pool. "He writes crime fiction, but I'm sure the actual process of writing is similar. You two should definitely have a chat sometime."

"Oh, that would be lovely," Pearl said, her gaze darting to the group. "It's always fun to talk to a fellow writer."

Bea made a mental note to introduce them later. For now, she had a mission: extracting Rich from Peter's clutches.

She interjected, "So do you come to this villa often, Peter? It's such a beautiful property."

Peter's eyes left Rich's and then narrowed, his lips twisting into a sneer. "I had…er, have a studio set up here. The light, the energy... It's inspiring. Essential for my work."

Pearl jumped in, her voice soothing. "We often come to look after the place for Ella and JT. It's the least we can do, considering their generosity."

"Generosity?" The question escaped out of her before Bea could stop it, curiosity getting the better of her.

Pearl's smile faltered. "I… er, we're going to live in a cottage on the grounds of Ella's LA estate." She clutched her half-full glass. "It will be handy when they start filming my book."

Bea's brow furrowed. *If Pearl's a successful author,*

surely they can afford their own home? Why were they living with Ella?

But before she could probe any further, Ella glided over to them, her smile as dazzling as the sun's rays. "My sister is very talented, you know." Her voice was honey-sweet, but Bea detected a hint of strain beneath the surface.

"Er... yes. Pearl mentioned your husband was turning one of her books into a film. That's exciting," Bea said.

"Oh, yes! JT and Derek think it has real potential to be a tremendous hit." Ella's eyes sparkled with pride as she reached out and squeezed her sister's hand.

Peter huffed, then giving Ella a filthy look, he threw the remains of his drink down his throat. "If you'll excuse me, I need a refill." His tone was petulant, like a child whose parents had told him there was no dessert because he hadn't eaten all his dinner. He stalked off without waiting for a response.

Bea exchanged a glance with Rich, who raised an eyebrow. There seemed to be no love lost between Peter and his sister-in-law. Pearl's worried gaze followed her husband's back as he disappeared into the villa.

"Don't mind him," Ella said, putting her arm around her sister. "Artistic temperament, isn't that right, sis?"

Pearl offered a quick gesture of agreement and continued to sip her drink.

"Anyway, Richard. I hear you were checking out the security around the place yesterday?" She smiled sweetly at Rich, a glint in her eye. "I hope you didn't find us wanting?" she asked coyly.

Bea pressed her lips flat. *Is she flirting with him in front of me? The cheek...*

Rich reached out and placed his hand gently on the small

of Bea's back. "It's impressive even for a gated community like this."

"You'll understand, Lady Rossex," Ella replied, looking from him to Bea. "I imagine you deal with the same issues I do concerning the press. They seem to be everywhere, don't they? Security really does an excellent job of keeping the paparazzi at bay here."

Well, I hardly think it compares to what I have to deal with...

Pearl cleared her throat. "I should probably go find Pete. Make sure he's alright." She gave a strained smile before excusing herself.

Ella watched her go, a flicker of annoyance crossing her features, then she turned to them and smiled. "More drinks?"

6

AT THE SAME TIME, TUESDAY 3 AUGUST

Perry followed Simon as they walked over to where Isla was waiting for them. Chloe was hunched over her phone screen. *Why are they so obsessed with their phones these days?* Perry's eyes shifted to the shimmering pool. When he was their age, you'd have had to drag him away from a swimming pool like that.

"Dad, this is Chloe Stone," Isla said to Simon as he and Perry stopped in front of the two girls. Perry spotted the look on Simon's face that said he still wasn't bored with being called 'Dad'. He suppressed a happy sigh. Who would've thought when Isla had first appeared and revealed herself as Simon's daughter from a holiday romance twenty years ago, that four months later, she would be so integrated into their lives that it both felt as if she had always been there, and yet was still so new that it still took him by surprise? "Chloe, this is my dad, Simon."

Simon smiled at the petite, dark-skinned woman standing next to his daughter. "Hi, Chloe, nice to meet you."

Chloe looked up from her screen and flashed him a brilliant smile.

Are they her real teeth?

"Hi," she said, then after a few seconds pause, she went back to her phone.

Rude!

Isla turned to Perry. "And this is my other dad, Perry."

Other dad? Perry's heart fluttered. He grinned at Isla, who grinned back. Bea had been right when she'd pointed out a couple of months ago when Perry had been struggling to accept Simon's daughter as a permanent addition to their family, that Isla would bring so much into their lives if only Perry would embrace the change. He had done, and now he was an 'other dad'. He couldn't be happier.

A barely perceptible sigh came from Chloe, then she raised her head and tilted it to one side, staring at Perry.

Be nice, Perry. She's only young. Be a good role model… "Hi, Chloe. I hear you're a big hit on social media."

Isla rolled her eyes and gave him a look that said, "Please don't embarrass me."

"You could say that," Chloe replied, looking smug. "I have over three-and-a-half million followers."

Three-and-a-half million? Perry couldn't imagine why that many people would be interested in what this slightly stuck-up girl was up to. He stifled the urge to shake his head.

"So you're staying with Lady Rossex?" Chloe asked. Without waiting for an answer, she carried on, "So is it true that if, like, the King of England dies or something, she will be queen?"

Perry stifled a sigh, then smiled. "It would take a blood-bath, but yes, technically, if sixteen of the more senior members of the *British* royal family died, then she would be queen."

"Awesome!" Chloe said, looking over at Bea by the side of the pool as she talked to Ella. She raised her phone.

"Stop!" Perry hissed.

Chloe paused, her phone half-way up to her face, and raised a well groomed eyebrow. A look of undisguised disdain flashed across her face.

"Please don't take a picture of her ladyship at a private event." *Did that sound a tad pompous?*

"Why?" Chloe sneered.

Perry's stomach dropped. He wasn't sure he liked this girl. "You don't have permission." *Does she need permission? Probably not. But hopefully she doesn't know that.* "And you don't want to get on the wrong side of the royal family," he added for good measure. "They can have you locked up in The Tower of London!"

Chloe hesitated for a moment, looking unsure about whether he was being serious or not, then with a little huff, she dropped her arm. Her attention immediately shifted to Simon as if she'd only just noticed he was here. "You're a crime writer and a chef, aren't you?" she asked. Simon responded with a faint incline of his head. "So you must have lots of followers?"

Simon shot Perry a look. "Er... not really."

"Dad doesn't do social media," Isla added.

Perry was happier with how this conversation was going now. He smirked at Simon. "How many times have I told you to get yourself online?"

Chloe's mouth fell open. "So how does anyone know to buy your books?" she asked, her voice tinged with incredulity.

"Exactly!" Perry cried. "Isla even set him up an account on Instagram, but he won't use it."

"Alright, alright," Simon replied, lifting his hands. "Look, it's simply not my thing, okay?"

"So we need to make it your thing, Simon," Chloe said in

a matter-of-fact voice. "Let's start by posting a selfie of us all, and I'll tag you. That will bump your followers up." She quickly jumped in between Perry and Simon, dragging Isla with her, and shouted, "Smile!"

Perry grinned into the camera. *Snap!*

As Chloe studied the resulting photo, Perry looked over her head at Simon and grinned. "We're going to make you a star!" he mouthed. Simon wrinkled his nose.

There was a short cough, and Perry spun around to see JT, Ella's husband, standing next to them, holding a tray of cocktails. "I thought you might like another drink. These are Ella's own concoction," he drawled, shoving the tray at Perry. "Some sort of fruity cocktail, I believe." *I won't say no…* Perry quickly drained what was left of his drink and took a fresh one. "Thank you."

"Ladies?" There was a slightly creepy look on JT's face as he looked at Chloe and Isla. Perry shivered.

"No thanks," Isla said, barely looking up. Chloe, on the other hand, hesitated, putting a finger to her lips.

"Can I tempt you, Chloe?" JT asked, his voice low and slightly husky.

Yuk! She's young enough to be his daughter. In fact, she *was* the daughter of his business partner.

"Maybe?" she said coyly, raising her eyes to meet his.

Perry shot a look at Simon, but he was perched on Isla's shoulder, studying a photo on her phone, so he was oblivious to what was going on.

Perry swallowed hard, then grabbed a drink from the tray and thrust it into Chloe's hand. "I'm sure they're very nice," he said. "You'll love it."

She stepped back slightly in surprise as she took the drink. "Er, thanks."

"And how did the selfie turn out?" Perry continued, inching his way towards Chloe and blocking JT.

"Oh, let me show you." Suddenly, she was animated, taking his arm and pulling him over to where Simon and Isla were.

Behind him, Perry heard JT huff and then move away. Perry smiled to himself. *Scuppered!*

————

Fifteen minutes later, Perry stood next to Simon, trying to contain his excitement as Chloe introduced her parents, Derek and Vanessa, who they'd moved to join by the pool. Nessa Stone was, as Perry had expected she would be, a striking woman. The photos he'd seen of her during her modelling days still barely did the statuesque woman justice. *Has she had a lot of work done?* Her skin seemed incredibly smooth and devoid of wrinkles for someone in her... what... mid-forties?

He hoped they would be friends. She'd moved from modelling into interior design and was now considered the go-to designer for the rich and famous. *We should have a lot in common*, he reasoned. And perhaps when he'd got to know her a little better, he would ask her what her secret was to looking so young. As she took his hand, he looked up into her striking eyes, her long lashes fluttering as she glanced at him. "It's great to meet you, Vanessa. I'm a big fan of your work."

"Of course," Nessa murmured, the words slipping out as if they were an afterthought. She shook Perry's hand, then dropped it quickly, a faint smile flittering over her face for only a few seconds. Her brown eyes, once the highlight of countless magazines, now flickered away, uneasy and distant as they rested just over his shoulder.

Perry pressed his lips tightly together. *Rude!* He could see now where Chloe had got her manners.

"And, Mom, Dad, this is Isla," Chloe said. "We met down at the beach. She's a college student." She slightly wrinkled her nose.

"Oh, whereabouts?" Derek Stone asked Isla as he took her hand. While Isla and Simon chatted with Derek and Chloe went back to her mobile, Perry opened his mouth to try again with the ex-supermodel, but he stopped. He followed Nessa's gaze as she stared at JT disappearing through the bifold doors leading into the villa. Her expression was a mixture of fear and excitement. *What's going on there?*

"So, Perry." Derek's voice grabbed Perry's attention. His broad shoulders and strong jawline contributed to his imposing presence. "What do you do for a living?"

"I'm in interior design," Perry replied, trying to muster up some enthusiasm now that he'd realised Nessa wouldn't be interested even if he said he'd met the King of England. Which, in fact, Perry had, as the king was Bea's uncle.

"Ah, Nessa here does that sort of thing too," Derek said, nudging his wife. The ex-model managed a brief smile, her gaze lingering on Perry for a moment as if she'd never seen him before.

"Indeed. We should talk about that some more sometime, but right now, please excuse me. I need to check on something inside," she said, leaving them with a slightly forced smile.

Perry's curiosity was piqued further. *Is she going after JT?*

While Derek turned to Simon to ask him what he did, Perry watched Nessa glide towards the villa. Before she reached it, a woman, who Perry recognised as Lucy Harper, Ella's personal assistant, came storming out of the villa, her face twisted in anger. She sidestepped Nessa, her head now down, and disappeared around the side of the building. *Oh my, what's going on with her?*

Chloe suddenly announced that she was off to film some content and headed towards the bifold doors. Isla watched her go, disappointment etched on her face. Perry's heart fluttered. *Poor Isla, I really think she thinks she and Chloe will become friends.* But as much as he felt his stepdaughter's distress, he wasn't sure Chloe was the right sort of person for Isla to spend time with. *She seems utterly selfish to me.*

He leaned over and whispered in Isla's ear, "If you want to go back to the villa and join the boys, no one will mind." She looked up and smiled at him. "And remember to put some more sunscreen on your face," he added as Isla made her excuses and left.

While what appeared to be a genuine interest from Derek in crime writing sparked a deeper conversation between him and Simon, Perry's attention drifted away from their chat to observe Bea, Rich, and Ella on the opposite side of the pool.

Bea seemed unusually clingy towards Rich, her hand gripping his arm a touch too firmly. Perry's brow furrowed, concerned that something might be wrong with his friend. Then he caught sight of Ella playfully touching Rich's other arm, a flirtatious smile on her face. *Oh, Bea*, Perry thought with amusement, *jealousy doesn't suit you, my dear!*

As Perry was settling into his role as a silent observer of his best friend's discomfort, Nessa re-emerged from the villa. She looked... *unsettled.* With a furtive glance, she skirted around the cluster of pots on the patio and followed the path Lucy Harper had taken earlier, disappearing around the side of the villa without so much as a farewell. *What's going on with these people?*

Whatever it was, he'd had enough now. Nessa had turned

out to be a tremendous disappointment, and he'd not got to ask Ella anything about acting. It was time to rescue Bea and go home. Perry's gaze rested on Simon, silently pleading for an escape. As if on cue, Derek asked, "How about another drink?"

"Actually," Simon replied with a well-timed glance at Perry, "we should probably get going. We've left two sixteen-year-old boys alone at our villa. Who knows what trouble they've got into already?"

Perry shot him a grateful smile.

"Of course, of course!" Derek agreed with a grin. "It's been great to meet you both. No doubt we'll see you again soon."

As Derek peeled off towards the villa, presumably to refill his drink, Perry leaned in and whispered to Simon, "We need to rescue Bea before she burns a hole in Ella with her jealous laser-beam glare."

Amusement dancing in his eyes, Simon gave a brief dip of his chin as he followed Perry over to where Bea, Rich, and Ella were engaged in conversation. Bea's expression shifted from tightly restrained irritation to palpable relief as they joined them.

"We were just thinking it's time to get back. We promised not to leave the boys alone for too long, remember?" Perry said, throwing Bea a lifeline.

She looked at her watch in a slightly exaggerated gesture, then gave a thoughtful tilt of her head. "I'd no idea that was the time. Yes, we really should be going."

Ella's face fell, the disappointment clear in her eyes. She scanned the empty garden, remarking bitterly, "It seems everyone needs a siesta today."

Oh dear. She looks like someone who's had all her toys taken away at once...

Turning her attention back to the four of them, Ella said, "Would you like to join us for drinks on Thursday night?"

Feeling a little sorry for her and hoping that it would give him a chance to talk to her about his up-and-coming role as Algernon, Perry said, "Yes. We'd love to."

"That's very kind, but unfortunately, Rich and I have plans with the boys," Bea interjected, trying to sound disappointed but failing badly.

———

The low Portuguese sun cast a golden glow on them as they retreated from Villa Sol. Simon and Rich were slightly ahead. Bea hooked her arm around Perry's as she let out a loud sigh of relief. "Good grief," she uttered. "What an odd bunch of people."

Perry snorted. "And there was me thinking you were having a great time."

She shot him a look. "Did *you* have fun?"

He dipped his head in acknowledgement. "Not really. I never got time to talk to Ella about acting. Ness Stone was aloof and disinterested. And that JT fellow gives me the creeps. And I fear Chloe is a bit of a cow."

Bea nudged him as they continued to walk. "Well, at least you didn't have to suffer Peter Mitchell, the misunderstood and criminally underrated artist, and his sweet but total mouse of a wife, Pearl. I thought Peter would bore Rich into a coma before I rescued him."

Rich turned his head and looked at them over his shoulder. "Yes, thanks for that. Although, you could have been quicker."

She laughed. "But where would the fun have been in that?"

He grinned. "Next time—"

"Next time?" Bea cut in. "As far as I'm concerned, there won't be a next time. I've done my bit. I've been sociable. Now I hope to not see them again while we're here."

"I agree," Rich said, opening the gate that led to Villa Mer. "I'm done with the Hollywood crowd too."

Perry watched Bea's expression soften with relief as they walked into their own grounds.

"You're the lucky ones," Simon said. "I have to do this all over again the day after tomorrow."

"You have my commiserations, mate," Rich said as he closed the gate behind them.

Perry's heart sank. He hurried to catch up with his husband. "If you'd rather not—"

But Simon cut him off with a wink.

You rotter!

As they emerged from the bushes lining the walkway, laughter and splashing reached Perry's ears, and he relaxed as the tension and disappointment of the party dissolved into the warm afternoon air. He was glad to be leaving the drama of Villa Sol behind.

7

TWO DAYS LATER. JUST AFTER 8PM, THURSDAY 5 AUGUST

"What can I get you to drink?" Maria, Villa Sol's maid, asked as she led Perry, Simon, and Isla into the vast open sitting room. She took their drink order and indicated a table full of fancy canapés along the back wall. "Please help yourself to the food, and if you need anything else, please let me know."

"Thank you, Maria," Perry said as he smiled at the young girl, pleased to see her looking a lot more composed than she'd done Tuesday afternoon when she'd been serving drinks at the pool party. She returned his smile, then left the room.

As Perry followed Simon and Isla towards the delicious looking spread sitting on top of the counter, the room unfolded before him like a photograph from an upscale-life-style magazine. Sleek modern furniture was arranged in sociable clusters on a highly polished hardwood floor, and the warm hues of pink and gold from the setting sun streamed in through the expansive windows, which framed a postcard-perfect view of lush gardens that stretched out towards the sea in the distance. The background music had clearly been carefully selected to suit the ambiance of casual luxury. *It sounds like something you'd hear in the lift of a posh hotel.*

"Very Hollywood," Simon murmured as he looked up at a contemporary chandelier resembling a constellation of multi-coloured tiny suns that dominated the high ceiling.

Perry's eyes were drawn upwards. The polished chrome and sleek glass gave off a look-at-how-expensive-I-am vibe, its colours reflecting the light and creating a dazzling display. Literally. He diverted his eyes. *Not really my style...* "It's way too flashy for me," Perry whispered back as his eyes continued to sweep the room. They stopped on JT, who was standing by the window, his back to Perry as he leaned in close to the person in front of him, blocking them from view. Then suddenly, a face popped out from around his tall frame.

"Oh, there's Chloe." Isla tried to catch the eye of the pixie-looking social media star, but she was listening to something JT was saying, her camera-ready smile revealing a perfect set of glowing white teeth.

Has she got veneers? She's too young, surely...

Isla sighed as Chloe continued to stare intently into JT's face, her head cocked provocatively to one side. Perry shook his head and looked around to see where Derek and Nessa were. Surely, they wouldn't be happy to see Derek's best friend flirting with their young daughter? But before he could locate them, Maria arrived with their drinks. She handed a gin and tonic to Perry, a bottle of fruit cider to Isla, and a glass of red wine to Simon, then left.

While Simon and Isla chatted, Perry surveyed the rest of the room. His eyes rested on each familiar face in turn. Ella, looking stunning in a fitted red dress, stood with Pearl and Peter Mitchell over on the other side of the room. Peter, drink in hand, was loudly lecturing her and Pearl about something. Their expressions seemed tense, but whether that was due to

Peter's monologue or something else, Perry was unable to tell. Over along the huge expanse of windows, Lucy, Ella's PA, sat on a sleek contemporary white leather L-shaped couch, her legs crossed. High-heeled sandals poked out from underneath her black trousers as she busied herself with her phone.

Close to the windows, Derek Stone, in a shirt and shorts, and his wife Nessa, in a long flowing purple maxi dress, were standing side by side in stilted silence. Both of them watched JT as he leaned in to whisper something in Chloe's ear. Derek's narrowed eyes suggested he was less than happy at their behaviour. The expression on Nessa's face was one of pain. *If she's that concerned about her daughter, why doesn't she go and break it up?* Why didn't they both go over? He would if it was JT acting like that around Isla.

He turned to ask Simon if they should interfere just as Isla said, "Would you mind if I went back to the villa to watch *Emily in Paris*?" She glanced over at Chloe, who was still cosying up to JT. "I don't think this is my sort of party."

Simon shook his head as he leaned in to kiss her cheek. "No, you go ahead."

Perry gave her a hug. "If it doesn't liven up, I might come and join you later," he said, only half-joking. He loved the TV show *Emily in Paris*.

Isla smiled, then headed towards the door.

Simon chuckled as he glanced around the room. "Same cast, slightly different location?"

"I'm afraid so," Perry agreed. "I was hoping for some fresh faces." He opened his mouth to suggest they joined JT and Chloe, but they were no longer there. JT had joined his wife, sister, and brother-in-law, and Chloe was nowhere to be seen. *I wonder where—*

"Well, on the upside," Simon continued, gesturing

towards Ella, who was now walking across the room towards the sofa. "With so few people here, you might get some quality time with Ella to talk about acting."

"True," Perry said, Chloe forgotten as a flicker of hope ignited in his chest. "Maybe I can pick her brains about how she prepares for a role."

"Exactly! Now go and hover by her," Simon encouraged, giving him a reassuring smile. "I'll distract the others."

Perry grinned at Simon as he lifted his drink in a salute. "And *that* is why I love you."

His mood lifted, Perry sauntered over towards the window, nonchalantly looking at the vibrant artwork on the walls as he went. But a few minutes later, when he looked over to see exactly where Ella was, she'd moved and was now deep in conversation on the sofa with Lucy. *I'm too late!* Not wanting to stand in front of the couch like a dummy in a clothes shop, Perry casually inched towards the window and gazed out into the now dark sky. In the reflection of the glass, he saw Simon had joined Pearl, Peter, and JT. *My hero!* JT was, of course, talking loudly. Perry could clearly hear him from where he was standing.

"But you know what really kills me?" JT leaned towards Simon as if he was about to share a deep secret. "These *streaming* services," he sneered. "Everyone thinks they can make movies now! Netflix, Amazon—anyone with a camera thinks they're Spielberg! It's a jungle, I tell you. Real cinema is dying, and we're left picking up the pieces, trying to make something authentic. Do you know what it takes to get a movie made these days—"

With a pang of sympathy for his poor husband, Perry tuned JT out and turned his attention to Derek and Nessa, who were a little further along the floor-to-ceiling windows. Again, using the reflection of the windows to spy on them, he watched as Derek jerked his hand up and rubbed it back and forth across his shaved head. Perry could just make out what he was saying to his wife as she stood in front of him, her head bowed as she stared at the floor.

"You can't have everything your own way, Nessa. You're the one who wants out of our marriage, not me." He lowered his hand, and with a huff, he moved away from his wife to join the group where JT was boisterously bellowing about a recent yacht purchase he'd made.

Oh… so Nessa and Derek's marriage is on the rocks, is it? Perry remembered how, at yesterday's drinks party, Nessa had seemed so distracted. *Perhaps that explains it…*

A movement in the window attracted his attention, and he watched as Ella and Lucy rose from the sofa. He spun around. Was this his chance to pick the brains of the award-winning actress? As Lucy, pushing up her glasses, headed for the opposite door to the one he and Simon had come in earlier, Perry glided swiftly across the wooden floor to intercept Ella.

"Ella, how nice to see you again! Thank you so much for inviting us tonight," he said, stopping in front of her.

"Hey, Perry! Good to see you too." Her voice was warm, but her gaze shifted past him, towards the group that included her husband.

"Ella, I don't know if I told you, but I'm soon to be on the stage in a leading role—"

"That's nice," she jumped in, her smile tight, a blend of politeness and distraction. Her eyes, however, remained partly on JT.

"Er, yes. Thank you. Anyway, can I ask you about how you get into character and—"

"Perry, I'm so sorry." She tilted her head to one side and rested her hand on his arm. "But I need to get my husband another drink—"

I really don't think you do!

"— so if you can give me five minutes, I'll be back and then we can have a proper chat about it. Is that okay?"

No, not really. Your husband has had too much to drink already, and I only came here tonight so I could talk to you about acting. I could have stayed at home, you know!

"Thank you, Perry. I'll be faster than a jackrabbit on a hot day!" She hurried off towards the bar before Perry could respond.

Rude!

Smarting slightly, Perry looked around to see where Nessa was. She was the only other person in the room who he was vaguely interested in talking to. He spotted her hurrying towards the exit Lucy had used.

Is she alright? Perhaps I'd best follow her and check....

8

A FEW MINUTES LATER, THURSDAY 5 AUGUST

Perry's forehead puckered. *Where did she go?* By the time he'd exited the room and walked down the corridor, there'd been no sign of her. He was now in a large empty lobby with a terracotta tiled floor and a sloped glass ceiling. He stopped. *What now?* He tapped his fingers on the half empty glass in his hand and looked back along the hall. He'd not gone past any doors. Swivelling on his feet, he continued to look around. There was an imposing chrome staircase in front of him leading upstairs and another, less ornate, set of stairs leading to what he presumed was a basement. To the right of the stairs was a door. This layout was nothing like Villa Mer's.

Has Nessa gone downstairs?

He hesitated. He should probably return to the party. *But it's so boring...* With a shiver of excitement, he edged towards the stairs and gingerly descended a few steps.

He stopped. The sound of a woman's voice singing above the clatter of pots and pans rose to meet him. *Maria? It must be the kitchen down there.* He sighed softly. He couldn't really go poking around—what would he say if Maria saw him? And anyway, Nessa wouldn't be in the kitchen, would she? *No.* He climbed back into the lobby. His only other option was the door. It had a glass panel in the middle, and Perry peered through. There was another hallway with a tall, wide archway at the end. That must lead to the side of the house where the pool is. *Should I—*

"Can I help you, sir?"

Startled, Perry spun round. Maria was standing behind him, an expectant look on her face.

Now what do I say? Think, Perry! "Er, I'm looking for the bathroom." *Who takes their drink to the bathroom with them, idiot!*

She smiled. "Of course, sir. It's through that door and on the left."

Perry acknowledged her words with a soft murmur. He had no choice now… He opened the door with his free hand and went through. Concerned that Maria was watching him through the door's window, he dashed down the hall and dived through the first door on the left.

Closing the door behind him, he let out a deep sigh of relief. *I'll hang out here for a few minutes, then go back.* Taking a sip of his drink, he looked around the room, all marble and chrome, then moved to the mirror. He adjusted his blond hair a little and gave himself a smile. *Okay, back to the party.*

He tugged on the handle, but before he was able to open the door fully, he heard voices. A man and a woman. They seemed to be in the middle of a heated exchange.

Oh my goodness! He slowly pushed the door until there was just a sliver open. He rested his ear on the edge so he could hear through the gap. *Well, I need to know when they're finished, don't I?*

"And what the hell do you think you were doing with my

daughter?" the woman hissed. Perry recognised her voice. It was Nessa Stone. "How dare you use her to get to me!"

"Oh, please!" the man sneered.

There was no doubt about that slightly slurred response. It was JT.

"I've no interest in anything to do with you any more! I've told you already, we're done." His tone was harsh. "And I'll talk to whoever I want!" he threw at her.

"But not my daughter, JT." Her voice cracked with emotion. "Look, I'm sorry. Please can we just talk about it?" The anger had gone from Nessa's voice. Now she was pleading.

"I'm done talking!" JT barked. "Leave me alone, Nessa. Go back to Derek and be grateful that there is someone out there who will put up with your diva behaviour and constant whining."

Perry's mouth fell open. *That's harsh!*

Nessa's voice trembled as she responded, "You can't ignore what happened, JT. You know I love you."

Perry's stomach dropped. *Nessa's in love with JT?* From what he'd seen of the man, it was hard to believe, but she sounded genuine.

There was a heavy silence before JT spoke again, his voice lowered to a dangerous growl. "What happened was a mistake. A series of stupid, drunken mistakes that you need to forget. I don't love you, Nessa. I never did."

The words hung in the air like a heavy fog. Perry's pulse quickened. He almost felt Nessa's heart shatter through the thin door separating them.

"Now go before someone—" JT's words stopped abruptly at the sound of a door opening, followed by a strangled cry from Nessa as her footsteps hurriedly retreated.

Perry swallowed. *If this is Ella or Derek...* He stayed

frozen behind the bathroom door, his heart now pounding fast. He squashed his ear closer to the gap in the door, not wanting to miss a single detail of this unexpected drama unfolding before him.

"What do you want, Pete?"

Perry's shoulders dropped a little.

"Was that Nessa?" Peter Mitchell asked, sounding intrigued. Perry sensed a hint of triumph in his tone, as if Ella's brother-in-law had caught JT in a vulnerable position he could exploit.

JT's voice was tight with irritation. "It's none of your business, Pete. What are you doing here?"

Perry's stomach dropped to his feet. *What if Peter is here to use the bathroom?* His mind raced, torn between the urge to eavesdrop further and the fear of being discovered. Should he risk it all and continue to listen? He glanced down at the lock underneath the door handle. *Will I have time to shut the door and lock it if I have to?*

"We need to talk."

Perry stifled a gasp of relief.

"What is it with everyone today?" It was obvious from JT's tone that he was losing whatever shred of temper he had left. "I've made my decision clear," he spat out, his speech still slightly slurred. "I want you gone by next weekend. End of."

There was a pregnant pause. Perry inhaled slowly through his nose.

"We'll see about that!" Peter snarled. His footsteps retreated, then a door slammed behind him. JT swore before he walked away in the opposite direction.

Perry's breath came out in a *whoosh*. "Good grief," he muttered under his breath, looking down at his hand gripping his glass. His knuckles were white. He was surprised he hadn't shattered it into pieces. He relaxed his muscles. *Okay. So that was fun!*

With another deep breath, he took a large gulp of his cocktail, emptying the glass, then he steeled himself and cracked open the door. He poked his head out and looked up and down the hallway. It was clear. He popped out into the corridor and scurried back the way he'd come. *I need another drink!*

———

"Where have you been?" Simon asked as he joined Perry by the food, handing him a drink. The music playing was now more upbeat and a little louder. *Trendy bar music,* Perry thought as he took the glass from his husband with a grateful smile and popped a delicate chicken dumpling into his mouth. "You wouldn't believe me if I told you," Perry answered, pulling a face, then swallowed. He turned back to the table, selecting a tiny round cheese scone filled with cream cheese and onion marmalade.

"Try me," his husband said, moving to stand closer to him, a grin hovering on his lips.

Perry finished the tasty morsel. "Well—" He stopped. Over his husband's shoulder, he spotted JT. He frowned. *He must have come back in through the other door.* Without even pausing for breath as he carried on talking at Derek Stone, JT grabbed a glass of something amber from a tray Laura was holding as she passed by. Does the man have no shame? Perry felt an urge to shout over, "He's been having an affair with your wife, Derek!"

Perry's eyes continued to flitter around the room. Peter was back with Pearl; both of them stood with Ella. But no Nessa. *Where has she disappeared to?*

"Er, Perry?" Simon prompted gently.

Suddenly, Perry was weary of all the drama. "Do you think it would be too rude if we left now?"

"But you haven't talked to Ella properly about acting yet," Simon pointed out.

Perry scoffed. "I know, but honestly, I don't think she's that interested…"

"I don't agree. She was asking after you. She said she wanted to hear about the role you were going to be playing."

Perry straightened up. "Did she?"

"Yes. Why don't we go over and join her?"

Perry grinned. "Okay."

Simon touched his arm. "But you will tell me later what you've been up to."

"Up to?" Perry's eyes widened.

"Perry, I know you. Something's happened."

Perry raised his hand to his chest. "I don't know what you—"

Simon raised an eyebrow.

"Oh, alright. I promise I'll tell you later," Perry said, giving his husband a cheeky grin.

9

10:30AM, MONDAY 2 AUGUST

"Ah, Perry, there you are." Ella smiled as Perry and Simon joined her, her sister, and her brother-in-law. "I'm so sorry I left you earlier. Now please tell me all about this important role you're going to be playing."

Peter grabbed his wife's arm. "We'll leave you to your actor talk." He pulled Pearl away, leading her towards the couch. Perry watched them go. *Is Peter going to tell his wife about his encounter with JT?*

"Perry is going to be Algernon in *The Importance of Being Earnest* by Oscar Wilde at our local theatre in Windstanton. Do you know the play?" Simon said as he reached out and subtly nudged Perry.

Perry returned his attention to Ella.

"Of course," Ella replied. "He's an interesting character. Based on Wilde himself, I believe."

Perry's toes tingled. She knew the part. *This is more like it!* His eyes opened wider. "Yes. I really want to understand the character, you know?" *Check me out, sounding like a professional actor.*

Beside him, Simon made a noise, then jerked his drink up to his face.

Ignoring him, Perry asked, "So what's your process for getting into character, Ella?"

Ella smiled. "Okay, so first, I would read up as much as you can on Wilde himself. Research is really important. Then read the play. Repeatedly. Try different voices, ways of standing, walking. See if you can find what feels right for your character. Then tweak it in rehearsals. See how it fits with the others. With the set. Really test it, you know?"

Perry agreed enthusiastically. This was great. He was getting proper acting advice. *My Algernon is going to be the best Windstanton has ever seen!*

"I often…" Her voice trailed off as JT let out a raucous laugh, and she winced.

Perry stifled a sigh. *That man is a pain in the—*

"I'm sorry," she said to them. "JT can be... a handful when he's had a few drinks," Ella admitted, her eyes flickering back to her husband.

I don't imagine he's a pussycat sober either.

The weariness Perry had felt a short while ago washed over him again. Ella was too distracted by her husband to be really interested in what Perry was up to. Perhaps it was time to go. Bea and Rich would still be up at Villa Mer, and he had so much to tell them…

Perry glanced over at JT, whose face had grown a shade redder since he'd last seen him, and his movements were unsteady as he flapped his hand at Derek. Then Perry caught a glimpse of Peter, who had left his wife on the sofa and was heading for the exit. Pearl slumped in her seat, her head bowed, seemingly staring into her drink. She looked defeated. *Is JT chucking them both out?* Pearl took a deep breath and rose, placing her half-full drink on a table, then headed towards them.

Perry returned his gaze to Ella. *Does she know her sister and brother-in-law have been told to leave?*

"I'm off to bed, darlin'," Pearl said as she approached her sister, her tone laced with forced cheerfulness. She leaned towards Ella and kissed her on both cheeks. "Pete's retreated to his studio. The muse calls."

Is she being sarcastic? Perry studied Pearl's face, but it was impossible to tell. *Perhaps when you're married to someone like Peter, you learn to hide your real feelings....*

"Goodnight, Pearl," Ella said, hugging her. She whispered something into her sister's ear, but Perry wasn't able to hear what she said. Pearl offered a quick gesture of agreement as she broke from Ella's hold.

"Goodnight," she said, turning to Perry and Simon. *She looks so sad...* Then she swept out of the room.

Is she alright? Before Perry had a chance to ask Ella, Derek appeared in front of them.

"I must go too, I'm afraid. Early meeting in the morning," he said, tapping an expensive-looking watch that probably would've funded the whole of Windstanton Theatre's production of *The Importance of Being Earnest*. "Time zones, you know?"

"Where's Nessa?" Ella asked, her voice betraying a hint of concern.

Does she know about Derek's wife and her husband?

"She had a headache and left," Derek said.

And for that matter, do you know about your wife and JT?

Leaving his glass on the sideboard, Derek made his way out of the room just as JT staggered over with the unsteady gait of a man struggling to keep his balance.

Talk of the devil...

"Time for my nightly dip, cutie pie," he slurred slightly as he grabbed onto Ella's arm.

Swimming now? Really?

She responded with a faint incline of her head and patted his hand. "Enjoy, honey," she replied with a smile that didn't quite reach her eyes.

Perry couldn't help himself. "Should he really be swimming in that state, Ella?" he asked as they all watched JT weave across the room and through the doorway like a ship without a rudder.

Ella sighed, her shoulders drooping ever so slightly. "I've learned over time which battles are worth picking, and this" —she gestured vaguely towards the exit JT had taken— "is not one of them. He won't give up his evening swim no matter how much he's had to drink." She managed a weak smile. "He'll be fine."

Lucy Harper swept into the room then, her movements brisk and efficient as she began collecting the empty glasses and half-eaten snack bowls that littered various surfaces. Approaching them, she asked, "Does anyone need anything before I check on the kitchen?"

Ella and Perry shook their heads. "We're fine, thank you, Lucy," Simon said, echoing the sentiment with a polite smile.

As Lucy left, Perry glanced around the now almost-empty room, sensing the energy of the evening dissipating like smoke. *We should go too.* He didn't want to outstay their welcome. And anyway, he'd been ready to leave for the last half hour. "I think it's time we headed home too," he said, barely able to disguise the weariness in his voice.

"It's not even late," Ella said as she glanced at her watch.

Perry looked down at his half-full glass and hesitated. He really wanted to get back and tell Bea about his night. *But it'll be rude to desert Ella like everyone else seems to have done, won't it?*

"We really haven't talked about your play properly. I want to know all about who has been cast in what role," Ella said.

Perry stifled a sigh. *Oh, alright then.* "Well," Perry said, his eyes sparkling. "The casting has been quite controversial, hasn't it, love?"

"Yes," Simon said simply, a slow smile spreading across his features.

10

A LITTLE LATER, THURSDAY 5 AUGUST

Perry suppressed a yawn as he shifted his weight on the uncomfortable white leather couch that was definitely more style over substance. His eyes darted between Simon and Ella. He looked down at his phone. Ten o'clock. *It feels so much later.* He longed to be back at Villa Mer with Bea, laughing over a bottle of wine rather than sitting here listening to Ella. It hadn't taken her long to lose interest in Perry's local theatre production, and she was now droning on about her latest film's release. She glanced at her watch for the tenth time without seeming to catch her breath. *She looks like she wants us to go. So stop talking then!*

Simon, bless him, was at least feigning attention, nodding along with an encouraging smile at Ella.

I should have insisted we leave when everyone else did. He stifled a sigh. He'd had enough.

Ella lifted her arm to look at her watch yet again, but this time, she waved a manicured hand. "Oh, is that the time? I hadn't realised it was so late. I—"

"We really should go!" Perry blurted out, putting his now empty glass firmly down on the table.

"Yes, of course," Ella said. "It's been swell having you—"

A blood-curdling scream shattered the night air.

Perry bolted upright, his heart pounding. "What was that?"

Simon was already on his feet, his ex-police officer's instincts kicking in. "It came from outside."

Without saying a word, Ella jumped up and dashed out of the room, surprisingly nimble in her high-heeled sandals.

Perry exchanged a worried glance with Simon before they both hurried after her. Swiftly moving along the corridor, they passed the main entrance and burst into the spacious living area on the other side of the villa. The space was lit up by the soft glow of the recessed lighting, the bifold doors flung wide open, the pool beyond them sparkling invitingly.

As Ella disappeared through them, Perry and Simon darted after her, heading towards a figure just visible by the side of the illuminated pool as they let out another heart-stopping shriek.

The cool night air sent a shiver down Perry's spine. As he got closer, he squinted, trying to make out who it was. *Lucy Harper?* She looked smaller than he remembered. *Yes. It was Lucy.* She was running along the side of the pool, her hands clutching a lifebuoy. She turned towards them and shrieked, "Help! Someone help!" Her voice was raw with panic as she threw the float into the water.

Ahead of him, Ella stopped next to her PA and peered into the water, her face a mask of horror.

Perry's gaze followed hers. His heart stopped as he spotted a figure wearing a bright Hawaiian shirt face-up in the water. Even in the dim light, he recognised the broad shoulders and salt-and-pepper hair. JT. The surrounding water was rapidly turning crimson.

Oh my giddy aunt! A twinge of guilt pricked at Perry's conscience. He'd known it'd been a bad idea for JT to go swimming when he'd been so clearly drunk. *Why didn't I stop him?*

Simon appeared beside him and frantically grabbed Perry's arm, his grip urgent. "Call an ambulance—now!" He yanked his shoes off and dived into the pool, landing to the right of JT's limp form on the bottom.

Perry fumbled for his phone, his muddled brain trying to recall the emergency services number for Portugal. *Think, Perry!* His fingers clumsily dialled one-one-two. He took a calming breath of air in through his nose, then relayed the situation to the dispatcher, grateful that the woman on the other end of the line spoke English.

As she took the details, Perry's gaze swept the poolside. Ella stood stock-still, her piercing blue eyes wide with shock, watching Simon's rescue mission as if hypnotised by the gruesome scene. Next to her, Lucy was clutching Ella's arm as she, too, stared into the pool, her free hand fluttering by her side.

"Someone will be there in two minutes, sir," the dispatcher reassured Perry.

"Two minutes!" Perry shouted to Simon, who had surfaced grasping JT under the arms and was now hauling him towards the pool edge. Perry made a move to help, but before he'd even registered the sound of footsteps echoing on the tiled patio, Derek Stone had appeared from nowhere. He leaned over the pool's edge, his powerful arms reaching out to aid Simon with JT's limp form.

"Oh God, oh God!" Perry looked across to see Nessa, her statuesque frame wrapped in a long silk robe, trembling as she took in the scene. "JT," she whimpered.

Derek and Simon heaved the movie producer's body onto

the concrete, then worked in grim silence in an attempt to get him breathing again. Perry averted his eyes, then turning around, he walked away from the pool. He knew with a sinking certainty that it was already too late.

Perry carried on moving forward foot by foot, eventually ending up on the grass slope that led to the path they'd used to get here on Tuesday. *What happened?* Had the fool dived in and cracked his head on the bottom? Or had he lost his balance and struck the edge? He slowly pivoted around, taking in the entire scene. And that was when he saw it. The four-foot-tall stone statue that had stood sentry over the pool now lay on its side, detached from its plinth. Had JT somehow collided with the statue in his drunken state? He hadn't heard the statue fall when they'd been at the party, but then, they'd been in the sitting room, which was over on the other side of the villa. *But surely it must have had something to do with JT's death...*

Perry slipped his phone from his pocket. Moving slowly so as not to attract any attention, he tapped on his camera app, then noiselessly snapped photos of the scene. *Just in case...*

By now, Nessa's sobs had taken on a hysterical edge, her slender frame shaking as she stood watching Simon's and Derek's efforts. Lucy appeared at the woman's side, murmuring soothing words, then led the ex-model away from JT's body and towards the villa.

Suddenly, Pearl emerged through the doors. She stopped and spoke briefly to Lucy, then with a cry, her dressing gown flapping behind her, she made a beeline for Ella, enfolding her sister in a comforting embrace. Ella clung to her, her usual poise shattered. "I think he's dead..." She buried her head into Pearl's shoulder.

Vehicles arriving on the driveway heralded the medics. They swarmed the scene, their movements efficient and practiced. But even as they worked, Perry saw the resignation in their eyes. Simon, having made way for them, looked up and caught Perry's gaze. He slowly shook his head as he made his way to join him, his wet clothes clinging to his stocky frame. "There was nothing we could do," he said sadly.

Perry reached out and took Simon's hand. "At least you tried, love. I'm proud of you."

The local police arrived. Perry watched as they conferred with the medics, their expressions grim.

"He took quite a hit to his head," Simon said, wrapping his arms around himself.

Perry pointed to the statue on the floor. "Do you think he might have knocked that over, and it caught him? He was completely pis—"

Lucy suddenly appeared, a stack of fluffy towels in her arms. "I've taken Nessa home," she said, her voice strained. "Poor thing's in shock." She held out a towel.

Perry took it, then draped it around Simon's vibrating shoulders. "Did you see what happened, Lucy?" he asked, keeping his tone casual.

She shook her head, blinking rapidly. "I… I'm not sure. It all happened so fast. There was a thud, then a splash, then… screaming?"

That was probably you! But before Perry could push her for more, she said, "I need to get a towel to Derek," and left them.

"We should probably get home," Perry said to Simon, who was gripping the towel around himself, a slightly glazed look on his face.

"Let's go!" Simon replied as he dragged the towel off, then balled it up and handed it to Perry.

Er…thanks…

He hurried off, leaving Perry frowning at the wet towel in

his hand. His energy was flagging now. He wanted to go—
Bea! He hadn't told his best friend yet. Dropping the towel on
the floor, he fished his phone out of his pocket, then rapidly
typed a text to her and pressed send.

Grabbing the towel from the floor, he hurried towards the
villa to deposit it inside. Doing so, he passed a police officer
who was talking to a damp-looking Derek Stone by the open
doors.

"...looks like he knocked into the statue," Derek was
saying. "It must've fell, hit him, and he tumbled into the
pool." He shook his head. "Terrible accident, I guess."

Perry sighed. He'd so desperately wanted the evening to
end. *But not like this...*

11

THE NEXT DAY. 9AM, FRIDAY 6 AUGUST

T*he Society Page* online article:

Is Another Royal Engagement Imminent as Lady Beatrice Holidays With Her Son And Boyfriend in Portugal?

The popular press is in full speculation mode this morning after it was confirmed that Lady Beatrice, the King's niece, is currently on holiday in Portugal with her sixteen-year-old son, Samuel Wiltshire, and a former Protection and Investigations (Royal) Services (PaIRS) officer, Richard Fitzwilliam. Although Lady Beatrice and Mr Fitzwilliam have been quietly dating for several months now, the move to go on holiday together, especially with her son is, according to The Daily Post, *'a sign that the seriousness of their relationship has been dialled up a notch'.*

. . .

Lady Beatrice, whose husband, James Wiltshire, the Earl of Rossex, was killed in a car crash six months before their son, Sam, was born, has not dated much since her husband's death. Last year, according to The Daily Post, *it was rumoured she was on the brink of an engagement to celebrity chef Sebastiano Marchetti, although this was strenuously denied by her at the time, with friends of the countess insisting that the couple had only been casually dating for a short while before Lady Beatrice had called it off.*

Divorcee Richard Fitzwilliam, whose wife is rumoured to have left him for another man, is an ex-army sergeant who previously worked for PaIRS, the organisation that protects the royal family. He has been involved in several high-profile investigations centred on Lady Beatrice and her family, including the death of Max Rhodes, the wealthy entrepreneur, and TV Chef Luca Mazza. He recently moved to a new role as a superintendent in City Police, leading the Capital Security Liaison team in a move that The Daily Post *suggests was made to enable him and Lady Beatrice 'to take their relationship to the next level'.*

The Daily Post *has also revealed that the couple are staying at a villa belonging to Lady Grace Willoughby-Franklin, wife of TV heavyweight Sir Hewitt, in Portugal, next door to the American actress Ella St Gerome and her family, who are reported to be in residence at this time, resulting in a swarm of paparazzi descending on the villa complex like proverbial locusts.*

12

A FEW MINUTES EARLIER, FRIDAY 6 AUGUST

"I'm just saying, it's asking for trouble leaving a top-heavy statue right next to a pool like that," Rich said, gesturing emphatically with a piece of toast. "It was an accident waiting to happen if you ask me."

The morning sun glinted off the polished marble terrace of Villa Mer as Bea sipped her coffee, relishing the moment of peace before the boys came down. Rich, Perry, and Simon were continuing their dissection of last night's unfortunate events.

As soon as Perry's text had landed, Bea and Rich had bundled the boys upstairs to the games room with drinks, snacks, and the promise of an hour of uninterrupted gaming time before bed. Shortly after, as Rich was opening a fresh bottle of wine, Perry and Simon had burst into the villa, and Perry had excitedly told them of JT's accident and all the tense conversations and sneaking around that had gone on beforehand. At one point, when he'd been recounting how he'd been caught by Maria in the hallway and had had to pretend he'd needed the bathroom, Bea had almost wished she'd gone to the drinks party just to have seen his face when he'd got trapped in the bathroom while JT had argued with Nessa and then Peter. Finally, much to Rich's and Simon's horror, Perry had then shared with them the photos he'd taken of the aftermath of JT's drowning. Bea agreed with Rich—a statue that close to the poolside was asking for trouble.

"Hmm," Simon responded to Rich, stroking his short beard thoughtfully. "I might have to borrow this setup for my next book. If I worked out a way for a killer to make a statue fall on someone like that, it would make a good murder method."

Bea's heart jumped. "You don't think—"

Simon put his hand up and laughed. "No, of course not, Bea."

"If you'd seen the state he was in, you can imagine him knocking into it. Even if he was conscious when he fell, he was probably too drunk to do anything about it once he hit the water," Perry added as his phone beeped.

Bea imagined how Ella was feeling today. In shock. In denial. Nothing prepared you for losing your partner in life, as she well knew. *But*, Bea thought, *at least she has her family and friends with her.* Bea knew at some point she would need to go over to Villa Sol to express her condolences but not today. Ella needed time to come to terms with what had happened.

Bea's gaze wandered to the lush landscape beyond the villa. What they needed was to get away from here for the day. "It would be lovely to explore some of the local sights today," she said, already imagining the quaint villages and hidden coves. "Do you think we could organise—"

A strangled noise from Perry snapped her attention back to him. His face had gone ashen.

Bea's stomach dropped. "Perry?" Bea asked, concern creeping into her voice. "What's wrong?"

Before he was able to answer, Sam and Archie burst onto the terrace, Daisy galloping behind them, both boys breathless and wide-eyed. "Mum!" Sam cried, his voice cracking with urgency. "There's something you should see."

Archie thrust his iPad towards Bea. "You should read this, Lady B," he blurted, his words tumbling out in a chaotic rush.

Perry cleared his throat. "I was about to tell you," he said petulantly. "There's an article... about you and Rich." He turned his phone towards Simon and Rich, who huddled around the small screen.

Bea's heart raced as she took the iPad from Archie. What on earth had got everyone so worked up? She steeled herself and read the *TSP* article published a few minutes ago.

Oh my goodness! Nausea washed over her as she read. Rich's wife had left him, and now the entire world knew. The words blurred before her eyes, each comment from *The Daily Post* a fresh blow. This was her worst fear realised. Her body tensed. Why hadn't her mother warned her? The advantage of your mother secretly owning *TSP*, as well as the princess's ability to correct any falsehood made against the family and promote Francis Court, was that she was an early-warning system for anything major that was about to drop in the press. Bea glared down at the table, looking for her phone. *Rats!* She remembered she'd left it upstairs by the side of the bed. *Sorry, Ma!* No doubt her mother had tried to contact her to let her know what was happening.

She sighed and closed her eyes for a second. As her hand dropped to her side, a wet nose nudged it. *Ah, Daisy.* Bea leaned down and picked the little dog up, holding her close. She couldn't bring herself to look at Rich, certain she'd see anger etched across his face. *It's all my fault. I've dragged him into the media circus that's my life, and now...*

Suddenly, she felt the warm pressure of his hand on her

back, gently rubbing circles. Surprised, she glanced up to find Rich smiling at her, concern etched on his face. "Are you alright?"

Me? She blinked, confused. "I... I'm so sorry, Rich. I never meant for..."

Rich winked, a mischievous glint in his eye. "Don't be silly. I was feeling rather left out."

"What?" she sputtered. *Has he gone mad?*

"Well, you know. Simon's a celebrity chef and crime writer. Perry will no doubt soon be the talk of Windstanton after his portrayal of Algernon. You and Sam are members of the royal family. All I've been until now is your boyfriend. But now I'm famous too in my own right..."

Bea lowered Daisy back to the floor, then stared at him incredulously. *He is mad.* Absolutely barking.

"I'm hoping my agent will get *that* call soon," he continued.

Agent? What is he talking about?

"I've always fancied a shot at *Strictly Come Dancing*. Have you seen the way I can move my—" He stood and shook his hips, but he couldn't keep a straight face any longer, and he burst out laughing.

She looked around at the others. Archie and Sam were bent over, holding their stomachs. Simon was wiping tears from his eyes, and Perry let out a snort.

She shook her head. *This isn't funny. The press won't leave it there...* But as laughter filled the room, a twitch tugged at the corner of her mouth, and she grinned. *They're all mad!*

Woof! Daisy ran off to greet the young girl who was stepping through the open doors of the villa. "What the—" Isla cried, her hands on her hips, a frown creasing her forehead as she stood in her pyjamas on the terrace, her eyes wide. She was looking from Perry to Simon and back, then her eyes met Bea's. She rushed over, a bewildered look still on her face. "I've just read the news," she said, stopping in front of Bea. Looking around the table, she added, "I wasn't expecting this... er, have you read it?" She adjusted the sleeve of her top.

Bea took her hand. "Don't worry. We've read it. As you can see" —she gestured towards the others, who were in the process of pulling themselves together— "it seems to have tickled some funny bones here."

"I don't care what they say about me," Rich said, wiping his eyes. "But I'm not so happy that they know where we are." His expression grew serious. "I've a horrible feeling it's going to curtail our plans to get off-site today if the press has arrived in force." His hand slipped around her shoulders, and he pulled her to him. "I'm so sorry, Bea. I know this is the last thing you wanted while we were here." He gently kissed her temple.

"I'm upset they found out you're here, Bea," Simon said as he took a large gulp of tea. "How on earth did that happen?"

Isla shifted uncomfortably. "I think it was Chloe, Dad. I've looked at her Instagram. She posted about the party last night, and even though she covered your faces, she kind of hinted there were 'royal guests'..."

Perry blurted out, "How dare she!"

Isla turned to Bea. "I'm so sorry, Bea. I didn't know, and I'm furious with her. I was really clear when we met her on the beach that she wasn't to post anything about you or Sam, and I—"

Bea reached out and took Isla's hand. She squeezed her fingers gently. "It's okay, Isla. It was never realistic to think that it wouldn't get out eventually, especially with so many others here at Marisol. It's not your fault, okay?"

Isla gave a weak smile and gave a brief dip of her chin.

"Is there any mention of JT's death?" Bea asked, surprised that it wasn't a headline in its own right. After all, he and Ella were huge names in America.

Simon's brow creased. "No. That news doesn't seem to have hit the papers yet."

"Chloe hasn't posted anything since about nine last night," Isla added.

Rich stood, pulling out his phone. "They must have decided to keep a lid on it until they're ready with a statement about the accident. But it can only be a matter of time, and then we'll be getting even more attention here. I'd better check in with security."

He stepped away, Daisy by his side. With his mobile to his ear, he spoke in a hushed tone. Bea strained to hear what was being said. "Extra personnel? How many... I see."

Rats!

Perry leaned towards her, his blue eyes full of concern. "You okay?" he asked.

"I'm fine," she lied, forcing a smile as her eyes shifted to Sam and Archie, who were helping themselves to toast. She didn't want them to worry about any of this. Her stomach fluttered.

Rich returned and shot Bea a rueful smile. "I'm afraid the press has set up camp outside the gates. But don't worry, security is on it. They've drafted in reinforcements."

Bea's heart sank, her plans of a carefree day of sight-seeing crumbling before her eyes. Her chest tightened. *Poor Ella.* She'd just lost her husband and now Bea had brought the press to her door!

"I think we all need to be prepared that we'll have to remain here at the villa for the moment," Simon said.

Sam and Archie exchanged glances. "Um, can we still go to the beach?" Sam asked hesitantly.

Bea's mouth went dry. "I don't know, darling. The press might be watching there too…" Her eyes prickled. *Have I ruined Sam's and Archie's holiday too?*

"There's no access, remember," Rich said, rubbing her back. "But why don't we take the boys to be on the safe side?" Rich offered, gesturing to Simon.

"I'm in," Simon said, rising. "We'll keep an eye out for any paparazzi lurking in the sand dunes."

What? Bea shivered involuntarily. Rich whispered in her ear, "He's kidding. They'll be fine."

Everyone's a comedian today! she thought, but her shoulders relaxed. Rich and Simon would keep the boys safe.

Perry clapped his hands together. "Looks like it's you, me, and Isla. Poolside chilling and margaritas anyone?"

Bea managed a half-hearted smile, while Isla giggled and went off to change into her swimming costume.

Bea puffed out her cheeks. There was nothing to be done. They would simply have to make the most of it, but Bea couldn't shake the feeling that this media scrutiny was going to put a serious damper on their holiday. *So much for a relaxing getaway… And,* she added to herself, *once news about JT's accident gets out, the press will* really *have a field day…*

13

THE NEXT DAY. 10:30AM, SATURDAY 7 AUGUST

T*he Society Page* online article:

BREAKING NEWS Woman Taken in For Questioning as Local Police Say JT Kenda's Death Was Murder

Police in Portugal this morning told reporters that a woman is being questioned in connection with the murder of the film producer Jason 'JT' Kenda, the husband of actress Ariella St Gerome.

Mr Kenda, who was found dead in the swimming pool of the villa he and his award-winning wife own in Portugal on Thursday evening, was initially thought to have died following an accident, but now police state that evidence found at the scene combined with the results of the post-

mortem have led them to believe the American was killed intentionally. No further details are available at this time.

Villa Sol, where Ella St Gerome and her husband have spent their summers for the last seven years, is part of an exclusive estate of three villas that includes the villa where Lady Beatrice, her son, Sam, and her boyfriend, Richard Fitzwilliam, are currently on holiday. It is not known if the King's niece knew the victim or not.

———

The sun-drenched terrace of Villa Mer sparkled like a jewel, but Bea couldn't ignore the listlessness that hung over their little group.

She nursed her coffee, savouring the bitter taste as she glanced at the others around the table. Perry fidgeted with his phone, his eyes darting across the screen as he scrolled. Simon appeared to be reading a manuscript, a pen poised in his hand, but his eyes weren't moving. Rich, with Daisy curled up on his lap, was hunched over a steaming mug and staring at the distant sea, seemingly lost in thought.

Bea gave a wry smile. *I'm sure there are worse things than being stuck in a beautiful villa overlooking the Atlantic...* But knowing they weren't able to leave because of the marauding gaggle of press outside Marisol made her *want* to leave that much more. Her gaze drifted to the pool, where Sam and Archie were engaged in what appeared to be an energetic splash war. Their laughter filled the air, a welcome respite from the despondency she felt. *At least they're having fun...*

Beep! Perry's phone interrupted the conversation. He glanced down, his eyes widening. "Oh my goodness."

Bea's heart dropped to her feet. *What now?* More sordid speculation about her and Rich? She braced herself for the worst as her own phone pinged. She swallowed and held it up. A message from her mother popped up.

Ma: *Darling, why didn't you tell me JT was murdered? It's about to break.*

Murdered? Her blood ran cold. She stared at the screen, her brain struggling to process. She looked up to tell the others, but Perry beat her to it.

"JT was murdered!" he declared, his eyes dancing with excitement.

"What?" Simon nearly choked on his coffee.

"It's all over the news," Perry added.

Bea tore her eyes away from her mother's text, her mind spinning. "But everyone said it was an accident!"

Rich leaned forward, shifting Daisy, his face grim. "What else does it say, Perry?"

They all studied Perry as he scanned the article he was reading. "According to *TSP*, a woman's been taken in for questioning—"

Who? Is it someone from the villas?

"But they're not releasing any details yet," Perry continued. "Oh, and there's also mention of the postmortem leading them to believe it's murder."

Just then Isla burst onto the terrace, her red hair flying wildly behind her as Daisy launched herself at the newcomer.

"Er, I think something's wrong. I went into the kitchen to get some juice, and Ana is in there crying her eyes out."

Without a word, the four adults sprang up. "Can you stay and keep an eye on the boys and Daisy, please, Isla?" Bea called over her shoulder as they hurried towards the open doors that led into the villa. Her mind raced. A woman being questioned about JT's murder. Ana in tears. *Are they connected?*

———

As they entered Villa Mer's sprawling kitchen, sunlight poured through the windows, illuminating gleaming stainless-steel appliances and pristine marble countertops. Bea's gaze was immediately drawn to Ana, who sat hunched on a sleek bar stool, her shoulders shaking with sobs. Her son, Enzo, stood beside her, his arm draped protectively around her trembling form.

"Ana, what's happened?" Bea asked, rushing over to the distraught housekeeper.

Ana lifted her head, tears streaking her olive skin. She opened her mouth, but no words came out. A fresh wave of sobs racked her body.

Enzo looked up, his dark eyes filled with anguish. "It's my sister, Maria," he said in a shaky voice. "They've taken her to the police station, something to do with Mr Kenda's death."

A collective gasp echoed through the kitchen. Bea felt as if the floor had suddenly tilted beneath her feet. *Maria? No, that can't be right...*

"What?" Perry looked as stunned as Bea felt. "There must be some mistake."

Ana shook her head vehemently. "*A policia*, they come...

They take her away... Maria would never hurt anyone," Ana choked out between tears. "*Ela é uma menina boa. I raised her right.*"

Rich drew near, addressing her son. "Enzo, do you know why the police think Maria had something to do with it?"

Enzo answered, his jaw tight, "*Minha garota...* my girl-friend... Matilde, she works at the station. She said they found a necklace in the pool. The necklace Maria was accused of stealing by Mr Kenda."

Bea's brow furrowed. *Hadn't Ana mentioned that before?*

"They think Maria and Mr Kenda argued about the neck-lace," Enzo continued. "That she... she pushed him into that statue and then ran away."

"They think she killed him?" Perry asked, astounded.

Enzo raised his eyebrows in silent agreement as Ana gave another loud sob.

Simon shook his head. "It sounds circumstantial at best. An argument, a necklace... hardly concrete proof that she intended to hurt him."

Bea turned to Rich, a spark of hope flaring in her chest. "Rich, is there anything you can do to find out what's going on?" Would his position as a senior British police officer allow him access to the team investigating JT's murder?

He met her gaze and gave her a brief smile. "I'll see what I can do." He pulled out his phone as he made his way across the room.

Grateful for his level-headedness, Bea tried to get her own emotions in check. She glanced over at poor Ana, who now had her head in her hands. *Is her daughter a murderer?* Her mother and brother clearly didn't think so.

But someone *had* killed JT, according to the police. So if Maria hadn't done it... then who had?

14

HALF AN HOUR LATER, SATURDAY 7 AUGUST

"**D**o you think they got through the press alright?" Bea asked Perry as she took the last of the forks and spoons from the dishwasher, and walked across the large kitchen at Villa Mer, and deposited them into the cutlery drawer. The police had been reluctant to say anything to Rich on the phone earlier, so he and Simon had gone to the station in person to try again. Rich had said he hoped once they saw his ID and realised he was a senior British police officer, it might convince them to talk. *I hope he's right. Maria must be frightened, and her poor family is so worried.*

After Rich and Simon had left, Bea had insisted that Enzo take the distraught Ana home, reminding them that Rich had promised to update them as soon as he learned anything more about Maria. Ana had been reluctant to leave, worried that there were the remains of breakfast to clear up and lunch and dinner to prepare. Bea had reassured her that they were able to look after themselves for the rest of the day.

Perry, wiping the surface down, shrugged. "Well, they haven't come back, so I guess they made it through. Maybe we'll read about it in the papers." He put down the cloth, and taking a theatrical stance, he raised his hands in the air and then spread them like he was revealing a banner. "Celebrity Chef and Royal Niece's Lover Leave Villa on Secret Mission," he proclaimed in a voice-over type manner.

The corners of Bea's mouth tugged into a grin. It sounded exactly like the sort of headline *The Daily Post* would come up with.

"Come on," Perry said, gathering the cloth up and returning it to the sink. "Let's see what the youngsters are up to. I think I might even have a swim while we wait."

Grabbing a couple of bottles of water, Bea followed him out of the room. She wasn't in the mood to swim, but she hoped the warm sun on her face would calm her nerves as they waited for Rich and Simon to return.

Twenty minutes later, she was sitting in a chair on the terrace, her eyes closed as she let the morning heat wash over her. Her limbs were loose, and a sense of calm languidly flowed through her veins. *Buzz!* She nearly jumped out of her skin as her phone rang on the table beside her.

Daisy, who had been happily snoozing under the table, sprang up as Bea glanced at the screen. Her heart sank. "It's Lady Grace," she said to Perry, who sat at the other side of the table to her, drying himself with a towel.

A call from Lady Grace was a bit like a call from her mother—Bea was either in trouble, was going to be given some unwelcome advice (which would irritatingly turn out to be good advice), or it would involve a request (no, not a request... a demand) to do something she wouldn't want to do!

"Go on then, answer it!" Perry urged, gesturing frantically.

Daisy gave a sigh and lowered herself onto the floor again

as Bea took a deep breath, then swiped to accept the call. "Lady Grace, what a pleasant surprise."

"Beatrice." The older woman's crisp voice crackled in Bea's ear. "I'll get straight to the point—"

Don't you always?

"I hear poor Maria's in trouble with the police. I've known the girl since she was a baby, and I can tell you now she's innocent of whatever they think she's done. I want you and that policeman chap of yours to investigate this dreadful business with the American who was killed next door and clear her name."

Investigate? Bea's stomach dropped, and she licked her lips. It was one thing to get involved in an investigation back home, but this was different. They were in another country with different laws. And on top of that, they barely knew the victim.

"I… I'm not sure we're the best people for the job—"

"Nonsense." Lady Grace sniffed. "You and your friends have a knack for these things. And what's the point of being courted by a senior detective, Beatrice, if you can't pull a few strings when you need to?"

That's hardly the reason I'm dating him!

"I know you're there to have a holiday, but events have overtaken that now, and it's not as if you'll be going anywhere, what with the press swarming like vultures outside Marisol."

She's right, but… Bea bit her lip, her mind racing. She needed time to think and talk to Rich. "I'm sorry, Lady Grace, but it's a… terrible… reception…" she said, slowly, raising her voice slightly. "I'll have… to… call you… back." She swiftly stabbed at the red end call icon, then blew air through her lips as she returned the phone to the table, placing it down carefully, as if it were an unexploded bomb.

She turned to Perry, her eyes wide. "She wants us to investigate JT's death..." she whispered, as if by not saying it too loud, she could pretend it wasn't really a thing.

"She does?" Perry asked, his blue eyes dancing.

"Well, she wants us to prove Maria didn't kill him, so it's the same thing."

Perry leaned forward, his expression serious. "Then I think we should do it. First, I wouldn't want to be the one to say no to Lady Grace, would you?" He gave an involuntary quiver, no doubt remembering when they'd investigated the murder at Fawstead Manor, Lady Grace's country home in Fenshire. She was a force to be reckoned with. "And second, we don't think Maria did it, so that means the killer is most likely someone on this estate."

It was Bea's turn to shudder as she looked over towards the pool, where Sam and Archie were engaged in another raucous water fight while Isla sat sketching on a lounger, wisps of ginger hair escaping her messy bun. Bea's blood ran cold. A killer on the loose meant they could be in danger.

"And finally, we're rather stuck here now thanks to the press, so we may as well do something useful with our time."

Bea sighed, knowing he was right. "I'll need to talk to Rich and Simon, of course, but I think you're right." Still watching Sam, Archie, and Isla, she added, "It won't feel safe here until we've caught whoever killed JT."

———

As Rich and Simon strolled onto the terrace fifteen minutes later, Daisy ran up to greet them, her tail wagging. As each man took it in turns to bend down and ruffle the little white dog's wiry head, one look at their faces told Bea that their 'secret mission' had been unsuccessful.

"As we suspected, the press outside Marisol has doubled now that they know JT was murdered. It took us ten minutes to drive through them all to get back inside," Simon said, dropping into a chair with a huff.

Bea rubbed her forehead. *Why can't they go away and leave us alone?*

"Security is doing a good job in the circumstances, but if more press arrive, then the police will have to send reinforcements," Rich added as he grabbed a bottle of water from the table.

"So how did you get on?" Perry asked, dropping his wet towel on the floor.

"The police chief was polite, but he didn't tell us much. He wouldn't even confirm it's Maria Rodrigues they're holding there for questioning," Simon said.

Rich shrugged. "And unless I'm there in some official capacity, there's nothing more to say, apparently." He threw himself into a chair and took a large gulp of water as Daisy jumped into his lap.

Bea winced. "Did you find out what was in the autopsy or what supports their theory that it was murder?"

"No," Rich said, shaking his head. "They wouldn't say. However, they emphasised that the person they're questioning hasn't been arrested yet."

"So they're not one hundred percent sure that Maria killed JT?" Bea asked.

"It would seem that way."

So she and Perry were right to be concerned. There was a murderer somewhere in Marisol. With a heavy feeling in her stomach, she now knew they would need to get involved whether she wanted to or not. "Lady Grace called," she said, watching Rich's reaction. He cast her a dubious glance. "She's concerned about Maria."

He rubbed his chin. "She *is* her housekeeper's daughter, so…"

"Exactly. She says Maria is innocent and that we need to help her. She's asking us to intervene."

"Intervene?" Simon said, frowning. "What does she think we can do? As we've proven today, the local police aren't open to share—"

"She means investigate who killed JT, love," Perry said, patting his arm. "And I, for one, don't want to say no to her." He gave his husband a look. Simon acknowledged him with a flicker of understanding in his eyes.

Rich's eyes sparkled with interest. "If we say yes, do you think that will get me in her good books?"

Bea tilted her head back with a groan. She knew Rich was convinced that Lady Grace didn't approve of their relationship, even though that belief was based purely on how she'd dealt with him when he'd still been with PaIRS and sent to investigate the death of a visitor at her country retreat, the same case Bea and Perry had become embroiled in while working at Lady's Grace's house. Bea suppressed a smile when she recalled how Lady Grace had thrown Rich and his team off-site at Fawstead Manor and had appointed Bea to liaise with PaIRS on her behalf. Rich had *not* been happy.

"Bea?" Rich regarded her with a quizzical look.

"Oh, yes… sorry. I think, in the circumstances, Lady Grace's request notwithstanding, while there's potentially a killer here in the complex, then I want to do everything I can to protect Sam, Archie, and Isla. So, yes, I agree, we should do it." *I hope I'm not going to regret this…*

Perry gave a low, "Whoop!" that caused Daisy to jump down off Rich's lap and run to him to see what the excitement was. Seeing the look on Bea's face, Perry straightened his features and said, "So what do we do first?"

Rich ran a hand through his hair, his brow furrowed. "Due to the possible danger to Bea and Sam, PaIRS will probably want to get involved. I'll reach out to my old boss and see if he can smooth things over with the local police, allowing me to investigate officially on behalf of PaIRS."

Is that likely? Rich no longer worked for PaIRS. Surely, they would want their own people here. Bea bit her lip, a sudden thought occurring to her. "What if Nigel says no? Will they send—"

Rich put up his hand. "Let's not worry about that at the moment," he said as he rose. "I'll call him now and see what I can do." He took out his phone. Giving Bea a reassuring smile, he stepped away.

Bea twisted the rings on her right hand; the sunlight danced off the vibrant green emeralds framed by sparkling diamonds. Rich could ask by all means, but she wasn't as hopeful as he that his old boss would agree to him getting involved in JT's murder investigation. After all, Rich had left PaIRS because it was inappropriate for him to be officially involved in her protection once they were in a relationship. That hadn't changed. And with the added scrutiny of the press now camped out at the gates, surely Nigel wouldn't risk putting PaIRS in such a compromising position, would he?

Her chest tightened.

No. She had to be prepared that not only would he say no to Rich but that he might send one of her least favourite people over to head up the investigation...

15

TEN MINUTES LATER, SATURDAY 7 AUGUST

Bea's fingers tapped an impatient rhythm on the table by her side, her gaze flitting between the villa's gaping bifold doors and the cloudless azure sky. Fifteen minutes had crawled by since Rich had disappeared into the house. *Is it a good sign that it's taking so long? No is a quick word...*

Simon had gone back to his manuscript, but he didn't seem to be paying much attention as he stared at the same page, not moving. Underneath his chair, Daisy was curled up in the shade, gently snoring.

Next to him, Perry, his eyes narrowed against the sun, was chewing on the end of his sunglasses, peering out to sea. His stomach suddenly rumbled loud enough for her and Simon to hear. Bea looked down at her watch. It was lunchtime, and she'd forgotten that Ana wasn't here.

"I'll whip up some lunch as soon as Rich gets back." Simon looked over to her with a smile.

Lifesaver! Bea smiled at him gratefully. Neither she or Perry was a 'whipping up lunch' type of person. Her attention then strayed to the swimming pool, where Sam and Archie had abandoned their aquatic fun and were now sprawled on the sun loungers, glued to their phones. She narrowed her eyes. "I hope you've put more sunscreen on!" she called out, receiving a mumbled, "Yes, Mum!" in return.

"Should we start a bet on how many shades of red Archie will be by the end of the day?" Perry said, nodding at the boys with a wry smile.

"Oh, don't..." Bea trailed off. She didn't want to return Archie to his parents the colour of a ripe tomato. She scrambled up and walked over to them. "It's almost lunchtime," she said as she got closer. The mention of food got their interest. "Why don't you both get cleaned up? By the time you're done, Simon will have some sandwiches." *Will Simon make sandwiches? Burgers? Or maybe a big hearty salad?* "Or... well, something for lunch. Alright?"

The boys leapt to their feet, and grabbing their stuff, they ran off towards the house. As they crossed the terrace, Daisy woke up, gave an excited *yap,* and ran after them into the villa.

Isla ambled over to join Bea, her wispy sundress fluttering in the warm breeze. "Did someone say lunch?" she asked hopefully.

"Yes, your dad is going to rustle something up as soon as Rich is back," Bea told her as they ambled back to the terrace.

"I'll help if you want, Dad?" Isla offered as she stopped by Simon.

Giving up the pretence of working, Simon placed his papers under the chair and smiled up at his daughter. "That'll be great," he said as she sat down next to him, and they began to discuss lunch options.

"I hope Rich is not much longer," Perry muttered to Bea with a sigh. "I'm so hungry, I could eat a—"

Rich's silhouette materialised through the open doors. Bea knew instantly it was bad news. His shoulders drooped in defeat, and he strode slowly towards them with a heaviness that spoke volumes of his disappointment.

He sighed heavily as he sat down next to Bea. She reached out and took his hand. "Are you okay?"

"Sorry it took so long. I was on hold while he finished a meeting. He said no." Rich grimaced. "I tried, but apparently, someone from PaIRS is already on their way to take over the investigation."

Her breath caught in her throat. *Oh no, not...*

Perry's eyes widened, a look of horror crossing his face. "Not Hayden Saunders!"

Bea failed to disguise a groan. That was what she'd been dreading. Memories of their last encounter with the abrasive detective chief inspector came flooding back. He'd been the one PaIRS had sent during a high-profile investigation into the death of a famous TV baker.

Rich shrugged. "He didn't say, but..." His voice trailed off. It was clear he feared the worst.

Bea gave his hand a gentle squeeze. There was no love lost between Rich and Saunders, especially when Rich had, with their help, found the killer of the Queen of Bakes before he had.

They sat in silence for a few seconds, then the sound of Sam's and Archie's carefree laughter floated out of the villa. Bea gripped Rich's hand. She would do whatever it took to keep the boys safe. To keep all of them safe. Even if it meant facing off against Detective Chief Inspector Hayden Saunders again.

She looked up, meeting Rich's eyes. "We're not giving up. Saunders or no Saunders. We'll just have to work around him, do our own investigation."

Rich's lips twitched in a faint smile. "There's my girl!"

Bea's heart soared. They would all work together to get to the bottom of this murder like they'd done in the past.

16

THAT AFTERNOON, SATURDAY 7
AUGUST

T*he Daily Post* online article:

EXCLUSIVE! An Unromantic Workaholic Who Thinks That Everyone Lies: Richard Fitzwilliam's Ex-Wife Tells Us Why She Wishes Lady Beatrice Good Luck

Amber Moss, formerly Amber Fitzwilliam, sits on a wicker chair in Amber Sands, the beachside bar cum cafe she owns and runs with her husband, Dave. Tanned and petite, Richard Fitzwilliam's ex-wife looks much younger than her forty-five years. She puts this down to the relaxing life she and Dave have made for themselves here on Spain's Costa Del Sol since they left England fifteen years ago.

The petite blonde explains: "It's beautiful here, a little slice of paradise, and I never get tired of watching the sun setting over the water. Most tourists don't surface until after lunch, so we get the mornings to ourselves. We spend the day serving beer, cocktails, and tapas to beachgoers. By evening, the place is buzzing with tourists, and we don't close until the last partygoers have had their fill—usually around 2 a.m."

When asked if she misses her life in Surrey, Amber laughs. "What is there to miss? The cold and wet? The long hours? As a sergeant in City Police, my team was under-resourced and run ragged. It was so stressful. No. I don't miss it at all."

So what went wrong with her marriage to Richard Fitzwilliam, the superintendent in City Police who is now dating the King's niece? "Where to start!" she jokes, then frowns. "When we first met, we were both young, ambitious police officers. Rich had left the army, and the police was a natural fit for him. I'd been to university and was looking for a stable career where I could make a difference."

She sighs. "He was funny, and we laughed a lot in those early days. But after a while, I wanted more. I wanted a life outside of work with sociable hours so I could see my friends. I even wanted to start a family. But for Rich, it was always about his next promotion. When he got the move to PaIRS (Protection and Investigation (Royal) Services, the organisation that protects the royal family), it got worse. He started in the intelligence wing, but when a move to investigations came along, even though he'd never liked that side of things —he thinks everyone lies to the police— he took it because it was good for his career. After that, work became all-consuming for him. It was all he cared about."

She hesitates and takes a drink of lemonade. "I tried, I really did. I was worried we were growing apart, so as a last-ditch attempt to save our marriage, I organised a romantic getaway in a cottage on the coast." She gives a small shrug. "But at the last minute, Rich cancelled because of work. It wasn't the first time, and I knew it wouldn't be the last. It was clear his job mattered more than we did. That was it for me. We struggled on for a short while after that, but it was too late…"

How does she feel about the rumours that her ex-husband

and Lady Beatrice will soon announce their engagement? "I'm pleased for them," she says. "Things might not have worked out for me and Rich back then." She pauses and looks out to the ocean, a faraway look in her eyes, then she turns and smiles. "But then Dave and I came out here, and I couldn't be happier. I wish Rich and Lady Beatrice all the best for the future."

17

LATER THAT AFTERNOON, SATURDAY 7 AUGUST

The afternoon sun shimmered off the turquoise water, a blinding contrast to the whitewashed walls of Villa Mer. Bougainvillea cascaded in a riot of magenta, its perfume mingling with the salty sea breeze. Bea flipped aimlessly through a glossy magazine, her mind churning with unease.

Across from her, Perry scrolled through his phone, his brow furrowed. "Oh, I never knew that," he muttered, shaking his head. *What's he reading?* It was the second time he'd made a similar comment under his breath.

Bea huffed, tossing the magazine aside. *How much longer will he be?* Rich had been summoned to the security gate to greet the PaIRS contingent. Was Rich there now, trying to convince DCI Hayden Saunders to let them help? She would've been better off going with Simon and the boys to the beach rather than sitting here fretting over it all.

"Do you really think Saunders will let us help?" she asked Perry, worrying her lip with her teeth.

Perry glanced up, an impish glint in his eye. "After last time? I doubt it." *He's right.* Saunders had been furious over their interference in his investigation to find the killer of the popular judge of *Bake Off Wars*, Vera Bolt, earlier this year. "I think we should have started without waiting for him to tell us to keep our noses out," Perry added.

She drummed her fingers on the tabletop by her side. Again, she didn't disagree with Perry. She already had a plan to request Ana's son, Enzo, to ask his girlfriend, who worked at the local police station, to dig up a copy of the autopsy report on JT. But... "We promised Rich we'd wait. So we'll just have to be patient."

Perry huffed, took a sip of his piña colada, and went back to his phone.

Bea leaned over the table to scoop up her bucks fizz at the same time as Isla sauntered onto the terrace with Daisy in her arms.

"Daisy is bored," Isla announced as she handed the little white dog to Bea with a sigh.

Bea suppressed a grin. *Really, it's Daisy who's bored is it?* She placed Daisy under the umbrella next to her and gave her a quick fuss, relieved to feel that she was still cool to the touch. The terrier licked her hand. "Alright, you can stay out here for a little while, but then you're going inside where it's cooler for you, Daisy-doo," Bea said to her.

Isla plopped down beside Perry and eyed him curiously. "Watcha reading?"

Perry glanced up, turning his phone over as he shrugged noncommittally. "Oh, nothing much."

Bea watched the exchange, sensing Perry's evasiveness. Isla seemed unperturbed, stretching languidly. "So did Ana's daughter *really* kill JT?"

Perry's brow's shot up. "We don't know. But it's nothing for you to worry about."

Aw, he's so protective of her...

"You say that, Perry. But if JT was murdered, and it

wasn't Maria that killed him, then it could be someone here at Marisol. Are you going to investigate?"

Bea smiled. Isla was nobody's fool.

"Well, er," Perry spluttered. "We're waiting to see who PaIRS send to oversee it, then—"

Isla's eyes widened. "It's not going to be that rude man from last time, is it?"

"We hope not," Perry replied, rubbing his hand over his forehead.

"Because if it is, you'll definitely have to get involved. He was rubbish."

Bea smirked. She had to agree with Isla's blunt assessment. DCI Hayden Saunders was inexperienced with investigating murders but too big-headed to admit it and ask for help. Her tummy fluttered. *Please don't let them have sent Saunders.*

"So if you do have to investigate, I want to help."

She rose at the same time as Perry's eyebrows. "I'm not sure your dad will—"

"Then you'll have to persuade him, won't you?" she replied with a cheeky grin. "I'm gonna go and join the boys at the beach."

"Er, hold on," Perry said, shifting in his seat. "I'm not sure that he will—"

"Oh, Perry," she said, leaning in and kissing his cheek. "Don't underestimate your charm. He's putty in your hands." She peeped over Perry's head and winked at Bea, then waved goodbye as she headed across the grass towards the break in the bushes that led down through the sand dunes and to the beach below.

Bea laughed as Perry fumbled for words. "I'm not sure... I mean... He might not..." He turned to Bea. "What do I do now?"

Bea shrugged. "Hope they send someone who will find the killer without us?"

Perry rolled his eyes, then with a sigh, he went back to reading from his phone.

What's he reading that's such a secret? Bea cleared her throat. Perry looked up expectantly. "Come on then. What's so secret that you didn't want Isla to see what you were reading?" she asked him.

"It's nothing, really." Perry fidgeted under her intense gaze.

I don't believe you...

"Perry..." Bea's tone held a warning as she lowered her sunglasses and peered over them at him.

Perry bit his lip and raised an eyebrow. "Are you *really* sure you want to know?"

Bea's mouth went dry. She had a bad feeling that perhaps she didn't. "Is it about me and Rich?"

He dipped his chin.

Bea sipped her drink. "How bad is it?"

Perry sighed. "This is exactly why you don't look at the press, Bea."

That bad? Her hand reached out and rested gently on Daisy's furry body.

"In fairness, it's mostly speculation about the two of you getting engaged." He gave her a wry smile. "There's even talk of you and Fred having a joint wedding."

Really? She breathed in through her nose. *That's ridiculous.* She met his gaze and sensed he was holding something back. "And the rest?"

"Er... *The Daily Post* has interviewed Amber, Rich's ex."

What?! Heat rose up Bea's neck, stinging her cheeks. *How did they even find Amber?* She was somewhere in Spain running a bar, according to Rich.

Her shoulders tensed. "Is it awful?"

"Not really. She even wishes you both well at the end…"

That's jolly nice of her! Bea blinked. *What exactly had Amber said about her relationship with Rich?* "Read it to me," she said, surprising herself.

"Are you sure?"

No. But I need to know now… "Yes, please."

"Okay." Perry had a mouthful of his cocktail and cleared his throat. *"Amber Moss, formerly Amber Fitzwilliam, sits on a wicker chair in Amber Sands, the beachside bar cum cafe she owns and runs with her husband, Dave. Tanned and petite, Richard Fitzwilliam's ex-wife looks much younger than her forty-five years—"*

Of course she does! As Perry carried on reading, Bea listened, imagining a small, slim woman with long, beautifully curled blonde hair, draped over a chair, dressed in a bright-coloured bikini and thin coverup, looking like Kate Moss posing for a photo shoot in the Maldives. Bea tucked a strand of her straight red hair behind her ear and sucked her stomach in.

"He was funny, and we laughed a lot in those early days. But after a while, I wanted more. I wanted a life outside of work with sociable hours so I could see my friends. I even wanted to start a family—"

A family? Bea's eyes widened as her jaw clenched. *Did Rich want children?* Up until this moment, it had never occurred to her he might. It wasn't something they'd discussed. She swallowed noisily. *Yet…* She'd been drifting along on this happy wave of growing love, and their future life together—it was something in the distance that they would get to eventually. *Is that 'eventually' now?* A slight shiver ran down her back despite the afternoon heat.

Daisy stirred next to her as Perry continued, "*It was clear his job mattered more than we did. That was it for me—*"

Daisy jumped down and stretched.

"*Things might not have worked out for me and Rich back then—*"

Daisy gave a little *woof* and scampered off.

"*I couldn't be happier—*"

"Hello, little girl. Shouldn't you be in the shade?"

Bea's chest tightened at the sound of Rich's voice behind them.

"*I wish Rich and Lady Beatrice all the best for the—*" Perry stopped abruptly.

An awkward silence descended. Bea turned around, searching Rich's face to see if he'd heard what Perry had been saying. It was clear he had. As he straightened up, Daisy gave a sharp *yip* and dashed towards the open bifold doors.

Bea cleared her throat. She spoke, her voice small, "Rich, I'm so sorry. Perry was... I mean, there's this interview... er, with Amber... and—"

He held up a hand, stopping her. "It's fine, Bea. I've already seen it."

He has? He'd not mentioned it to her...

Perry turned around in his chair. "And are you alright about it?"

Rich shrugged, his jaw tight. "It's basically true. From her point of view, at least." His gaze met Bea's, and she saw something there, but what was it? *Anger? Disappointment? Embarrassment?* She longed to go to him, to wrap her arms around him and tell him none of it mattered. But she knew he wouldn't want her to do that with Perry watching.

Seeming to sense her predicament, he quickly changed the subject. "Anyway, I've got a surprise for you both." He gave a sly smile. *What's he up to?*

"Let me guess," Perry said. "Saunders has agreed to let us do all his dirty work for him again, and he promises to take all the credit like he did before?"

Rich barked out a laugh. Bea's shoulders relaxed a tad. "Even better." He turned and darted into the villa, leaving Bea and Perry exchanging curious glances as they rose from their chairs.

A moment later, Rich reappeared with a familiar blonde woman, Daisy contentedly nestled in her arms.

Bea hurried forward, a genuine smile spreading across her face. "Tina!" She held her arms out wide. "What a lovely surprise. What are you doing here?"

Detective Inspector Tina Spicer grinned as she handed Daisy over to Rich and accepted a warm hug from Bea. "I'm here to oversee the investigation into JT Kenda's death on behalf of PaIRS, my lady."

Perry greeted Tina enthusiastically as Bea stepped back. *What a stroke of luck!* Someone they knew and trusted. Having worked with her on several cases when Tina had been Rich's sergeant, before her recent promotion to inspector, Bea was so happy to know she was on the case. "Where are you staying?" Bea asked. "We've got plenty of spare rooms here at the villa."

Tina waved away the offer. "They're putting us up in one of the houses used by the security team. But thanks, my lady."

"Tina, please. It's Bea now, remember?"

Tina gave a shy smile and inclined her head.

"I'm heading to the local police station with Tina now," Rich said, handing Daisy over to Bea. He gave her a reassuring smile.

Bea offered a quick gesture of acknowledgement, then

turned to Tina with a hopeful smile. "Will you join us for dinner tonight?"

"Absolutely…. my, I mean, Bea," Tina replied eagerly. "See you later."

Bea smiled as she hugged Daisy to her. The cloud of DCI Hayden Saunders that had been hanging over them all afternoon now lifted. *Maybe we can actually get properly involved in this investigation, after all…*

18

EVEN LATER THAT AFTERNOON,
SATURDAY 7 AUGUST

Bea stretched out on a lounger, enjoying the warmth of the golden glow of the late afternoon sun on her skin. A swim was what she'd needed. Slowly moving through the water had loosened up her limbs and relieved the tension in her neck. Now drying in the sun, her body felt lazily content. Her mind, on the other hand, was still awash with concerns about the impact Amber's interview with *The Daily Post* had had on Rich. Clearly, the arrival of Tina had been a welcome distraction, but was he *really* as fine about it as he would have her believe? *I need to talk to him.* When she was able to find five minutes for them to be alone…

Across the garden, Simon and the boys were laughing as they appeared from the beach access path.

Sam waved, and Bea blew him a kiss. "See you later, Mum. We're going to get changed," he called out as the teenager duo disappeared into the villa, leaving Simon to stroll over to the pool alone.

"Did you have fun?" Perry asked, sitting up from the lounger next to Bea and running a hand through his wet hair.

"As always," Simon said, plopping down on a chair. "The water was perfect—calm and warm. Like the best bath you can imagine. I don't understand why you didn't want to come with us."

Perry looked over the top of his sunglasses at his husband. "I have two questions. Have all sharks in the world been eradicated yet?"

Bea smirked, shaking her head. Perry's fear of being attacked by a shark was based on nothing more than having read too many stories of people being attacked by sharks.

"Perry, we went through this before we came. Shark sightings here are rare, and there have been no recorded shark attacks in Portugal. Ever!" Simon replied as if dealing with a young child.

"So that's no then." Perry's response was curt. He continued, "And secondly, has sand stopped getting in between people's toes?" He noticeably shivered as he asked the question.

Bea clamped her hand over her mouth to disguise a snort of laughter.

"No. But that is why we have showers after we've been to the beach." *Simon really would be good in a kindergarten.*

Perry huffed. "But it doesn't get rid of it all, does it? There's always still some there days later... even weeks."

Simon reached out and laid his arm on Perry's. "How about if I get you some beach shoes?"

A look of horror spread across Perry's face. "What, those ugly black things made of rubber?" He glanced down at his Dior thong sandals tucked under the sun bed and wrinkled his nose. "I hardly think it's my style, love."

Simon smiled indulgently as he patted Perry's arm. "Perhaps you *are* safer up here by the pool." He did an exagger-

HELEN GOLDEN

ated sweep of the poolside, then added, "As long as there are no heavy statues around just waiting to tumble down…"

Perry shook his head. "Too soon, Simon. Too soon."

Bea's stomach was hurting with trying to contain her laughter. *I love these two so much!* They never failed to lift her spirits. Wiping her eyes, she shaded them with her hand and scanned the garden. "Where's Isla?"

Simon shrugged. "We bumped into Chloe at the beach. I thought Isla would ignore her. She seemed to have gone off her after she found out Chloe was the one who'd leaked that you and Rich were here, but she made a beeline for her." He shrugged. "Now she's gone back to Chloe's villa for a bit."

Perry, his blue eyes wide with concern, said, "Is that wise? With everything that's happened... is she safe there? I mean, with a killer on the loose?"

Bea pressed her lips together. Perry had a point.

Simon frowned. "No one has a reason to kill Isla." He paused, seeing their worried faces. "But I'll text her and tell her to come back shortly and help me with dinner, okay?"

Perry and Bea nodded as Simon pulled out his phone and started tapping. Perry suddenly sprang up straight in his chair. "I can't believe we forgot to tell you. We have news!"

Simon looked up from his phone and lifted an eyebrow. "Go on."

"Guess who has arrived to oversee the investigation on behalf of PaIRS?" Perry asked, practically bouncing in his seat.

Simon put his phone away and looked between them both. "I'm guessing from your faces that it's not Hayden Saunders."

"Correct," Bea said, grinning.

"Er, well—"

"It's Tina Spicer!" Perry wasn't able to contain himself any longer. "She's an inspector now."

Simon gestured subtly in response, smiling. "Yes, I remember Rich telling us she'd had a promotion. That *is* good news."

"She and Rich have gone to the police station," Bea added. "In fact, they should be back—"

There were footsteps on the terrace, and the three of them spun around. "Talk of the devil…" Bea finished as Tina and Rich headed towards them, looking less than thrilled. *Oh dear…*

"So that was a waste of time," Rich grumbled as he sat down next to Bea. "They wouldn't even let me in with Tina. I had to wait in the lobby!" he said indignantly.

Tina sighed as she joined them, her usually vibrant eyes dulled with frustration. "I didn't have much luck either. The local police chief made it crystal clear that this is his investigation, and their only responsibility is to keep me informed and cooperate on security matters for you and Sam, Bea."

"So it's not a joint investigation?" Simon asked.

Tina shook her head, then seemed to notice who had spoken. A grin transformed her face. "Simon, good to see you." Simon rose, and they greeted each other warmly.

"So we're on our own, after all?" Bea asked Rich.

"Not quite," he replied and glanced at Tina.

"They grudgingly provided copies of the statements, autopsy, and crime scene reports before showing me the door," she told them. "I've left them inside on the table." She indicated back to the open doors of the villa.

Bea licked her lips. *Okay, that's useful.* "Did they give any indication of their leading theories? Suspects? Anything like that?"

"Only that they're still holding Maria. The implication

was heavy that they consider her their prime suspect," Tina said.

"But they can't formally interview her yet," Rich chimed in, an edge of amusement in his tone. "Apparently, some hotshot lawyer is jetting in from Lisbon to represent her."

A lawyer from Lisbon? That had to cost a fortune. *How can Ana afford it?* She recalled the conversation she'd had earlier with Lady Grace. Bea had called to tell her they'd do everything they could to find JT's killer and prove Maria innocent. Lady Grace had mentioned that she and Sir Hewitt would do everything they were able to do to help too. *Was that what she'd meant?*

"They're not happy," Tina added.

"So what now?" Simon asked.

"For me? I have to keep Bea and Sam safe and wait," Tina replied. "And hope the local police know what they're doing."

Perry shook his head. "But—"

"I cannot be seen to be *officially* investigating, you understand," Tina continued. "But you, on the other hand. You do whatever you think is best…" She trailed off with a shrug.

Bea smiled at Rich. Tina was clearly giving them her permission to investigate along with an implied promise that she would help them as much as she could. Unofficially.

"I'll be back for dinner," Tina said, then with a quick wave, she hurried off.

Perry leapt up. "Let's set up an incident room like in the TV shows. We can then go through all the paperwork there." He rubbed his chin. "We'll need a whiteboard, some red string, and some of those fat coloured marker pens."

Bea rolled her eyes, her lips twitching. Of course he'd want an incident room. "We can use the basement," she suggested. "I'm not sure if there's a suitable board there, but there *is* a large table." They all stood and followed Perry, who had already scampered off towards the villa.

———

"I've already looked over the autopsy report while we were driving back from the station," Rich announced as Simon started laying out the documents Tina had given them on the table in the make-shift office in the basement. Crime scene photos, witness statements, the autopsy report—all were spread out like pieces of a jigsaw puzzle. "The key point is that JT had ketamine in his system when he died," Rich continued. "That's why the police believe it's murder rather than a simple accident."

So JT wasn't drunk?

Bea looked over at Perry, who was frowning. "So do you think rather than being drunk, he'd actually been drugged?" Bea asked him.

Perry shook his head decisively. "No. He was definitely drunk. I saw him neck at least ten bourbons during the evening, and I wasn't even there for a chunk of it, remember?"

Simon agreed. "He was drunk, no question. But it seems he was also drugged." He scratched his chin. "That might explain why he was so unsteady on his feet, I suppose. He was high *and* drunk."

Bea's head was already full of questions. *Had JT taken the drug willingly or had someone slipped it to him? And if so, who?*

"But I don't understand why the police think it's murder. He could've taken it himself. That would make it even more likely it was an accident," Perry said.

Rich shrugged, picking the report up from the table and

flicking through it. He stopped when he found what he was looking for. "It says here in the autopsy report there were no obvious signs of a struggle, nothing to suggest he was pushed hard enough to leave marks."

So no signs there was a fight? But if the evidence pointed to an accident, why are the police so convinced it was—

"Which begs the question—what on earth is making the police so sure it's murder?"

Exactly!

"They must know something we don't," Simon said.

"Or they're jumping to conclusions?" Perry suggested.

"Maybe there's some crucial detail in here somewhere," Rich said, gesturing to the pile of papers.

Bea heaved a deep sigh. *So we'll need to go through them all.*

Simon glanced down at his watch. "I agree, but I'm afraid we'll have to leave it until tomorrow now. Dinner will be ready in twenty minutes. I need to go and see how the youngsters are faring."

Sam, Archie, and Isla, under Simon's supervision, were cooking dinner for them all.

"I think our best bet for the morning is to split up the work," Rich said, his tone businesslike. "Simon, if you can go through these statements with a fine-tooth comb and try to piece together a timeline of the night in question, that would be very useful."

Simon gave a brief dip of his chin. "Good idea. We need to know who was where and when."

Rich continued, "And I'll have a chat with the security guys. They might have noticed something that evening, and there must be some CCTV footage too."

Bea turned to Perry. "Why don't we go to Villa Sol

tomorrow? We can check on Ella and see who we can talk to there."

Perry rubbed his hands in glee. "It's my favourite bit—time to start interviewing witnesses."

As they left to get ready for dinner, Bea felt a surge of relief. They had a plan of attack for tomorrow. Soon, they would find out what had *really* happened on the night of JT's death.

19

THE NEXT MORNING, SUNDAY 8 AUGUST

Bea strode up to the imposing front door of Villa Sol with a spring in her step. The warm sun shone on her face, and as she slid her sunglasses on her head, she briefly closed her eyes and enjoyed the heat. She turned to Perry, who was at her side. "Now remember, we're supposed to be here to express our condolences, so don't go charging in asking questions about JT's death straightaway, okay?"

Perry held his hand up to his chest. "I'm fully aware of the delicate nature of our visit," he said in a slightly affronted manner. "I'll be the soul of tactfulness."

"Um," Bea said as she reached out and pressed the bell. *Well, that'll be a first!*

After a moment, the door swung open, revealing Lucy, Ella's assistant. The young woman's eyes were red-rimmed, and her face was blotchy. *Oh, no. Have I got the timing wrong? Is it too soon?* "Er, hello, Lucy. I'm sorry to trouble you at this time, but we wanted to check on Ella and offer our condolences."

"Lady Rossex, Mr Juke, that's kind," Lucy said, attempting a smile. "Please come in. Ella is out on the deck."

The cool interior of the villa was a relief from the growing heat outside. Bea, having never been inside the villa before, took in the minimalist décor—white walls, glass surfaces, a few abstract sculptures. It was the kind of place that screamed 'expensive'. Lucy led them through, into the modern living cum dining space and out through the bifold doors leading onto a spacious terrace overlooking the pool, its blue cover stretched tightly over it. *The police must have emptied it.*

Ella St Gerome reclined on a plush lounger facing the distant ocean. Even in grief, the actress was a vision—her dark hair spilling across the cushion, oversized sunglasses shielding her famous blue eyes. She wore a flowing black sundress that accentuated her slim figure.

Bea noticed the statue and its plinth were nowhere to be seen. Had the police taken it away or had Ella understandably had it removed?

Ella lifted her head as they approached. "Lady Rossex, Perry," she said, her usually confident voice wavering slightly as she pushed herself up to a sitting position and removed her sunglasses, revealing tired red eyes. "How good of y'all to come."

Bea's heart went out to the woman. She knew all too well the shock of suddenly losing a husband. "Ella, I'm so very sorry. We don't want to intrude, but we also wanted to express our condolences and ask if there's anything we can do."

"Ah, bless your heart." Ella gestured to the cluster of chairs to her left. "Please sit down," she said. "What can we get you to drink?"

Bea asked for iced water and Perry for a lemonade. Lucy picked up Ella's empty glass on her way back to the villa.

"How are you holding up, Ella?" Bea asked.

Ella leaned over and squeezed Bea's hand, her perfectly shaped brows drawing together. She gave a dramatic sigh. "I'm... in a state of disbelief, honestly. It doesn't seem real that JT is gone. It's like a nightmare I can't wake up from."

Bea gave a thoughtful tilt of her head. Looking down at the tiled floor, she recalled those first few weeks after her husband's death when she'd still expected to see James walk through the door any minute. Every time he hadn't, a fresh wave of pain had ripped through her. "I'm so sorry..." She really didn't know what else to say. She glanced up into Ella's face to find the woman was staring at her intently. Bea's skin prickled as she caught a flicker of something in Ella's eyes. *What is that?* It wasn't shared grief or pain as Bea would have expected. It was more like fascination. Like she was a subject being studied to see how she'd react...

Ella quickly turned away and addressed Perry. "I didn't have time to talk to you after... you know, after everyone arrived, but please thank Simon for trying to—" She hesitated, seeming to compose herself. "I want him to know I appreciate it," she finished in a low, unsteady voice as she rested her hand on her chest.

Perry mirrored her glance with quiet understanding. "Of course."

The terrace door opened, and Lucy emerged, carrying a tray of iced drinks, her round glasses glinting in the sun. Her hands shook slightly as she set the tray down on the glass-topped table next to Ella.

"And of course I'm without Maria." Ella smiled at Lucy. "Lucy has been a massive help."

Lucy dipped her head in acknowledgement, then turned to leave.

"Please stay, Lucy," Ella said mournfully, gesturing at an empty chair.

The assistant hesitated, then sat, twisting her hands in her lap. "Yes, of course," she mumbled.

Is there a reason Ella doesn't want to be alone with us? This was all beginning to feel a bit off to Bea.

"Maria's with the police, I understand," Perry said, leaning forward to take his drink from the table. "Their number one suspect, in fact."

Bea suppressed a smile. Trust Perry to move them onto the other reason they were here.

Ella took a deep breath. "I still can't wrap my mind around Maria being a suspect. Accused of murder? It's crazy. She would never harm JT—or anyone else for that matter."

"But didn't she steal a necklace?" Perry asked.

Ella exhaled, her shoulders slumping. "Maria always denied stealing that necklace, you know. And I believed her; truly, I did."

Perry leaned forward. "Whose necklace was it?"

Ella took a sip of her drink, which looked like champagne to Bea. *But at this time in the morning?* It was probably a fizzy apple juice or something similar. "It was mine. JT bought it for me to say... er, I mean as a present. It went missing about a week ago." She rubbed her temples as if the memory pained her.

Bea frowned. "Why did suspicion fall on Maria?"

"JT." Ella's voice was flat. "He got it into his head that she must have taken it. He bumped into her coming out of our room the day it disappeared, but she was only dropping off the laundry," Ella said, her voice catching. "He accused her outright of stealing and wouldn't listen to reason." She absently scratched at a red, irritated patch of skin on her hand. "This entire ordeal... It's been incredibly stressful."

Bea's gaze flickered to Lucy, who sat unnaturally still, her face a mask of tightly controlled emotion. The assistant seemed to vibrate with nervous energy, like a coiled spring ready to snap.

"And there's another thing. Where would Maria even get her hands on ketamine?" Ella asked, her brow furrowed. "I can't imagine there's a ready supply around this area."

She has a point. Bea made a mental note to mention this to Rich and Simon.

Perry raised his hand to his mouth, considering. "Is it possible JT took it himself?"

"No, no, that's impossible," Ella said, shaking her head vehemently. "JT was allergic to ketamine. It made him terribly ill."

Did it? That's interesting...

Ella nodded, her gaze distant as if lost in a memory. "He found out back in college. Had a dreadful reaction—broke out in a helluva rash. Felt sick as a dog, apparently. It wasn't life-threatening, but it was enough to put him off the stuff for good. He wouldn't have taken it willingly; I'm certain of that."

So that must be why the police think someone gave it to him...

The sound of approaching footsteps drew their attention, and Bea turned to see Pearl and Peter Mitchell walking out onto the terrace. Peter shuffled towards them, looking even more unkept than the last time Bea had seen him. Next to him, Pearl's shoulders were low, and she had her head down, watching the ground as they approached.

Lucy glanced at Peter, and her eyes widened. Then she immediately leapt to her feet, mumbling something about having work to do before scurrying away.

"I was just telling Lady Rossex and Perry," Ella said as her sister and brother-in-law settled into seats nearby, waving her sunglasses in the air, "that I simply don't believe Maria is a killer."

Peter snorted, his face twisting into a sneer. "She stole the necklace, didn't she? It's not a gigantic leap to think she'd kill for it too."

Bea wrinkled her nose. He was as bad as she remembered him being at the pool party a few days ago.

Pearl's face crumpled, her eyes shimmering with unshed tears. "I don't believe Maria took the necklace," she said, her voice trembling. "I'm sure this is all some terrible misunderstanding. It has to be."

Bea studied Pearl, taking in the raw emotion etched across her delicate features. She seemed utterly distraught over JT's death, which struck Bea as odd. She hadn't got the feeling when she'd seen them together that they'd been close.

Perry leaned forward, his blue eyes locking on Peter. "Speaking of relationships—"

Were we?

"How was yours with JT? Were you close?"

Subtle as always, Perry! Although, Bea was curious about how Peter would answer. They knew from what Perry had overheard the night of JT's death that they'd been anything but. Would Peter admit it?

Peter stiffened and folded his arms across his chest. "We got on fine," he answered tersely. "I don't know what you're implying, but—"

Perry held his hands up. "I'm not implying anything," he said, his voice all innocent.

With another sigh, Ella slumped back against her lounger, her eyes fluttering shut as her hand holding her sunglasses dropped by the side of her chair.

Pearl reached out and patted her sister's arm. "I think Ella needs to rest now," she said, her voice soft but firm. She rose. "Thank you both for coming."

Bea caught Perry's eye and rose. "Of course. We understand. We'll let ourselves out." As she took a last glance at Ella, she could've sworn she saw the actress had one eye open before it snapped closed.

Once they were outside, Perry said, "Do you feel what we just saw was one of her better performances?"

Bea blinked. "I thought you were her biggest fan."

"I admire her as an actress, but I also think she's not as cut up about her husband's death as she'd like us to believe. And," he said, giving her a look, "she was drinking champagne. That's not drowning your sorrows; that's celebrating!"

Bea pushed her sunglasses up her nose. "So at least we now know why the police think JT didn't take the ketamine himself."

Perry nodded, a sly grin tugging at his lips. "And we know Peter is lying about his relationship with JT. I rather fancy him as the murderer, you know..."

20

NOT LONG AFTER, SUNDAY 8 AUGUST

B ea kicked off her sandals as she stepped onto the sunwarmed tiles of Villa Mer's terrace. *That's better.* Daisy bounded up to greet her, her tail wagging furiously. "There's my girl!" Bea bent down and ruffled the terrier's scruffy ears. Daisy tried to lick her nose. She laughed as the white dog moved on to Perry, this time successfully landing a gooey *slurp* on the side of his face as he bent down to fuss her.

"Mum!" Sam cried as he waved from the pool where he and Archie were floating on inflatable beds on the shining blue water. Bea straightened up and waved back. "Have you put sunscreen on, you two?"

"Yes, Mum!" they wailed back in unison.

Bea laughed. "We're going down to the basement. See you later," she told them as she scooped Daisy up. "It's too hot for you out here, Daisy-doo," she said, then followed Perry into the villa.

As they entered the cooler interior downstairs, Simon was standing in front of two whiteboards next to each other. *Where did he find them?* On one were photos of all the residents from each of the other two villas clustered together and a grouping of Ana, Maria, Enzo, the three gardeners, and what looked like another maid in the bottom corner. On the second board, there was a long line penned across the top that snaked across the board and was divided into time slots with writing beneath. Bea suppressed a grin. *Very professional.*

Simon turned around and smiled. "There's a pot of coffee over there." He indicated towards a work surface along the wall where mugs, sugar, and a plate of biscuits were clustered around a coffee pot and a kettle. "Rich should be back any minute and then we can share what we've learned so far."

As Bea made her way to the countertop, her stomach fluttered. *Is Rich alright?* After their conversation last night, she was both elated and apprehensive. *You really should stop worrying!* After all, he'd finally said what she'd wanted to hear...

Her mind wandered back to the evening before. After saying goodnight to Sam and Archie, she'd found Rich brooding over a brandy in the sitting area, staring at something on his tablet. As she'd got closer, she'd seen it was Amber's interview with *The Daily Post.*

"Are you okay, Rich?" she'd asked as she'd gestured at the article and settled beside him on the sofa. At first, he'd shrugged it off, mumbling something about press gossip. But she'd known him too well. "You seem like it's still bothering you."

"It's the not being able to tell my side. That's the frustrating part," he'd finally admitted, his jaw clenched. He'd held up a hand as Bea had opened her mouth to speak. "I get it. I really do. Engaging adds fuel to the fire." He'd let out a deep sigh. "But it feels like she's rewriting our entire history, and I'll never have a chance to... I don't know, set the record straight, I suppose."

Bea had responded with a faint incline of her head. The unwritten royal rule—never complain, never explain.

"How do you deal with it?" Rich had turned to her, his eyes searching. Bea's heart had sunk. He had always been the confident and so-sure-of-himself one, and yet, now he had turned to her for help.

She'd stared deep into his eyes. "Honestly? It's hard." Her mind had flashed back to the tabloid rumours that had swirled when James had died — and the horrible insinuations about his relationship with the female passenger who had been killed in the car crash with him. Bea had known her husband hadn't been having an affair, but she'd never been given a chance to declare it publicly. She'd squeezed Rich's arm. "The important thing is that the people who really know and love you… well, they know the truth. That's what matters in the end." She'd tried for a small smile. "And you can always rant to me if it helps."

He'd leaned in and kissed her gently. "Thanks. It does." Then he'd taken her hands, his brown eyes searching hers. "I mean, nothing she actually said was untrue. It's just... I really thought I was doing it for us, you know? All the hours. Chasing the next promotion. For our future. But it seems she still can't see that."

"She mentioned wanting children. Did you two ever discuss that?" The question had slipped out before Bea had been able to stop herself.

Rich had blinked at her, surprised. "No. Actually it was weird she brought that up—we never really went there."

Bea's heart had jumped as she'd bitten her bottom lip. *Should we go there?* Her heart had pounded. Ever since Perry had read the article to her, she'd been thinking about what she would say if Rich had asked her if she wanted more children. And she still had no idea how she felt about it. She loved Sam more than anything in the world… but the thought of doing it all over again… *oh my goodness.*

A silence had descended as Rich had turned to stare out into the darkness, his arm now resting along the back of the sofa.

Should I say something? This is dangerous territory—the uncharted waters of our future, the conversations we need to have. She'd coughed. "Er, what are you thinking about, Rich?"

Bracing herself for a response along the lines of, "I want three children. How many do you want?" or "I feel ready to be a father now," her heart had felt as if it was going to burst from her chest.

The "Nothing," he'd replied with had taken her by surprise. *What does he mean, nothing?*

"Really?"

He had turned to her in earnest. "I'm not going to let it bother me anymore," he'd stated firmly. Some of the tension had left Bea's body. "She didn't say I was an awful husband, did she? In fact, she said I was funny." He'd twisted his head sideways and winked at her. "And we both know that's true." He'd grinned.

Even in her confusion, Bea hadn't been able to stop herself from grinning back. "Hilarious," she'd agreed. Her heart rate had returned to near normal. *He seems happier. I don't want to ruin it…*

Rich had continued, "I was young and foolish then. Now I'm older and—"

"Still foolish?" Bea had suggested.

He had made a sudden grab for her, and laughing, he'd enveloped her in an enormous bear hug. "What do they say about a fool in love?"

Bea had frozen. *Did he say the L-word?* He'd kissed her just below her ear, then whispered, "Then, yes, I'm a fool…" Bea's heart had stopped beating, and everything had seemed to move in slow-motion. *Breathe!* She'd taken in a gasp of air. *He loves me*….

They would discuss that other little matter another time… "And so am I…" she'd replied as they'd kissed.

"Bea?" Simon stared at her, his head to one side, dragging her back to the present. He held out a mug of coffee to her.

"Er, thanks." She took it from him as Rich came bounding down the stairs.

Daisy ran to meet him, and he bent down to greet her. He looked up and caught Bea's gaze. He grinned. "Hey, you," he said as she rose. He moved towards her, stopped in front of her, leaned forward, and kissed her.

"Um… hey, you too," she mumbled.

Perry cleared his throat loudly. "When you two have quite finished, can we get on? We've stuff to tell you."

"Of course," Rich replied, taking Bea's hand and giving it a squeeze. "Tell us all, Perry."

Perry briefly summarised his and Bea's visit to Villa Sol, including the news that JT had been allergic to ketamine.

"That explains a lot," Rich said, nodding.

Perry finished by saying, "I think Peter is our number one suspect."

Simon's forehead creased. "Because he lied?"

"Not only did he lie about his relationship with JT, but we also know JT was throwing him out. That's an excellent motive for murder."

Simon dipped his chin. "Good point." He moved over to the first whiteboard and wrote something beneath Peter's picture, then he shifted to the second board: "I've been going over the witness statements. I've mapped out a timeline as best as I can, but there are still some blanks." He glanced up at Perry, quirking a brow. "First, your little solo adventure after ducking out of the party."

Perry squirmed slightly under his husband's knowing gaze.

"And second, who was on- and off-site during the day? Rich, did you find out if anyone not on this board had access to Marisol the evening of JT's death?"

Rich dropped Bea's hand as he reached into his pocket and took out his phone. "Okay, so there's CCTV around the estate, but it only faces outwards. That's to afford the owners their privacy. Recordings show no one came in or out that day except the staff and Lucy Harper."

Simon, a pen paused above the second whiteboard, said, "Give me the times, and I'll check them against my timeline."

"Ana and Enzo arrived at seven-thirty in the morning. Enzo drove Ana to go food shopping later. They left at ten-thirty and returned two hours later. Enzo left at six, and Ana went off-site for the day at six-thirty. The maid at Villa Luz arrived at eight that morning and left a tad after six in the evening."

Simon wrote it all on the board. Rich continued, "Miquel, he's the head gardener, and the two other gardeners arrived at eight-thirty in the morning and left at around five. Maria arrived at five to noon and departed at around eleven that night. One of the security lads took her home as she was understandably shaken up after JT's death. And that's it for the staff. Which just leaves Lucy. She went off-site at eight that morning, telling the security staff she had errands to run, and returned three-and-a-half hours later at around eleven-thirty."

Simon finished writing, then moved over to the first board. He grouped Ana, Enzo, Miquel and the two gardeners along with the maid from Villa Luz together at the side of the board and wrote above them 'Off-site at TOD'. "We can rule these six out."

A heavy silence fell as they all digested the implications. Bea's mind raced ahead, connecting the dots… It wasn't an outsider then… "So…" She met Rich's gaze. "The killer has to be someone staying at Villa Sol or Villa Luz."

He acknowledged her words with a soft murmur.

"Or Maria," Simon added. "We can't dismiss her yet, I'm afraid."

Bea raised her eyebrows in silent agreement. A few years ago, she would've smarted at Simon's comment, pointing out that the whole point of their investigation was because they thought Maria was innocent, but now, like an old hand, she recognised it was all about evidence. That was the only way to *prove* someone was innocent.

"Right. Let me go through the timeline then according to the witness statements, and Perry can jump in when we get to the part of the evening where he overheard the encounters between JT and Nessa and JT and Peter. Unsurprisingly, neither of them mentioned these meetings in their statements." Simon stood in front of the board. "So let's concentrate on the time from the party onwards to make it easier. It started at seven-thirty, and Perry, Isla, and I arrived at about eight. All the others—Ella, JT, Pearl, Peter, Derek, Nessa, Chloe, and Lucy were already there. Isla left at just after eight-twenty and came back here, and Chloe says she left and went back to Villa Luz at about eight twenty-five and was there for the rest of the evening. Nessa Stone says she left the party at eight-thirty because she had a headache and went home to Villa Luz. Perry, does her time seem about right to you?"

Perry nodded. "That's the time she left the party. I followed her out a couple of minutes later. I wanted to see where she was going, but she'd disappeared by the time I'd got into the corridor."

"Who did you see next?" his husband asked.

"I heard Maria in the basement kitchen as I looked for Nessa. Maria found me outside the door leading to the corridor about... Er, five or six minutes after I left the party."

"So by eight thirty-seven, say, you were in the bathroom?"

"Yes. I waited in there a few minutes, then as I was leaving, I heard the argument between Nessa and JT."

Simon mumbled as he wrote, "So about eight-forty?"

"Then not more than three or four minutes later, Peter appeared, and Nessa ran off. Peter and JT then exchanged words. It wasn't a long conversation, four minutes tops, then Peter stormed off. I waited another minute or so just to make sure the coast was clear, then I bolted out of the bathroom and returned to the party."

"That was a few minutes after nine," Simon confirmed as he wrote. "I remember looking at my watch at nine and wondering where you were." Simon stood back and turned to them. "Derek says in his statement that JT left to take a call at about twenty to nine, returning fifteen to twenty minutes later. So that fits in with what you've said, Perry. But no one seems to have seen Peter leave the party or reappear."

"I find that hard to believe," Perry said. "Pearl rarely leaves Peter's side from what I've seen of them since we've been here."

"I agree," Simon said.

So Pearl is lying.

"Maybe she knows Peter went off to tackle JT, and she's covering for him," Perry jumped in. Then he frowned. "Which suggests she knew they were being thrown out of the villa by JT."

And if so, then Pearl, too, had a good motive to want JT dead...

21

A FEW MINUTES LATER, SUNDAY 8 AUGUST

"So let's go back to the party," Simon said, turning back to his timeline on the board. "Peter says he left at nine thirty-five to go to his studio. That's confirmed by his wife, Pearl. She then left about five minutes later. Perry and I can confirm that. Peter says he passed Maria in the foyer on her way to the sitting room with a tray of drinks."

Bea was confused. "But I thought you said Maria wasn't in the room?"

"She wasn't," Simon replied. "Lucy left just after Peter and took the tray from Maria, returning with the drinks shortly after and handing them out. Maria never came into the room."

But she could've put the drug in JT's glass before she handed the tray to Lucy...

Simon continued, "Derek left a few minutes after that, and then, hot on his heels, JT came over and said he was going for a swim. That would have been about nine forty-five," he confirmed, referring to the board. "Shortly after that, Lucy left the sitting room to go to the kitchen with the dirty glasses, which she washed up. That left us and Ella in the sitting room. Maria, who'd been in the kitchen clearing up, says she went to the bathroom about that time and returned to an empty kitchen around ten minutes later, where she continued to clean up." He pointed to the timeline on the board. "Lucy's statement says she was in the living room cum diner, checking it was all tidy when she heard a thud followed by a splash. She's unclear what time it was exactly, but it must have been around ten."

"I remember looking at my watch when you and Ella were chatting as I wanted to leave, and it was ten," Perry said. "We heard the scream just after that."

Simon added a note to the board. "Lucy says she rushed outside and saw JT's body in the pool. Then she can't remember much else until the three of us arrived, when she went straight to Ella. Perry made the call to the emergency services at four minutes past ten." He put down his pen. "So JT's death is estimated as a few minutes before or after ten."

Rich gestured subtly in response, his expression thoughtful as he studied Simon's meticulously crafted time-line. "This is great work, Simon. It really makes it easy to see where everyone says they were." He glanced up, his brow furrowing. "So let's think about the ketamine and when it was most likely administered. I know a bit about the drug from a case I was involved with a few years ago. It can be dissolved in liquids, so it's easy to mix ketamine into a drink, and although it has a slightly bitter taste, if you mix it with something with a strong flavour, the taste can be masked."

"JT was drinking bourbon," Simon said.

Rich dipped his chin. "That's what the autopsy said too. They're waiting for the blood results to see exactly how much alcohol and ketamine he had in his system. That will allow them to work backwards to narrow a time down as to when they think he was given it. But I know that the effects can take longer to appear when it's taken in a drink like that compared to being injected or snorted. The onset of symptoms might be as long as thirty minutes after ingestion. He'd feel drowsy, dizzy, perhaps confused, and probably unsteady on his feet. You both saw him when he left the party. How did he seem to you?"

Perry and Simon looked at each other. Simon tipped his head to Perry.

"He seemed drunk but not confused. A little unsteady on his feet but not dizzy, I would say," Perry told them.

"I concur," Simon added. "The witness statements from Derek and Lucy say he was drunk but not that much more than usual at a party. Ella told us and the police that he always swam around the same time in the evening, nearly always after drinking. She said he seemed no worse than normal."

He always drank before swimming? Bea shook her head slowly. It seemed to her that it was inevitable that he would get into trouble in the pool eventually.

Rich continued, "So if we assume for the moment that the effects of the ketamine hadn't really kicked in when he left the party, then he could have been given it as early as nine-thirty. Does that rule anyone out?" He looked at Simon, who referenced the board.

"Yes," he replied. "It rules out Maria, Chloe, and Nessa, who weren't in the room at the time."

"Well, there you go then. It couldn't have been Maria," Perry said decisively. His hand came up to his chin. "Or Ella," he added, rubbing it. "She was *in* the room, but she was with us the whole time, so she couldn't have done it either." His eyes lit up. "Though she did make it a point to get JT a drink earlier! And she kept checking her watch! Could she have done it then? Maybe put it in his ice?" He looked at Simon, his eyes shining.

"Whoa, slow down, Jessica Fletcher," Simon said, gently. "For a start, she got that drink before you went off on your big adventure, so around eight forty-five. That's way too early."

Rich nodded.

Bea's stomach fluttered. *But if it was in the ice?*

"And nice idea about putting it in ice. But JT didn't have ice in his drink. He had his bourbon neat. He made a point of telling me earlier that adding anything to it was sacrilege."

Bea's shoulders dropped. *That would've been too easy...*

"So we *can* rule out Ella?" Perry asked.

Simon dipped his chin. "If our timings are correct, then yes, I think we can."

So that's Maria, Chloe, Nessa, and Ella off the suspect list already. They were narrowing the list down quite nicely. *Except...* "Is it possible someone prepared the drink in advance though?" she asked.

Rich beamed at her. "Good question. Simon, was JT the only person drinking bourbon?"

Simon frowned. "It's not in the witness statements what they were each drinking. I think we'll need to dig a little deeper for that."

"Agreed. Anything else of note in those reports that's useful?" Rich asked.

Simon shrugged. "Honestly, I've not had a chance to go through it all. The crime scene report was my next job. There's a lot there and some of it has been translated from Portuguese to English, so you have to fill in the gaps a bit. My eyes were starting to cross."

Rich jumped in immediately. "What if Bea and I take over

here? It will give your eyes a break, and you two can pay Derek and Ness a visit?"

He winked at her, and Bea grinned impishly. "Yes. You can use the excuse of picking up Isla for lunch."

Bea had been surprised when Isla had informed them an hour or so ago that she was popping over to see Chloe. Last night at dinner, when Simon had asked her if she liked Chloe a bit more now she was getting to know her, Isla had replied that she didn't think they had a lot in common, and she suspected Chloe was only being nice to her now because of Isla's connection to Bea and Sam. Bea had considered that insightful and probably true. *So why does she want to spend time with her?*

Perry clapped his hands together. "I like that. I'm keen to see what the interior designer to the stars has done with her place."

Simon hesitated, glancing between Bea and Rich. "Are you sure you don't mind? It's tedious work."

"Not at all." Rich waved him off. "We'll manage just fine. Right, Bea?"

Yes, please! "Absolutely. You two go play detective. We've got this."

As Perry and Simon headed up the stairs, Bea felt a flutter of nerves in her stomach as she looked at Rich.

"Alone at last!" he whispered as he put his arms around her and pulled her close. She nestled into his powerful chest. "I don't know about you, but I could use some fresh air before we dive in. Shall we take a quick break and have a romantic stroll on the beach?"

Romantic? Mmmm... She leaned back and gazed up into his eyes. "You wouldn't be trying to prove a point, would you, Rich?"

He smiled sheepishly. "I don't know what you mean."

"Does it have anything to do with Amber's accusation that you were unromantic?"

"Of course not!" he cried in mock indignation. "I simply want to walk hand-in-hand along a deserted beach with the woman I love. What's wrong with that?"

A smug smile spread over Bea's face. *Nothing. Absolutely nothing!*

22

TEN MINUTES LATER, SUNDAY 8 AUGUST

P erry adjusted his sunglasses, squinting in the bright sunlight as he and Simon strolled along the winding path to Villa Luz. The air was thick with humidity. He reached up and patted his spiky hair. *It'll be all frizz soon if I don't get inside.*

As they passed Villa Sol, the front door burst open. Lucy came hustling out, a set of car keys gripped in one hand.

"Oh, hello!" she chirped, her voice strained despite its cheeriness. "Off to the supermarket. It's a bit chaotic without Maria, I'm afraid."

Simon and Perry acknowledged her words with a soft murmur of sympathy. Although Maria's lawyer had arranged her release within a few hours of arriving, according to Tina, the police had made it clear that the maid was still their number one suspect, and it was only a matter of time before they would have sufficient evidence to haul her back in for further questioning. The lawyer had advised Maria not to return to work until the police inquiry was completed and to talk to no one. So for the time being, she'd been shipped off to an aunt who lived about fifty miles away to escape the attention of the media who still overran the small town outside Marisol's gates. They'd all been disappointed they wouldn't get Maria's side of things in person, but Tina had promised them a copy of the transcript from the police interview with her later today.

A thought suddenly occurred to Perry—what better person to ask who'd drunk what at the party than the person who'd served and cleared up most of the drinks? "Er, Lucy. Do you remember what everyone was drinking at the party on Thursday?"

Lucy blinked, clearly caught off guard. "What? Why on earth would that matter?"

Why had he asked that? *You idiot!* What possible excuse could he have for such a specific question? He opened his mouth, but nothing came out.

"We are thinking of throwing a small pool party once this is all cleared up, you know, to take everyone's mind off the tragic events, and we wanted to make sure we have the right drinks available," Simon said, smiling at her.

Brilliant! Well done, love.

"Ah, I see." Lucy visibly relaxed. "Okay... Ella's easy. She only ever touches champagne — Veuve Clicquot or Taittinger, preferably. Pearl goes for gin and tonic. Peter bounces between beer and rum. Derek favours rum too or a bourbon."

Perry's eyebrows rose. So if Derek was drinking bourbon that night along with JT, then it would've been hard for anyone who hadn't been in the room to be sure a drugged bourbon would end up with JT and not Derek.

Lucy was still reeling off people's drinks. "Nessa sticks to white wine—chardonnay or pinot grigio. And Chloe, bless her, drinks those awful fruit ciders."

"I didn't realise Derek drank bourbon," Perry butted in. "I thought he had something longer on Thursday night."

Lucy frowned at him, and Perry held his breath while she seemingly decided whether to answer or not. She folded her arms. "He started off the evening with rum and coke but moved on to the bourbon later." Her eyes challenged him to question her further.

"Oh, I see... of course. And you?" he asked with a placating smile.

"I don't drink when I'm working," Lucy replied curtly. "Now I really must dash!"

As Lucy scurried off, Perry turned to Simon, a triumphant gleam in his eye. "Bingo!" he whispered. "If JT wasn't the only one drinking bourbon that night, then our killer must have been in the room…"

———

A uniformed maid ushered Perry and Simon into Villa Luz's expansive sitting room. Floor-to-ceiling windows showcased a glistening infinity pool with a stunning coastal panorama beyond. Inside, pristine white sofas flanked a sleek glass coffee table, while abstract art in bold primary colours adorned the walls. Undeniably chic but lacking in lived-in warmth.

More like a show home than a family abode, Perry thought as he took it all in.

Derek Stone sat hunched over a laptop at a massive glass dining table. He flipped down the screen and rose to greet them, his face etched with weariness. "Perry, Simon. Welcome. What would you like to drink?"

Simon smiled. "Thank you for the offer, but we're here to fetch Isla for lunch. But we also wanted to extend our deepest condolences on JT's death. I can't imagine how difficult this has been for you and your wife."

"Thank you." Derek sighed heavily. "It still doesn't feel real, even now." He gestured for them to sit.

As they settled onto the stiff sofa, Perry, sensing an opening, asked, "You and JT had known each other for a long time, I understand?"

"Since high school in San Jose. We stayed best mates through all these years." Derek's eyes clouded over. "JT—he can... I mean was... a bit of a show-off in a crowd, you know but one-on-one? He was a completely different man. Well-read. Generous. And a brilliant producer—he knew in his bones what would kill at the box office and what would flop."

Perry remembered the article about Ella being passed over as lead in JT's next film. "Is that why he wanted Ella to transition into character roles? Because he thought her star was fading?"

Derek's eyebrows shot up. "It's not so much that her star is fading, more than she needs to... diversify. JT believed it was time for Ella to stop relying solely on her looks, take on more challenging character roles."

Perry recalled the heated argument he and Bea had overheard at Villa Sol the day before the pool party. *Something about an ultimatum, wasn't it?* "And Ella? How did she take the news?"

Derek shifted uncomfortably. "She wasn't thrilled, naturally."

Not thrilled enough to kill JT?

Then Perry checked himself. Ella couldn't have drugged JT's drink. He and Simon had been with her from before nine-thirty until they'd heard Lucy scream.

"Her agent's been... er, persistent." Derek paused, then added with forced lightness, "It's made this trip a touch awkward, to be honest." His gaze flickered to the window, then he rose abruptly. "I'll let Nessa know you're here. Excuse me."

Derek paused at the doorway, his stocky frame filling it. "Nessa!" he called out, his voice tinged with forced cheerfulness. "We have visitors!"

Turning back to Perry and Simon, Derek lowered his voice. "She's taken it all rather badly, I'm afraid. A bit overemotional. You know how women can be."

What! Perry's eyebrows shot up, grateful that Bea wasn't here. But before he could open his mouth to say a scathing, "No, I don't know how women can be," Nessa glided into the room. Her statuesque figure was impeccably dressed, her makeup flawless, but there was something off about her eyes. They looked... hollow. Perry and Simon rose.

"Hi," she greeted, her voice shaking slightly. "How lovely to see you both."

Perry offered his most sympathetic smile. "Nessa, how are you holding up?"

She attempted a smile that didn't reach her eyes. "Oh, you know. One day at a time."

As Nessa spoke, Perry recalled the heated exchange he'd overheard between her and Derek at the party. *"You're the one who wants out,"* Derek had said. Was it possible Nessa had been hoping to leave Derek for JT? If so, no wonder she was taking it badly. Her future dreams had been shattered. *But, wait!* Whatever Nessa had wanted, JT had made it very clear to her later, when they'd been arguing outside the bathroom, that he'd no such desires. She'd sounded devastated to Perry.

What was it about JT that had two stunning, successful women like Ella and Nessa vying for his affections? Perry wondered.

But then later, when Nessa had realised that JT didn't

want her, had she gone back and killed him? *Oh, hold on.* She hadn't come back to the party, so how would she have drugged him? Perry suppressed a deep sigh. It seemed that almost everyone who'd been there that night had a reason to want to kill him. But unless Perry was missing something, not all of them had access to JT's drink. *At least we're narrowing down the suspect pool...*

Derek cleared his throat. "Er, Simon. I'm glad I've got this opportunity to thank you for what you did that night. You know, getting JT out of the pool and trying... Well, it was good of you."

Simon dipped his chin. "I only wished I was in time. But with the ketamine and alcohol in his system, not to mention the blow to the head, I'm not sure he stood much of a chance."

Derek's head snapped up. "You know about the ketamine?"

And so do you, clearly. Had Ella told him or the police?

"Our friend Richard Fitzwilliam, you met him at the pool party? He's a senior police officer back in the UK. He's been liaising with the local force," Simon said.

Perry marvelled at his husband's smooth delivery and the way he implied an insider's knowledge without saying too much. *I should let Simon take the lead more often...*

"It's just so shocking," Derek said, shaking his head. "To think someone wanted JT dead. I can hardly wrap my mind around it. When I said goodnight to him... Well, I never imagined it would be the last time I saw him." His voice wavered slightly. "I keep thinking about that moment, you know? Wishing I'd said something more meaningful."

Perry's gaze shifted to Nessa, who stood with her arms crossed, radiating tension. *Let's test the waters.* "Nessa, how's your headache now? Feeling any better?"

Her large brown eyes widened in surprise. "My... headache?"

"I thought someone mentioned you'd left the party early because of a headache," Perry said, watching her reaction closely.

Recognition flickered across her face. "Oh, right. Yes, I... I came back here and went to bed to sleep it off."

The door swung open. Chloe sauntered in, her trendy outfit perfectly coordinated. Isla was close behind her.

Chloe's eyes locked on to her mother. "Did you, Mother?"

Perry's eyes widened. *What's going on here then?*

"Because I didn't hear you come in that night," she sneered.

Nessa's perfectly manicured hand tightened on the arm she had wrapped around her. "You were probably too engrossed in the TV to notice," she snapped back, lifting her chin.

"Umm," Chloe exhaled slowly, but her eyes never left her mother's face.

The tension in the room was palpable. Perry made a mental note to ask Isla about it later. There was clearly something more than simply grieving for JT going on here.

Simon glanced at his watch. "We should probably head back to Villa Mer for lunch," he said, breaking the uncomfortable silence. "Ready, Isla?"

———

The sun beat down on Perry's neck as they strolled along the winding path back to Villa Mer. He tugged at the collar of his polo shirt, grateful for the sea breeze that offered the occasional relief.

"So, darling," Perry said to Isla, his voice casual. "What's the deal with the Stones? The atmosphere back there was pretty tense."

Isla's blue eyes darted to Simon, who gave her a quick nod. "It's awful. Chloe says her parents barely speak to each other these days. She blames her mum."

That was clear from that little exchange back there. "And why is that?"

"Chloe overheard them arguing the day before the pool party. Nessa told Derek she wanted a divorce." Isla lowered her voice. "Then Derek said something like, 'He won't want you, so you're wasting your time.'"

Perry's mind raced. "He? Who's he?"

Isla shrugged. "Chloe thinks her mum's been having an affair, but she doesn't know who with."

JT! The same man Chloe had been oh-so-flirty with that same night.

"But," Isla continued, "Chloe is so mad about it. Like, so much more than seems reasonable. So I think…" She trailed off and looked at Simon.

Simon put his arm around his daughter's shoulders. "Isla, anything you know that may help us catch JT's killer before anyone else gets hurt, well, we'll be really grateful."

Isla stopped dead in her tracks. "So you're definitely investigating it then? Like you did the death of that TV judge?" Isla asked, her eyes shining.

Perry's throat tightened. He'd not said anything to Simon about Isla wanting to investigate with them. Isla had been with Perry and Simon when they'd apprehended a killer on an earlier case. She'd appeared to have taken it all in her stride at the time, but Perry knew Simon had been worried that she'd been putting on a brave face. But Perry saw the excitement in his stepdaughter's eyes right now. *She wants to be part of this…* He mirrored her glance with quiet understanding.

Simon dipped his head to the side. "Let's just say that we're unofficially helping Tina."

"In that case… I think it was JT she was having an affair with. And that's why Chloe's so mad because she had designs on him too."

And she's hit the nail on the head! Good girl.

"Really?" Simon asked. "But he was old enough to be her father."

"I overheard an argument just as I arrived," Isla admitted. "Chloe and her dad were outside by the pool. They were both shouting. She said, 'Why would you need to say anything about me to him? I bet you never warned him off Mom, did you?' and he replied, 'Your mom's an adult. She can make her own stupid mistakes. But you're my daughter. I couldn't let him take advantage of you like that.'"

Perry's heart stuttered for a moment as he let out a low whistle. *Had Derek killed JT?* "And then?" he asked Isla.

"Sorry, there's no more. The maid came up behind me and coughed. They both looked around, and I pretended I'd just arrived."

Perry's mind whirled. *This is huge.* So Derek had known of Nessa's affair with JT.

Isla then turned to Simon. "Do you think Derek killed JT?"

Simon took her arm, and they began walking again. "I've no idea, but let's not worry about it, alright? You did the right thing by telling us. Thanks."

Derek was now not only a suspect with a motive, but he'd also had the opportunity to drug JT. They needed to tell Rich and Bea immediately.

Perry sped up just as Isla eagerly asked Simon, "Do you want me to carry on spying on them?"

Perry grinned. *She's a chip off the old block!*

23

AFTER LUNCH, SUNDAY 8 AUGUST

"So what you're saying is that as both Derek and JT were drinking bourbon towards the end of the evening, only someone in the room would have been able to put the ketamine in JT's glass?" Bea asked. Simon and Perry had finished briefing her, Rich, and DI Tina Spicer, who had joined them for lunch before they'd moved down to the basement to show her their progress.

"Yes." Perry nodded. "It's the only way the killer could've made sure the drugged drink didn't go to Derek by mistake."

He has a point... So that means—

"Unless," Rich pointed out. "It *was* Derek. He would know which glass he'd put it in."

Also a good point... Perry had told them what Isla had overheard between Derek and Chloe.

Daisy, who'd been perched on Bea's lap enjoying a back rub, gave a low *woof* and jumped down.

"Hello?" Isla slipped into the room, her ginger ponytail catching the dim light. Daisy ran to greet her. The young woman bent down to fuss over Daisy, but her wide eyes were looking around the room until they rested on the whiteboards standing along the wall in front of the large wooden table strewn with papers that they were sitting around. "So this is Murder HQ, is it?" she asked, cocking her head to one side.

Perry grinned. "Yes, what do you think? Your dad set it up. Professional, heh?"

Isla straightened. "It looks good." She hesitated, then said in a firm voice, "I want in."

In what?

"Want in what?" Rich echoed, frowning.

"I want to be involved in investigating JT's murder."

Simon's eyes widened. "I thought we'd talked about this, Isla. Absolutely not. It's not safe."

"Dad, come on." Isla crossed her arms. "I'll be fine. Plus, I might hear something important when I'm hanging out with Chloe. You know, a young person's super hearing and all that." Her blue eyes darted around the room, landing on each face in turn. The girl's jaw was set, determination radiating from her slight frame. Her gaze stopped when it landed on Perry.

Perry cleared his throat. "She's got a point, love. She's already told us about something she overhead that has proven to be really helpful. A set of ears on the inside will be useful."

Simon opened his mouth to argue, but Isla cut him off. "And I'll feel safer if I know what's going on. Please, Dad?"

They all looked at Simon, whose face gave away the battle going on inside his head. Bea understood. Simon would be torn between wanting to protect Isla, who at nineteen was only three years older than Sam, and allowing his daughter to spread her wings as a young adult. *Poor Simon.* Bea discovered recently that older teenagers were a whole new level of worry—the need to stop them doing anything that could get them hurt, physically or mentally, balanced against letting them make their own mistakes and learning from them.

After a long moment, Simon sighed. "Fine. But the deal comes with some conditions, okay?"

Perry shot Bea a look and rolled his eyes. She smirked.

Isla nodded. "Shoot!"

"First, you're never to be on your own with Derek Stone."

Oh, does Simon suspect Derek in particular?

"Okay."

"Second, you must always have your phone at least fifty percent charged and on vibrate but never off. Don't leave it lying around at their house; make sure it's always on you. Got it?"

Good advice. I really should be more careful to make sure I always have mine...

"Yes, Dad."

"Thirdly, don't go poking around for evidence. Just be there and keep your ears open."

Bea's cheeks burned. The number of times she'd gone poking around during previous cases and got into trouble!

"Got it!"

"And finally, make sure you don't do anything without discussing it with one of us first. Deal?"

Isla's face lit up with a triumphant grin. "Deal!" she said and plopped down next to Perry.

Bea couldn't help smiling. *The girl has guts!* She caught Rich's eye, and he winked at her before rising. "Your dad and Perry can bring you up to speed later, Isla, but in the meantime, let's carry on. Spicer... Sorry, I mean Tina, do we have anything more from the local police?"

"Medical records sent from JT's doctor in the States confirm he had a previous allergic reaction to ketamine," Tina began, her voice steady and professional. "So I think it's fair to say he wouldn't have voluntarily taken it himself."

Although they'd been confident this was the case, it was good to have it validated.

"Blood tests confirm both alcohol and ketamine in his system. His BAC, that's the blood alcohol concentration, was zero-point-fifteen percent. That's over twice the legal limit to drive over here."

"Do they know when the ketamine was administered?" Rich asked.

"The pathologist estimates around twenty to thirty minutes before death," Tina replied.

Bea dipped her head at Rich. He had been accurate with his guesstimate earlier.

"So sometime between nine-thirty and nine-forty?" Simon clarified.

Bea's breath caught in her throat. "So he was definitely still in the room when it happened."

"And so was the killer," Perry added, his eyes shining. "So we really can narrow the suspects down now. It was either Peter, Pearl, Derek, or Lucy. Chloe had already left, Ella was with me and Simon during that time, so she wouldn't have been able to slip anything into JT's drink. Nessa had also left not long after her daughter, and Maria didn't come into the room."

Bea frowned and turned to Tina. "So if that's the case, why are the police still considering Maria as the prime suspect?"

Tina shrugged. "It's beyond me. I can only assume now that they have all the evidence here, they will have to back off her and consider someone else."

"Well, after what Isla told us, Derek has to be up there now," Perry said with a tip of his head.

Has he changed his mind? "I thought Peter was top of your list?"

Perry gave a wry smile. "He was. And I still think he has a powerful motive, *and* he was in the room. But Derek was also in the room, so he could've drugged JT. We know he confronted or at least planned to confront JT about Chloe at some time. What if he went back later? He could be the one who pushed him into the statue."

"There were no signs on JT's body to suggest he was shoved hard," Tina reminded him. "However, when someone is that unsteady on their feet, even a gentle push might be enough to unbalance them."

"And what about motive?" Rich asked.

Perry crossed his arms. "His wife was having an affair with JT, and JT was making a play for his daughter. Take your pick."

Rich cleared his throat. "So next, Bea and I went through the crime scene reports and made a note on the board." He pointed to a list underneath the timeline Simon had laid out earlier. "The police seem to have taken everything that wasn't nailed down in and around the garden and pool that night."

Bea had written all the items that had been catalogued, although it had seemed a random collection of things to her. She glanced up at it now. A skimming pole used to clean the pool had been found in some bushes near the pool. *Would the gardeners have left that lying around?* A large roll of gaffer tape and a pair of scissors had been found in the unlocked pool house—*someone was probably fixing something in there and left them behind*—along with clean towels, pool toys, a wooden chair in front of a long mirror, a fully stocked drinks fridge, goggles, nose clips, more swimming gear. Nothing *really* out of the ordinary.

Rich continued, "There were no footprints as the ground

was too dry. There was one thing that we thought might be relevant. The statue, the one that hit JT, wasn't secured properly. The bolts that should have attached it to the plinth are missing."

Simon started, his brow creasing up. "Missing? How does that even happen?"

"According to the police report, the statue was taken away for cleaning six months ago," Rich explained. "They're trying to contact the company who reinstalled it to see if they remember bolting it back onto the plinth properly."

"Six months ago?" Bea asked. "Surely, someone would have noticed?"

"Not necessarily. How often does anyone look at a statue that closely?" Simon replied.

I suppose so…

"And that explains why it fell on him," Perry said. "Is it possible it was part of a plan?"

Tina leaned back, crossing her arms. "The police aren't focusing on the statue at all. They think it's irrelevant. Their current theory is that the killer drugged JT, planning to push him into the pool. They think if he didn't overdose from the mix itself, then he would've drowned because of the ketamine incapacitating him."

"And it would've looked like an accident?" Isla asked.

"It would if everyone thought he took the ketamine himself," Simon told her.

A thought popped into Bea's head. *So does that mean the killer didn't know about JT's allergy?*

"But that's not what happened," Perry said slowly.

But who, apart from Ella, knew?

"No," Tina agreed. "They believe there was a confrontation. The killer pushed JT, he fell into the unsecured statue, and it toppled over, striking him. An unintended consequence but with the same result."

"Oh, and I almost forgot, there's the necklace found in the pool when they drained it. Ella has confirmed it's hers—the one that went missing," Rich said.

"The one JT accused Maria of stealing?" Simon asked.

"There's something about that in the transcript from Maria's interview." Tina interjected, pulling a file towards her and flipping it open. "She's adamant she didn't steal the necklace but confirms JT accused her of it. She was upset about the incident, but says Ella reassured her, telling her she didn't believe JT's allegations."

Perry frowned. "Wasn't he threatening to sack Maria over it though?"

"Yes," Tina confirmed. "But according to Maria, Ella told her she wouldn't let that happen."

Bea remembered Maria's red-rimmed eyes and Ella being deep in conversation with the maid. *Is that what was going on at the pool party?*

"So what happens now?" Isla asked.

"We need to look at each of our suspects and consider means, opportunity, and motive," Perry replied like an old hand.

Bea rubbed her hands together. They seemed to be getting somewhere now…

24

___

A WHILE LATER, SUNDAY 8 AUGUST

The basement at Villa Mer was feeling muggy as Bea tapped her finger against her bottom lip and studied the grid Simon had drawn on the whiteboard. Along the top were the names of all their suspects and down the side were four words—means, opportunity, motive, and alibi. They had spent the last forty minutes completing all the boxes, but now Perry was layering Post-it notes with additional comments scrawled on them on top of the grid.

"Right," Perry said, tapping a manicured nail against a hot-pink Post-it with the number one written on it. "So Peter has a strong motive. We know JT was planning on throwing him off the property. He was in the room between nine-thirty and nine thirty-five when he then left to supposedly go to his studio. However, no one can corroborate that, so he might have waited until he knew JT was going for a swim, then went back and pushed him into the pool."

Bea frowned. "Don't you mean into the statue?"

"Er, yes. Sorry… into the statue, which then fell on him, causing him to fall backwards into the pool."

Why push him into the statue when it would've been so much quicker to push him into the pool?

"I think that puts him at the top of our list," Perry wrapped up with a flourish.

"And what about the ketamine?" Bea asked. "Where did Peter or anyone else for that matter get it from?"

"Did he bring it with him?" Simon suggested.

"Have the police searched Villa Mer for any signs that there's ketamine present?" Rich asked Tina.

She dipped her head. "As far as I know, they've been through the villa, but they've not personally searched individuals or Villa Luz. Their thinking is that it's such an easy drug to get hold of, anyone could do so, so they're not really focussed on that at the moment. But as Maria's lawyer pointed out to them, there's no known local supply of the drug, so they need to prove Maria had access to some, and they haven't been able to as of yet."

Simon's suggestion that one of the Americans had brought it with them made sense to Bea. So that didn't really narrow down their options much.

"Anyway, surely, whoever had it would have disposed of any extra by now, knowing it was used in JT's murder?" Perry added.

"Probably," Tina agreed.

"So if for the moment, we assume that any one of our suspects got hold of ketamine somehow, your money that was on Derek is now on Peter again, is it, Perry?" Simon asked, a wry smile on his face.

Perry screwed up his nose. "Well… I just feel Peter has an air of desperation about him."

"But," Rich chimed in, "Pearl possibly had the same motive as Peter, assuming she knew they were being moved on. She was also in the room at the right time to have added ketamine to his drink, and she left only a few minutes after her husband. Again, no one can confirm she went straight to bed, so she too might have snuck out to the pool and pushed JT."

Bea looked up at the board. Rich was right. Pearl, Derek, and Peter *all* had a motive, the opportunity to add the drug to JT's drink, and no alibi to confirm where they were when JT had fallen into the pool.

Woof! Daisy jumped off a large chair in the corner of the room and ran to the door with an excited *yap* as the doorbell rang.

"I'll get it," Rich said, rising and dashed up the stairs, Daisy on his heels.

Bea gazed back at the board. Something was nagging at her, but what was it? A niggle at the back of her right eye warned her that a headache might be on its way. *I need to get out in the fresh air…*

She rose. "I'm going to—" She was cut off by Rich's and Daisy's return. The little terrier danced around Rich's feet as he landed at the bottom of the stairs, a cream-coloured envelope in his hand.

"Oh, what have you got?" Perry asked, his eyes wide open.

"A summons from none other than the grieving widow herself." Rich handed Bea the note. "Ella requests my presence at Villa Sol as soon as is convenient."

Bea looked down at the elegant script. *Why does Ella want to see Rich?* A prickle of unease crept up her spine as she recalled Ella draping herself over Rich at the pool party. Batting her lashes. Hanging on his every word. And now with JT out of the picture... Bea's stomach clenched. "I'll go with you," she blurted out. Rich gave her a questioning look.

"For... investigative purposes, of course," she added hurriedly.

Perry coughed, then met her gaze, a knowing smirk playing on his lips. Bea shot him a warning glare.

"Okay. Shall we go now then?" Rich asked, seemingly oblivious to the undercurrents passing between Bea and her best friend.

———

Bea took a deep breath as she and Rich approached Villa Sol. The fresh air seemed to have worked, and the threatening headache had thankfully disappeared. Lucy greeted them at the door, her demeanour still subdued. Dark circles shadowed her eyes, and her smile didn't quite reach them.

"Ella's expecting you on the deck out back," she said, ushering them through the airy foyer. "I'll fetch some refreshments."

As Lucy scurried off, Bea leaned close to Rich. "Is it me or is she looking very frazzled?"

Rich shrugged. "Maybe the stress of having to cover Maria's job is getting to her."

They stepped onto the sun-drenched terrace, where Ella sat at a huge wooden outside dining table, flipping through a glossy magazine.

Removing her sunglasses, she glanced up, a slow smile splitting her face as her piercing blue eyes zeroed in on Rich. "Richard, darlin'!" Ella purred, rising gracefully. "How good of you to come so soon." Her gaze shifted to Bea, a flicker of annoyance quickly masked. "And Lady Rossex. What a... an unexpected pleasure."

I bet! Bea gritted her teeth as she gave the actress a wry smile.

"Do sit, both of you," Ella said, setting aside her magazine and crossing her long legs. "Derek mentioned you were assisting with the investigation. I'm hoping you can enlighten me on the latest developments."

Who told him that? Oh... Perry, of course. But if she's after information, why not simply talk to the police?

Rich shifted, clearly surprised. "Ah, you know... I have... er, connections."

Ella leaned forward, her ice-blue eyes boring into his. "Good. So you must know more than those tight-lipped local police. I'm worried sick about Maria. Is she still in custody? When can she come home?"

Home or back to work? Bea chided herself. In fairness to Ella, she did look concerned for her maid.

At that moment, Lucy appeared, bearing a tray of drinks. "I have homemade lemonade," she told them. "But I can get you something stronger if you prefer?"

Bea and Rich opted for lemonade. The tart sweetness was refreshing in the heat of the afternoon sun. Lucy handed Ella a flute of champagne, then poured herself a glass of lemonade and perched on the edge of a chair opposite them, her knee bouncing.

Rich coughed. "Actually, the police have released Maria. She's staying with family outside of town for now."

Ella gave a grim smile. "That's great news. I hope she's recovering from the shock of it all."

"She's still a suspect," Rich advised her. "But without further evidence against her, the police cannot charge her."

"And do they have any other suspects?" Ella asked, her breezy voice not reflecting the keenness in her eyes.

"Not that I know, although they seem to have narrowed it down to someone within the complex," Rich replied.

Bea studied Ella's reaction, but the actress' face remained

an inscrutable mask. *Was she hoping it was an outsider, or did she suspect it was someone she knows? Time to see if I can find out...* "Ella, was there any issue between JT and anyone staying here, do you know?"

"Not that I know of." Looking away, Ella took a delicate sip of champagne.

She's cool, this one. "What about Derek and JT?"

Ella's lips tightened. "They were the best of friends, like brothers. Sure, they had their disagreements, but what friends don't? They always worked it out. Why do you ask?" Her gaze swivelled to Bea, sharp and assessing.

Rich deflected Ella's attention away from Bea. "We have reason to believe Derek and JT argued at some stage that evening."

Ella gave an elegant shrug, but Bea's attention was drawn to Lucy, who shifted in her seat, worrying her bottom lip. She looked like a volcano about to blow.

She knows something. "Lucy? Did you see Derek and JT have an argument?" Bea's tone was gentle.

Lucy's eyes widened, darting between Ella and Bea. "Er, no, not exactly, but... I did see him. Later. After he left the party."

Bea's fingers tingled. "And where was that?" Bea asked.

She hesitated, then said, "He was, er... walking past the window... I was heading down to the kitchen."

"Did you tell the police?" Rich asked.

"No, I..." Lucy twisted her hands in her lap. "I forgot. Until just now. At the time, I thought he'd left something behind, but now..." Her voice trailed off, and she swallowed loudly.

Ella waved a dismissive hand. "That's probably all it was." Her eyes slid to Bea's face. "Just because he came back doesn't mean he saw JT," she said firmly.

Lucy was still mumbling, "With everything that's happened, it completely slipped my mind."

"What time was this, Lucy?" Rich asked.

"Er… it must've been about ten to ten. I'd left the sitting room a few minutes before."

Rich and Bea exchanged a look. *Did he go back to confront JT about Chloe, and things had got out of hand? And* it meant Derek had lied to the police. They needed to tackle him about it as soon as they were done here.

Ella's voice cut through Bea's thoughts. "So thank you for the update on Maria." She smiled sweetly at Rich. "You will keep me informed of any developments, won't you?"

Rich shifted in his seat, clearly uncomfortable. "I'll do my best to—"

"Of course," Bea cut in, not entirely sure why she felt the need to interrupt. Perhaps it was the way Ella's gaze lingered on Rich or the memory of her flirtatious behaviour at the pool party. "We'll let you know if anything significant comes up."

Ella seemed satisfied, though her eyes still held a calculating gleam. *I bet she's already planning to ring Maria and ask her when she can come back to work.*

But hold on, there is one more thing…. "Did either of you use the skimming pole that day?" Bea asked. It had been bugging her since they'd read the crime scene report that said it had been found in the bushes. She was sure the gardeners wouldn't have left it lying around.

Ella's hands fidgeted in her lap. A slight flush crept up her neck. "No, I didn't touch the skimming pole," Ella said, her voice sharp with disdain. "It's not my job to clean the pool. That's what we have gardeners for."

Lucy, on the other hand, seemed completely unfazed by a question for the first time since they'd arrived. She simply shook her head and said, "No, I didn't use it either."

Ella suddenly leapt up. "Well, I'm sure you both have a lot to do. Please don't let me keep you."

As they stood to leave, Bea glanced at Lucy, who had turned away and was staring at her feet. Bea had a feeling the PA had more to tell them…

25

A FEW MINUTES AFTER THAT, SUNDAY 8 AUGUST

Bea squinted against the sun's glare as she and Rich stepped out of Villa Sol. She dragged her sunglasses down from the top of her head and made her way down the front steps.

"It feels like Derek's really moving up the list to suspect number one," Rich said, catching up with her and taking her hand.

Yep! She looked over to her left, where Villa Luz, Derek and Nessa's home, stood, its white facade adorned with vibrant orange bougainvillea flowers and delicate pale-pink blooms of jasmine. *We can pop over there now...* "Should we go see him while we're here?"

Rich's forehead wrinkled. "I think I'd prefer to consult with Tina first—"

As if summoned by their conversation, Derek rounded the corner, a beach bag slung over his shoulder and his flip-flops slapping against the pavement.

"Speak of the devil," Bea murmured to Rich, plastering on a smile as they let go of each other's hand.

Derek grinned, his tan emphasising a set of startlingly

white teeth. "I've just come from the beach via the main gate," he said as he stopped in front of them. "I wanted to check out how busy it was out there. Nessa's been nagging me to take her out of the complex. Retail therapy, she calls it. But I didn't fancy it with all the press around, you know?"

"And how bad is the press situation?" Rich asked, his tone casual, but his eyes focused intently on Derek's face.

Derek shrugged. "There's still a fair contingent of paparazzi, but the TV crews and large news outlets seem to have gone, so it's nowhere near as bad as before."

Bea responded with a faint incline of her head. Rich had received a similar report from security this morning. She was trying not to get her hopes up too much, but she was optimistic that they were losing interest in her and Rich, although speculation around JT's death was still making the news regularly.

"I expect I'll have no excuse now not to take Nessa out shopping," Derek said, rolling his eyes in the I'm-a-poor-man-being-dragged-off-shopping-by-my-wife way that men had.

As he made to move on, Bea took a deep breath, channelling her inner Perry. "Actually, Derek," she said, her voice steady despite her racing heart, "there's something I'd like to ask you." Rich shot her a surprised glance, but Bea pressed on. "Why did you lie to the police?"

Derek's relaxed expression morphed into one of shock. "Excuse me?" he sputtered, his stocky frame tensing. "What are you talking about?"

Bea stood her ground, her eyes locked on Derek's face. "You were seen returning to Villa Sol after you'd left the party. Did you return to see JT? Did you two have an argument by the pool?" *Oh my goodness, have I gone too far?*

They didn't know if Derek had been with JT poolside that night.

Rich's eyebrows shot up, but he remained silent. Bea shot him an apologetic look.

Derek's mouth opened and closed a few times before he finally spoke. "I… How did you know?"

Bea's breath caught in her throat. She hadn't expected him to admit it so readily.

Not prepared to give away Lucy as their witness, she pressed him, "So it's true then?"

His shoulders sagged. "Yes, I went back to see JT before his swim," he said, his voice barely above a whisper. "But I swear JT was alive when I left."

"Why did you go back?" Rich asked, his voice level.

Derek's jaw clenched, and he shook his head. "There was something I needed to say." Then his eyes narrowed. "I'm not saying any more than that." He raised his chin.

Why not? He'd told them he'd gone back to confront JT. Why was he clamming up now? Assuming it was about Chloe, was he worried it would incriminate him further?

"Look, JT had had too much to drink. He was completely wasted," Derek continued, his words tumbling out. "I couldn't get any sense out of him, so I left." He took a deep breath. "Then I heard the scream as I was about to go through my door at home. That's when I ran back and…" He trailed off, swallowing hard.

She studied his face, searching for any sign of deception, but he looked genuinely distressed thinking about his friend's death.

"I have nothing to hide," Derek insisted, his voice cracking slightly. "I would've never hurt JT. We were best buddies."

Except he was having an affair with your wife and

appeared to be hoping to move on to your daughter next! Surely, that was a no-go between 'best buddies'? Bea opened her mouth, ready to bring up it up, but when she caught Rich's eye, he subtly shook his head. *Spoilsport!*

"Thank you for your honesty, Derek," Rich said smoothly. "We appreciate you clearing that up."

Derek nodded, looking relieved and exhausted. "If there's nothing else, I should get going." He hurried off towards Villa Luz without a backwards glance.

"So I think I'll start calling you Perry," Rich said once he was out of earshot.

Bea gave him a mock exasperated look as a smile tugged at her lips. "I don't know what you're talking about. It seemed a shame to waste the opportunity to ask him some more questions."

Rich chuckled as he draped an arm around her shoulders and pulled her close. "You'll be telling me Subtle is your middle name next."

She gave him a gentle elbow in the ribs.

"Ouch!"

"Well, I'm glad we ran into him," Bea said, pushing her sunglasses up on her nose with one hand while she snaked the other around Rich's back. "Despite his evasiveness, I believed him when he said he wouldn't have hurt JT." Another thought struck her. "Also, why would he have drugged JT if he'd wanted to talk to him seriously? It seems counterproductive."

Rich dipped his head. "I agree, but we can't rule him out completely. His confession places him at the pool just before JT died. He might have been the last person who saw him alive."

When they arrived at Villa Mer, a furry missile of excitement hurtled towards them. Daisy, her tail wagging furiously, greeted them with enthusiastic barks.

"Hello, little girl," Bea cooed, bending down to scratch behind Daisy's ears. She glanced up to see Ana hovering in the kitchen doorway, her expression tense.

"*Olá,* Ana." Bea straightened. "How's Maria doing?"

Ana's shoulders sagged slightly. "*Olá.* She's back at the police station for more questioning. I hope they will leave her alone after this."

Bea met her gaze with a knowing look. As Maria had not been in the sitting room during the time window when someone had drugged JT's drink, she was in the clear.

Rich nodded, trying to offer a reassuring smile. "I'm sure they have it all in hand."

"*Si.* I hope so, *se Deus quiser,*" Ana murmured, her eyes distant for a moment, then, as if remembering her duties, she asked, "Would you like a drink?"

They both declined and thanked her as she retreated into the kitchen. With Daisy trotting at their heels, they walked through the villa and out onto the terrace, where they found Sam and Archie huddled over a tablet, engrossed in something.

Rich flopped into a recliner and, with an enormous sigh, removed his boat shoes and waggled his toes while Daisy crawled under the chair and curled up. Bea walked over to the boys. "What are you two up to? I thought you'd be back in the pool by now."

Sam jumped slightly, looking sheepish. "Oh, um, just looking at Chloe's feed."

Bea's curiosity piqued. "Chloe Stone's social media? May I see?" She'd still not got around to looking at anything Chloe had posted yet. She hadn't been sure that she'd wanted to. But now it was here...

Blushing, Sam leaned back and let Archie hand over the tablet. "This one's from a few days ago. You and the super are in it, actually," Archie told her. Bea's eyes widened as she recognised the gardens of Villa Sol on the screen. *This is from the afternoon of the pool party.* Her pulse quickened. Maybe there would be something in the background that would help them. JT arguing with someone perhaps? *Now that would be perfect evidence to take to the police...* She watched intently, searching for any clues or suspicious behaviour. But it was only Chloe posing and preening for the camera, showing off the luxurious villa and grounds.

Wait a minute! Bea frowned, noticing something odd in the background. "Can you play that again?" she asked Archie. He obliged, and Bea leaned in closer, her heart now pulsing in her ears. There, behind Chloe, the camera panned across the pool area. Something wasn't right. Then she saw it. "Stop!" she cried, her hand shooting out.

Archie's finger jabbed the pause button, freezing the frame. Bea leaned in, her green eyes narrowing.

"What is it, Mum?" Sam asked, excitement tinging his voice.

"I'm not too sure, darling." Bea turned to Archie. "Can you take a still of this shot for me and send it to my phone?"

"Sure thing, Lady B," Archie replied, his fingers flying over the screen. "Do you want me to send you the link to the whole video too?"

Bea inclined her head absently, her mind whirring. "Yes, please. That would be brilliant." She rose. "Why don't you two have a swim? I need to find Perry and Simon."

The boys agreed and headed off towards the pool house as Bea hurried off to where Rich was now lying back, soaking up the sun with his eyes closed. Bea thrust the phone under his nose. "Look at this, Rich. The statue—I think I can see the bolts, and they were in place!"

Rich's eyes shot open. "What?"

She explained it was a still from the video Chloe had filmed the afternoon of the pool party. Bea pointed to the poolside scene.

Rich raised an eyebrow as he leaned over and zoomed in with his fingers. "I think you might be right, although it's too blurred to say for sure."

"Perhaps we can compare it to the photos taken on the night JT was killed?" she suggested.

Rich sprang up, nearly tripping over Daisy, who had clambered out from under his chair. "Sorry, little girl," he murmured, giving Daisy a quick pat before saying to Bea, "Basement?"

Bea's heart pounded with the thrill of a potential break-through as they moved inside. But as they passed the door to the kitchen, a woman's wail stopped them in their tracks.

Oh, no! Ana! Bea and Rich burst through the door to find her slumped at the table, her face buried in her hands, sobs racking her body. Enzo stood nearby, his face drawn with worry. Bea's shoulders tensed.

"What's happened?" Rich asked, his voice urgent as he rushed towards them.

Enzo's words hit like a punch to the stomach. "Maria's been arrested. For JT's murder."

26

IMMEDIATELY AFTER, SUNDAY 8 AUGUST

Bea's jaw dropped. "Maria? Arrested? That's ridiculous!"

The shocked faces around her mirrored her disbelief. Why did the police think Maria had anything to do with drugging JT? She hadn't even been in the room.

Rich was already dialling a number on his phone. "I'm calling Tina to find out what on earth is going on." His brow furrowed as he waited for her to pick up.

Bea glanced over at Ana, whose face was pale and drained of colour. Daisy trotted over and jumped onto the housekeeper's lap, resting her head on Ana's arm and gazing up at her with soulful brown eyes. Ana absentmindedly stroked the dog's wiry fur as she wiped her face with her other hand.

"Tina, it's Rich. Why have they arrested Maria Rodrigues?"

Bea leaned in, straining to hear Tina's response. Rich's frown deepened as he listened, then he hung up, shaking his head. "Tina has no idea about the arrest. She's going to call the local police to get details, then head over here."

Bea thoughtfully tilted her head, then turned to Enzo, who hovered nearby, looking shaken. "Enzo, why don't you take your mother home? She needs to rest. It's been a terrible shock. We'll let you know as soon as we learn anything more."

Daisy jumped off Ana's lap as Enzo gently guided the dazed woman out of the door. Bea rubbed her temples, a headache building behind her eyes. What had they missed? What clue had slipped past their notice? She clenched her fists, determination rising. *We have to prove Maria's innocence—and fast.*

Rich reached over and kissed her on the forehead. "Let's tell Perry and Simon what's going on, shall we?"

Bea's flip-flops made a soft, rhythmic *slap-slap* on the tiled stairs as she descended with Rich and Daisy into the basement. Perry grinned when he saw them. "Don't tell me, Peter confessed, and we can take all these down." He swung his arm at the whiteboards. Then he saw Bea's face and stopped, his arm dropping to his side. "What's happened?" he asked, his face etched with concern.

Rich stepped forward, his face grim. "They've arrested Maria."

Simon's pen clattered onto the table. "Arrested? Why?"

Bea sank into a nearby chair. "That's what we're trying to find out," she replied wearily as Daisy leapt onto her lap, circled twice, then curled up.

"I've called Tina, who's speaking to the local police," Rich said, lowering himself on the arm of Bea's chair.

Simon rubbed his short beard, a crease across his forehead. "There must be additional evidence… Or something we've overlooked."

"But it makes no sense," Perry insisted as he ambled towards them. "JT and Derek were both drinking bourbon that night. How could Maria have possibly ensured it would hit the right target?"

Exactly!

"I think we'll have to wait and see what Tina says," Rich said.

Simon nodded. "In the meantime, what did Ella want?"

Bea started. Hadn't they seen him since then? It seemed like hours ago that she and Rich had left to see what the actress had wanted, but glancing at her watch confirmed it had only been forty minutes ago.

Rich told Perry and Simon that Ella had wanted an update on the case, her main concern appearing to be around Maria's welfare, and then Bea jumped in and told them about Lucy's revelation that she'd seen Derek return after the party, and finally they recounted what Derek had told them when Bea had confronted him on the driveway.

"You *have* been busy," Perry said once they'd finished.

Oh, and there's the statue! Bea went to say something, but before she got a word out, Daisy jumped off her lap as hurried footsteps echoed from the stairwell. Detective Inspector Tina Spicer appeared in the basement doorway, slightly out of breath. Daisy bounded over, her tail wagging in greeting.

"I've spoken with the local police," Tina said, getting straight to the point as she hovered by the stairs. "They've arrested Maria but not formally charged her yet. Things are slightly different over here. She has to be brought before a judge within forty-eight hours, but then they can decide if she should be charged, released, or placed in investigative detention, which means they *could* hold her for up to eighteen months without charge. In the meantime, she's being held at the station." Tina's eyes darted around the room. "The police claim they have fresh evidence implicating Maria, but they wouldn't give me details over the phone."

"What about Maria's lawyer?" Bea asked. "Surely, that formidable woman is able to get her released?"

Tina shrugged. "She's not available apparently, much to the police's delight. I expect Maria will be allocated a local lawyer now."

Bea frowned. *But would they be up to speed?* She needed to contact Lady Grace and find out if she would make Maria's ace lawyer available again. She picked up her phone and sent a quick text.

"I'm heading to the police station now to find out more," Tina continued. "Do you want to come too, sir?"

Rich rose, his jaw set. "Absolutely." He reached out and squeezed Bea's shoulder. "We'll be as quick as we can." Then he joined Tina, and they left together.

Alright! Well, while he did that, she would see what more she could find out about the statue. "The statue," she said, turning to Perry and Simon as she got her phone out of her pocket. "I think the bolts were there at the time of the pool party."

"Now that's interesting," Simon said, scratching his chin. "How come?"

"Look." Bea got up and joined them by the table in front of the whiteboards. She showed them the still Archie had taken from Chloe's video. "This is from a video Chloe Stone posted online of the pool party two days before JT was killed." She zoomed in. "See the plinth? It doesn't look like there are any holes in it. Whereas—" She reached up and removed one of Perry's photos taken the night JT had died. She placed it to the right of the photo on her phone. "Here, in Perry's photo, there are holes where the bolts used to be."

Simon leaned over and squinted at the two photos. "You

might be right," he said slowly. "But it could simply be the effect of angles and shadows. This is a still from a video. We really need to see a clearer image to be sure."

Bea's heart shrank. *Is it just a trick of the light?*

Perry tried to zoom in even further on the image on Bea's phone, then shook his head. "It's too blurred. Is this the only snapshot you have?" he asked her.

"Yes. But Archie sent me a link to the video."

"Okay, I think it needs looking at properly," Simon said, straightening up. "So when Rich gets back, let's see if he or Tina can send it to the tech wizards at PaIRS. They might enhance it or take a better still from the video."

But how long will that take? Bea huffed out a breath, her frustration mounting. They had less than forty-eight hours before the police charged Maria with murder. She didn't want to let Ana and Lady Grace down. *We can't wait around...* But who could help?

Woof! Bea looked over to find Daisy but couldn't see her. She rose. "Daisy?" The little white dog appeared at the bottom of the stairs, then turned and hurtled herself up them again.

"I think she needs to go out to the garden," Perry said.

Of course! "Sorry, Daisy, I'm coming." Bea hurried across the room, her mind making connections. *Garden... gardeners!* "We should talk to the gardeners. See what they know about the statue." She looked at her watch. "They should be packing up about now."

"I'm in," Perry said, rising. "I can do with some fresh air."

Simon waved them off. "You two go ahead. I'll stay here and comb through the statements again. There has to be something I've missed."

27

TEN MINUTES LATER, SUNDAY 8 AUGUST

Perry held open the gate linking Villa Mer and Villa Sol as Bea and Daisy walked through it. "Are you sure this is where the gardener's shed is?" Bea asked him.

Perry gave her a cheeky smile. "Rich pointed it out to me when we came this way to go to the pool party. Did you know he's got a copy of the whole layout here that security gave him when we first arrived?"

Bea chuckled. "You can take the man out of royal protection, but you can't take royal protection out of the man. He wants to keep us safe."

"Talking of Rich, how did he take Amber's interview?"

"In true Rich fashion, of course," Bea replied with a smile.

"Wasn't he angry that she'd talked to the papers?"

"He didn't say so. All he admitted to was being frustrated that he has no right to reply. Overall, he focused on the fact that she said he was funny. He was quite pleased about that." Watching Daisy veer off to snuffle through some nearby bushes, Bea kicked herself for not having got around to addressing the elephant in the room with Rich yet...

Perry gave her a knowing look. "I'm sensing a 'but' here. Come on, spill!"

Bea huffed. She should've known better than to hide anything from Perry. "It's just, Amber mentioned children. It's not something that Rich and I've discussed. What if he says he wants them one day? I'm not sure I do."

"Not sure or fairly sure you don't?"

Be honest! "Fairly sure I don't," she replied, slowing down. "I know technically I'm not too old, but mentally... I'm not sure I want to do it all again. The sleepless nights, the worry, the not being able to do anything other than watch over this tiny thing that is totally reliant on you. I love Sam dearly, but I also love that he's old enough now that he does his own thing." She took in a deep breath. "I know this sounds selfish, but I want Rich to myself. To have adventures with him. I don't want the tie of a baby."

Perry stopped. She stopped next to him. He turned and took her hands. "Do you remember the advice you gave me last year when I was worried that Simon wanted children, and I knew I didn't?"

She looked down at her hands in his. "Tell him?"

"Exactly! And it worked, Bea." He shrugged his shoulders. "Well, except for the bit where we found out he already had a child and now she's my stepdaughter."

Bea looked up into his face. "But what happens if it's a deal breaker? I love him, Perry. I don't want to lose him."

"Then you'll figure it out somehow. We did, and now I love Isla as if she was my own. But I know this—not talking about it won't make it go away, Bea."

He's right. Of course he is. Bea felt a weight lift from her shoulders. "Thank you. I'll talk to him as soon as I get the right moment."

"So. Tell me. Do I take it from this conversation that he's

finally dropped the L-word?" Perry's grin was positively impish.

"Maybe," Bea mumbled, blushing. Since the whole 'fool in love' comment, they'd said the three little words to each other on several occasions. It felt like a natural thing to say.

As Perry stared at her face, she couldn't suppress a smile. He let out a whoop of triumph as he enveloped her in an enormous hug. "I knew it! I knew he loved you!" he cried into her auburn hair.

She hugged him back tightly. *I'm so glad I've got you.*

Her phone vibrated in the pocket of her shorts. She took it out.

Lady Grace: *What lawyer? We didn't have time to organise one. Ana told us Maria already had one. Do I need to ask Sir Hewitt to get one over to her now?*

Frowning, Bea replied: *Yes, please.*

"What is it?" Perry asked. She showed him the message.

So if it hadn't been Lady Grace, then who had sent a top-flight lawyer to get Maria out the first time? *And why had they now withdrawn her support?*

―――――

Bea pulled her sunglasses up and onto her head as they entered the gardener's hut. Miquel, the head gardener, stood wiping his hands on a rag while Enzo sat on a stool, holding a mug.

"Lady Beatrice, Mr Perry! I wasn't expecting you."

Bea quirked an eyebrow. "We weren't expecting to see you either. I thought you'd still be with Ana. Is everything alright?"

Enzo shrugged, his tanned face creasing into a weary smile. "My girlfriend, Matilde, is with my mother. So I thought I'd come back and help Miquel pack up for the day. *Eu preciso me manter ocupado...* How you say...? I need to keep busy."

"And how's Ana holding up?" Bea asked.

"*Ah, bem.*" Enzo scratched his head. "Lady Grace telephoned Mama and told her that a new lawyer, a good one, is on their way to help Maria. It makes Mama feel better, you know?"

Bea exchanged a glance with Perry. "And is there any word on this fresh evidence the police have supposedly found?"

"*Não faço ideia,*" Enzo sighed and slowly shook his head. "Matilde's off today, so we have no way of knowing."

Bea chewed her lip. Should she tell Enzo and Miquel what they were up to? It might make them more inclined to help them... "We're trying to prove Maria is innocent. So we're doing our own little investigation."

"*Sério?* With that nice blonde English *polícia*?" Miquel asked, his brown eyes sparkling.

Bea's lips twitched in mild amusement.

Enzo shrugged. "My friend here is a little sweet on her, you know?" he said with a wry smile.

Bea suppressed a grin. "Do either of you know anything about the statue at Villa Sol, the big one by the pool that was taken away to be cleaned six months ago? The one that..." She trailed off, not wanting to say, "Fell on Mr Kenda."

"*Ah, claro,*" Miquel met her gaze with a thoughtful look.

"All the statues in Marisol get taken away and cleaned every few years. The same company always handles it."

"Are they reliable? And safe?" Perry asked.

"*Sim*! Of course." He looked puzzled. "Why?"

"The statue that killed JT... it wasn't bolted down to the plinth when it fell," Bea told him.

Both men's eyes widened in shock. "*Madre de Deus*," Miquel muttered. "That... That makes sense now. When Lucy told me what happened, I didn't believe it. That statue, when it's properly attached, is as solid as a *montanha*... How you say...? Er, mountain."

Bea's eyes narrowed as she studied his face. "Is it possible the cleaning company forgot to bolt it back on properly six months ago?"

The head gardener shook his head emphatically. "*Nah*. They've been doing this for years. They wouldn't make a mistake like—"

He paused, and something flickered across his face. *He's thought of something.* Bea's pulse quickened. "What is it, Miquel? Did you see something?"

He hesitated, then shook his head. "It's more what I didn't see, you know?"

Bea's stomach fluttered. This could be it—the breakthrough they needed. "Go on," she encouraged gently.

"The morning of JT's death, I came back here at ten to get a *chave ajustável*...er..." He paused and typed something into his phone. "Ah...wrench, you know?" They nodded. "It was gone, along with a can of *uma lata de lubrificante*...er, WD-40?" Again, they both acknowledged his words. "They were here when I'd arrived at eight-thirty. Of course, I thought one of the others was using them, so I got on with other things. When I came back here at eleven for a tea break —we do that every day—they were both back on the shelf where they'd been before. I asked the other two if I could take the… er… wrench as I had jobs at Villa Luz to do, and they said, of course, we haven't touched it."

Bea's mind raced. Had someone used those tools to loosen the statue's bolts? And if they'd done it on the day of JT's murder, then it must have been deliberate and part of the plan to kill him.

"But you have no idea who took them?" Perry asked, his eyes dancing with excitement.

Miquel shook his head.

"And can anyone get into this shed?" Bea held her breath, waiting for him to answer.

"We lock the shed at night, but during the day, with all of us coming and going…" He shook his head.

She let out her breath. *Bingo!* Everyone in Marisol had access to the shed that morning… "Miquel, we'll need to tell DI Spicer, the blonde police officer, about this. She'll want to take the wrench and WD-40 and have them examined."

Miquel offered an enthusiastic gesture of agreement. "*Si.* Would you like me to wait here for her?" he asked hopefully.

Enzo stood and shook his head at his friend. "There's no need. When she's ready, she can ring me, and I will come and let her in."

Miquel huffed and dropped his rag on the bench.

"Thank you," Bea said as a soft whine drew her attention. Daisy was sniffing around a low shelf containing pool cleaning chemicals, her tail wagging low.

"Daisy, come here," Bea cried, patting her thigh.

The little terrier trotted over, and as Bea scooped her up, it reminded her of something. "One more thing. The pool skimmer that was found in the bushes near the statue at Villa Sol. Is that where it's usually kept?"

Miquel turned down his mouth. "No, we keep it in the pool house after we clean the pool first thing in the morning."

"And on the day JT died?" Perry prompted.

"I finished cleaning the pool at Villa Sol just before nine, and I put it back myself before heading over to Villa Luz." Then he added, "Thursday is the day we're at Villa Luz."

"So do you have set days when you are at each villa?" Bea asked.

He tilted his head. "It makes it easier for the residents if they know when to expect us. Although we clean the pools every morning for each of the two villas first. Enzo here cleans the pool for Lady Grace."

So everyone would have known that the gardeners would be at Villa Luz that day. Bea caught Perry's eye, and he smiled smugly in return. *Yes. We've done a good job.*

―――――

As they made their way back to Villa Mer, having thanked Miquel and told Enzo that they didn't expect Ana to come over in the evening, Perry turned to Bea, his brow furrowed. "So are you thinking what I'm thinking?"

"That knowing the staff would all be at Villa Luz until they returned for their tea-break at eleven, someone went into the shed and took the wrench and WD-40 so they could remove the bolts that secured the statue to the plinth, then—"

"They got the pole out of the pool house and hid it in the bushes, ready to use to push over the statue so it would fall on JT and kill him?" Perry added with a flourish.

She glanced down at Daisy, who was trotting happily between them as a chill ran down her spine despite the warm sun on her face. She knew they shouldn't jump to conclusions. Not yet. They needed proof, solid evidence to back up their theory. She quickened her pace, desperate to get back to Rich and the others to tell them what they'd learned.

Because if she and Perry were right, the ketamine hadn't been the murder weapon; it had been the statue all along....

28

FIRST THING THE NEXT DAY, MONDAY 9 AUGUST

The *Daily Post* online article:

A Daily Post EXCLUSIVE by Sarah Denby (Part 1) — The Troubled Family Ties of Richard Fitzwilliam, Suitor to the King's Niece

In the wake of intense public interest surrounding Richard Fitzwilliam, the man believed to be on the verge of proposing to Lady Beatrice, seventeenth in line to the throne and the King's niece, the mystery of his background has deepened. As speculation grows over the couple's future together, The Daily Post *has uncovered the shadowy past of Fitzwilliam's father, Eric Fitzwilliam, a man whose disappearances and debts have haunted his family for decades. The question now looming over Britain's elite: Is Richard Fitzwilliam, a man* with such a troubled family history, truly suitable for royal circles?

For years, Richard Fitzwilliam, a decorated police officer who served with the City Police and PaIRS (the Royal Family's protection service), has remained an enigma. The public knows little about his family life and with good reason. Fitzwilliam's father, Eric, abandoned them when Richard was only five years old, leaving behind a crumbling building business, mounting debts, and two young children.

The fallout was swift and devastating. Richard's mother, Dawn Fitzwilliam, faced financial ruin as their home was repossessed, forcing the family to move to a council estate in one of Leeds' toughest neighbourhoods. Dawn, struggling as a single mother, worked tirelessly to qualify as a nurse, but the scars of Eric's betrayal lingered.

Our investigation uncovered that Eric Fitzwilliam resurfaced when Richard was ten, begging for his wife's forgiveness. Dawn refused to take him back, although she allowed him to see Richard and his younger sister, Elise, once a month. For young Richard, the return of his father was a moment of excitement, but for Elise, according to someone who knew her at school, it was a source of mistrust and pain. While Richard embraced these sporadic visits, his sister remained distant, often refusing to see the man who had walked out on them.

.   .   .

Just as Eric rebuilt a semblance of a relationship with his children, he remarried to a woman named Joyce. Richard was twelve at the time. Unfortunately, Eric's newfound stability didn't last. Three years later, he vanished once again, this time leaving Joyce saddled with debts and the Fitzwilliam family with even more heartache. Sources told The Daily Post *that no one has heard from Eric Fitzwilliam since. Until now…*

COMING TOMORROW: In the second part of this exclusive three-part serial by Sarah Denby, we hear for the first time from Eric Fitzwilliam, Richard's long-lost father. Read it only in The Daily Post *TOMORROW!*

29

BREAKFAST, MONDAY 9 AUGUST

The sun warmed Bea's face as she sipped from a mug on the terrace of Villa Mer. Toast, pastries, and fresh fruit lay on the large dining table beside her. She shook her head, a wry smile playing on her lips. Trust Ana to show up for work this morning, insisting she "needed to keep busy".

But as normal, all Bea needed at this time in the morning was her coffee fix. She stretched out lazily and flexed her left ankle. A twinge of pain shot up her leg, causing her to catch her breath. She'd done the right thing not joining Rich on a run this morning, but she hoped this niggle would clear up soon. It was her own fault. She'd been so excited to get back late yesterday afternoon and tell Rich, Tina, and Simon their theory about the statue that she'd hared across the lawn and slipped on a patch of grass, which had been soaked from the sprinkler that came on late each afternoon to preserve the lushness of the garden. She'd almost gone flying, but Perry, his quick reactions having surprised both of them, had grabbed her arm before she'd fallen, and the only resulting damage had been a twisted ankle on her part and a red rash for Perry where he'd rubbed against a bunch of nettles and stung his arm while helping her up. A large packet of frozen peas administered immediately after she'd hobbled into the villa by an attentive Rich had reduced the swelling, and she was able to walk normally this morning but running on it would be reckless.

She yawned. The downside to not getting her morning exercise was that she'd planned to use the time alone with Rich to raise the subject of children. Now that would have to wait. *And with it, the chances of me getting a decent night's sleep…*

As she closed her eyes, her mind returned to yesterday and the bombshell Tina had dropped not long after Rich had settled Bea into a reclining lounger and instructed her to keep her left leg elevated. Tina's patient smile while Perry had told them, "We've cracked it!" before pouring out their theory based on what Enzo had told him and Bea should have been a sign that something had been wrong.

"That's great, Perry," Tina had said, her voice gentle. "But there's been a development."

Bea's stomach clenched at the memory. She set down her coffee cup with a soft *clink.*

"They found a bottle containing traces of ketamine in the kitchen bin," Rich had told them grimly. "Only Maria's prints were on it."

"But how?" Perry had protested.

"She claims the bin bag split when she went to throw it out that night after she'd finished clearing up. She said some rubbish had spewed out onto the floor, and she'd grabbed everything, including the bottle, and put it in a fresh bag." Tina had rubbed her temples. "Her new lawyer asked about evidence of the split bag. And they admitted that the rubbish was double-bagged."

"So that backs up her story," Simon had said.

Tina had shrugged. "Yes, it does, but coupled with Peter's and Lucy's statements that they saw Maria with the tray of drinks outside the sitting room just after nine thirty-five is enough as far as the police are concerned to prove she had the opportunity to drug JT's drink before Lucy took them into the sitting room."

"But how did Maria know JT would take the right glass?" Perry had asked.

"Both JT and Derek were drinking bourbon that night, remember?" Bea had added.

"The police believe she somehow manoeuvred the situation so that JT got the drugged glass." Tina had sounded as incredulous as the rest of them. "I agree it seems far-fetched, and the evidence seems too circumstantial at the moment for the judge to charge her, but the police still have a little over thirty hours to prove their theory."

"And that means we have thirty hours to find out what *really* happened," Rich had said solemnly.

"And I think the statue theory is a good place to start," Simon had said, patting Perry on the arm. "So let's make that our job for the morning."

A light-hearted feeling passed through Bea as she took another sip from her mug. *We did it before, and we can do it* — She nearly leapt out of her skin when Perry came barrelling onto the terrace, his blue eyes wide with alarm.

"Where's Rich?" he demanded breathlessly.

Bea sat up straight. "Running on the beach with Daisy. Why?" Unease prickled down her spine.

Simon appeared behind Perry, looking equally grim. "Is he here?" he asked, his eyes scanning the terrace.

"What is it? You're scaring me." Bea stood, her heart pounding.

Perry thrust his phone in her face. "Brace yourself."

Bea grabbed the phone with shaking hands, expecting to see another interview with Amber. But as she scanned the screen, she realised it was much worse. Her first thought was of Dawn, Rich's mum. Thank goodness she was safely in Scotland with Rich's sister, Elise, and her family, hopefully too tucked away for the press to find them.

Taking a deep breath, she scrolled down to continue reading. Her heart clenched as she saw it was a three-part serial, and the next one would feature an actual interview with Rich's dad. Bea's chest tightened. "This is all my fault," she said miserably. "No one would ever have tried to find his father if Rich wasn't with me."

"No, don't say that." Perry reached out and squeezed her shoulder. "It's the ruthless vultures at *The Daily Post*. Not you."

Simon nodded vehemently. "He's right, Bea. You can't blame yourself for this."

Bea's chin quivered. *But I do…*

Her phone pinged with an incoming text.

Fred: *Yikes! Did you see The Daily Post yet? Is Rich ok? x*

Before she had a chance to reply to her brother, another message popped up.

Ma: *Darling, I'm so sorry. I had no idea about this exclusive. I have told my editor not to reference it. Let me know if you or Rich want to comment. I can cite 'source close to the family' xx*

. . .

Bea's eyes prickled. She needed to find Rich.

As if summoned by her desperate thoughts, Rich appeared at the beach access point, Daisy trotting faithfully at his side. But instead of his usual easy lope, he drifted across the lawn, with his mobile phone pressed to his ear.

"It'll be okay, El," Bea heard him say as he drew closer. "Focus on your holiday and try to ignore it."

Perry squeezed Bea's arm again, whispering, "It will be alright," then he and Simon discreetly melted away.

Rich ended the call, and without looking at her, he dropped into a chair, his face a mask of exhaustion. Daisy padded past Bea and through the open bifold doors, into the kitchen. The sound of lapping water soon followed.

Rich sat up and grabbed the coffeepot, pouring himself a large black coffee without a word. Bea watched him, worry gnawing at her insides. She'd never seen him like this—so quiet, so defeated.

"Are you okay?" she finally asked gently.

Rich's brown eyes met hers. "No," he said flatly. Then, unexpectedly, a small smile tugged at his lips. He reached out, taking her hand in his. "But I will be. I just need time to get my head around this."

Bea squeezed his hand. "Have you read the article?"

"Not yet." Rich exhaled noisily. "Elise gave me the high-lights. Or lowlights, I suppose. I understand we'll have the joy of hearing his thoughts tomorrow." He huffed.

"How's your mum taking it?"

Rich dipped his head to the side. "Surprisingly well. Her only comment was that she hoped Joyce was okay."

Rich's mother was gentle-hearted, almost to a fault. "And Elise?"

"Furious!" Rich said, his voice heavy. "Says she doesn't want to know anything about him."

A pause stretched between them. Bea's heart ached for him. "And how do you feel?"

Rich's gaze dropped to their intertwined hands. "Honestly? I couldn't care less about him. But I *am* worried he will embarrass you and your family." He raised his eyes. "I'm so sorry, Bea."

You're sorry? Bea's free hand came up to cup his face. "Hey, look at me. You have *nothing* to be sorry about. If it wasn't for me, no one would be interested in your dad."

Rich leaned in, pressing a soft kiss to her forehead. "And you're more than worth it."

Her heart skipped with joy. *What did I do to deserve this man?* She smiled at him. "I may have to remind you about that over the next two days."

He smiled back.

"Fred and Mum have already reached out. All any of us care about is that you and your family are alright. Mum even offered you a right of reply via *TSP* under the guise of 'a source close to the family'," she added.

He shook his head and said firmly, "No. I won't engage with him or *The Daily Post.*"

Bea's phone buzzed with another text. She glanced at it and chuckled.

"What is it?" Rich asked, raising an eyebrow.

"It's Perry," she said, rolling her eyes affectionately. "He wants to know if it's safe to come back out now. Apparently, he's dying for coffee and a croissant."

30

SHORTLY AFTER, MONDAY 9 AUGUST

The early morning sun bathed the terrace of Villa Mer in a warm glow as Bea sipped her coffee, enjoying the soothing, aromatic warmth. Daisy, lounging at her feet, occasionally thumped her tail against the cool tiles. *Is Rich really alright?* He'd gone to shower and change, seemingly upbeat, but surely, he knew that tomorrow an interview with his father would be plastered all over the newspapers, and that must be weighing on his mind. Bea twisted the rings on her right hand. *What will Eric Fitzwilliam have to say?*

"Bea, pass the honey, will you?" Perry's voice cut through Bea's worries, his perfectly manicured hand outstretched expectantly.

Bea slid the jar across the table, watching as Perry meticulously spread the gooey golden nectar on his croissant. He dropped his knife and took a huge mouthful, sheer delight whipping across his features. *Where does he put it all?* Bea asked, not for the first time, as she regarded his slim body dressed in sand-coloured linen trousers and a crisp white linen shirt, open to expose his tanned neck, the sleeves rolled up to just above his elbows.

"So Rich is okay, is he?" Simon mumbled as he worked his way through a plate of ham, cheese, boiled eggs, and toast.

Bea sighed, pushing a stray strand of hair behind her ear. "He's putting on a brave face, but I'm worried. He says he doesn't want to respond even though Ma offered him the opportunity to do so via *TSP*."

Simon gave her a questioning look. "There's not much he can say, is there?"

"I don't know," Bea said, rubbing the side of her head. "I'm dreading the actual interview. Who knows what his father will say?"

As if summoned by their conversation, Rich appeared on the terrace, looking positively chipper. He plopped down on an empty chair next to Bea, immediately reaching for a croissant. "Any of that coffee left?" he said cheerfully, taking a hearty bite of the pastry.

Simon poured Rich a cup and passed it over. "Thanks, mate," Rich said. "So I have some interesting news from my PaIRS IT contact. He got a clearer shot of the statue in Chloe's video. Turns out those bolts were definitely in the plinth that afternoon."

Bea felt a jolt of excitement. "So the statue really could be our murder weapon!"

Perry leaned forward, his eyes sparkling. "This changes everything. We need to—"

A familiar bark interrupted him as Daisy suddenly perked up, her tail wagging furiously. Bea turned to see Detective Inspector Tina Spicer striding towards them. Daisy ran to greet her.

"I come bringing gifts!" she said, straightening up, then walking over to them, clutching a manilla folder with a thick, lumpy plastic bag balanced on the top. "The English translations of the transcripts of Maria's interviews over the last twenty-four hours." She took the plastic bag in one hand and dropped the folder on the table. She sank onto a chair opposite Bea and Rich while Daisy returned to Bea and curled up under the table by her feet.

"How is she?" Simon asked.

Tina shrugged. "I've been updating Ana and her son. Maria's worried, clearly, but she's being looked after well. The police are still treating her like their only suspect, while her new lawyer is poking holes in everything they have, which, at best, is circumstantial. If Maria's story is true, then anyone could have put that bottle in the kitchen bin."

Bea leaned back in her chair. *Really?*

She stole a glance at Simon, who sat opposite her, scratching his beard thoughtfully. "But wouldn't she have seen them?" he asked.

"Maria said she left the kitchen at about quarter to ten, remember? She needed the bathroom," Rich replied. "She was gone for about five minutes, so there would have been a chance for someone to pop in then and dispose of the used bottle of ketamine."

Bea's mind raced. "So Peter could've snuck in after he left the party?"

"Possibly," Rich told her. "But that was a good ten minutes before, so he'd have had to wait somewhere."

"Or go while Maria was handing over the drinks tray to Lucy," Tina pointed out.

"Or it could be Pearl, who left at nine-forty, or Derek, who left three minutes later," Simon added.

"And don't forget Lucy. She went into the kitchen to wash the empty glasses while Maria wasn't there," Perry said before popping his last morsel of pastry into his mouth.

Bea shook her head. *We're going in circles.* "This really isn't narrowing down our suspects at all."

Rich's brows knitted together. "What about the interviews with Maria? Any new insights there?"

Tina shook her head ruefully. "I've only just printed them off and haven't had a chance to go through them yet. I've been preoccupied with these." She held up the evidence bag, which Bea saw contained a wrench and a WD-40 can. She smiled slyly. "A very charming man assured me that no one had touched them since your visit to his shed yesterday."

Bea suppressed a grin. *I wonder how early Miquel got in this morning?*

Tina leaned forward, her blue eyes keen. "So tell me your theory about the statue. The one you mentioned last night in your text."

Bea tilted her chin, grateful to get back to it. "We think someone removed the bolts between eight-thirty and ten on the morning of JT's death."

"Oh, that reminds me," Tina murmured. "The cleaning contractors confirmed they bolted the statue down when they left. They even have after photos to prove it."

"Actually, we already know they were in the day before because Chloe took a video, and you can see them in it," Perry told her. "So that means anyone on the estate who knew the gardeners' routine, and therefore knew they would be at Villa Luz that morning, could've taken the bolts out using the wrench and the WD-40, and returned the items by eleven, when Miquel saw them back in their place in the shed."

Bea suddenly remembered something. She turned to Rich. "Except Lucy. Wasn't she off-site that morning, according to the security records?"

Rich met her gaze with a knowing look. "You're right. Good spot." He winked. Her tummy fluttered.

"So that rules Lucy out?" Perry asked, his eyes sparkling.

"And Maria," Rich added. "She didn't start work until lunchtime that day."

"Hold on a minute." Tina held up a hand. "Can someone please explain how the removal of the bolts is connected to the murder?"

"We think the person who removed the bolts left the pole in the bushes—you know, the one that the crime scene officers found—then came back later and used it to push the statue on top of JT," Perry told her eagerly.

"And the ketamine?" Tina asked.

"They gave it to JT so he would be disoriented and confused. Then when he fell in the water, after the statue hit him, he would be unable to react quick enough to save himself," Perry finished triumphantly.

Tina frowned. "I get why they'd want to use the pole, so if someone ran out after hearing the crash, they could stay hidden in the dark. Or even sneak back to the house maybe. But how did they ensure he'd walk between it and the pool so they could hit it with the stick in the first place? And then fall into the pool?"

Good question. Bea sighed. Tina was right. *How did the killer make sure JT ended up in the pool?* But then—

Simon cleared his throat. "I've been thinking about this. I wonder if they intended to topple the statue onto him when he was entering or leaving the pool. It was right by the steps, if you remember, and he was keen to go for a swim. He would then have fallen forward or backwards into the water and drowned after being knocked on the head."

Brilliant! Although… "Would it really have mattered if he didn't end up in the pool?" Bea said, a little hesitantly. She was thinking off the top of her head now.

They all looked at her.

"I mean, as long as the statue hit him and he was too drugged up to do anything about it, he probably would have died from the blow anyway, wouldn't he?" Rich cocked an eyebrow at her. She continued, "And once he was unconscious, then the killer always had the option of pushing him into the pool afterwards to finish the job if he wasn't dead already."

"Okay, so that's quite a theory," Tina said, nodding slowly.

"Tina, were any prints found on the pole?" Rich asked.

The detective shook her head. "It wasn't considered relevant to the inquiry, I don't think. But I can have it checked when I get these looked at." She tapped the bag in front of her on the table. She turned to Bea. "I think you're onto something here. I'll mention it to Maria's lawyer, and between us, we'll see if I can subtly suggest it as an alternative."

She rose. "Right, well, I need to get these things checked out as soon as possible, so I'll catch you all later." As Tina strode off purposefully, evidence bag in hand, a flicker of hope ignited in Bea's chest. If they were right, then Maria couldn't have killed JT...but now they needed to find out who had.

31

STILL AT BREAKFAST, MONDAY 9 AUGUST

D aisy's excited bark drew Bea's attention to the bifold doors as Isla strode onto the terrace at Villa Mer, a triumphant grin on her elfin face. Daisy, her tail going like the clappers, ran to meet her. Isla scooped up the little dog.

"I've been doing some digging," she announced, plopping down at the table, Daisy still in her arms. She reached over the table and snagged a croissant, holding it high in the air to avoid Daisy's open mouth.

Bea leaned forward, her heart quickening with anticipation. "What did you find out?"

"I came across a copy of an old article online from a now defunct American celebrity magazine." Isla took a bite of her pastry, her blue eyes sparkling. "Apparently, Ella called the police about JT three years ago, claiming he'd got very abusive. She told them she feared for her life."

Perry's eyebrows shot up. "Seriously?"

"Yep. They took him away but released him the following day when she declined to press charges," Isla continued. "JT checked into rehab a day later. Some super-exclusive place. I couldn't find out exactly what they treat there though."

Perry frowned. "If it was alcohol, then he well and truly fell off the wagon. He'd been drinking openly since we got here."

"So it must've been something else," Simon reasoned.

Bea's mind raced. *What other demons had JT been battling?*

"Anger management perhaps?" Rich suggested, shrugging.

"There's more," Isla added, her voice dropping. "A recent rumour about JT having had an affair with a young actress in his latest film. Ella found out and went mad at him. Their marriage has supposedly been on the rocks ever since."

And what about JT's affair with Nessa? Had Ella known about that too?

"What was it about him?" Perry asked, his brow furrowed. "A young actress. Ella. Nessa. Chloe." He turned to Bea. "What did they see in him?"

Bea shook her head. "Don't ask me! I thought he was rude and too full of himself." Although, there had been that moment at the pool party when he'd apologised to her for his behaviour the previous day. She remembered seeing a glimpse of charm. But then he'd got drunk and loud...

"Well, it certainly paints a different picture of their relationship than the one they portrayed in public," Perry said.

She nodded, remembering she and Perry had caught them arguing that first time they'd visited Villa Sol. Although, Bea had never been sure if JT had been angry at Ella or had been angry about whatever he'd been telling her about.

Perry's face lit up. "Is this our motive?"

Bea felt a pang of disappointment as she shook her head. "Ella has an alibi. She was with you and Simon when someone slipped ketamine into JT's drink, *and* she was with you when someone toppled the statue over. She can't be our killer."

The excitement drained from Perry's face. "Oh, yeah. So, really, it's not helped us at all."

"I think it's been useful for background," Rich said, smiling at Isla. "Abusive. Unfaithful. It paints the picture of a man who probably had enemies."

Simon rose, picking up the folder Tina had left on the table with one hand and refilling his coffee cup with the other. "Okay, so I'm going to take this and head down to the basement to comb through Maria's latest interview. Hopefully, there will be something new in there."

Rich stood too, stretching his arms above his head. "I'm going to contact Fred to ask if he can dig up any info on JT and our remaining suspects."

Bea gave a half-smile. Her brother's connections within MI6 and the CIA were definitely an advantage when they were investigating a case.

Isla placed Daisy gently on the ground, then rising, chimed in, "I'll pop over to see Chloe. You never know. I might find out more about JT from her."

Simon placed an arm around her shoulders as they walked away. Bea just caught him say, "Be careful, remember," as they disappeared into the villa.

A few seconds later, Sam and Archie bounded out of the villa and onto the terrace, their youthful energy palpable. Bea smiled at her son, with his tousled reddish-brown hair and his infectious cheeky grin. She was so proud of him.

"Super!" Archie called out to Rich, his voice cracking slightly. "Don't forget you promised to take us to the beach!"

Rich glanced up from his phone, where he'd been tapping out a text message. The ghost of a smile touched his lips. "I did, didn't I?"

"Yeah, and you said we could go snorkelling and every-thing," Sam added, his face flushed with excitement.

"Tell you what," Rich said, pressing send on his message. "By the time you gannets have finished eating, I'll be done, and we can head out. Does that sound good?"

The boys agreed eagerly, their faces alight with antic-ipation.

Bea listened to the exchange, her heart bursting. Rich was so good with them, so patient and attentive. It was one of the many things she loved about him.

The boys sat down and began gathering food onto their plates, but as she watched Rich move away to answer a call, she felt a twinge of unease. She still hadn't broached the subject of children with him.

But now isn't the time, she reminded herself. They had a case to solve. *After we clear Maria's name, it will be my priority,* she promised, ignoring the feeling of relief she felt at postponing the conversation a little longer.

Perry tapped her hand. "So what about us?"

Focus, Bea! "I think we need to concentrate on Peter, Pearl, and Derek. They're our prime suspects."

"Agreed," Perry answered, then his lips curved into a sly smile. "What about we talk to Lucy? Now she's off our suspect list, we can probe her for some juicy gossip about them. After all, she must see and hear things, don't you think?"

Bea's heart quickened. "Perry, you're brilliant! Let's find her now."

32

MID-MORNING, MONDAY 9 AUGUST

"So exactly how are we going to get Lucy on her own to talk to us?" Bea asked, voicing the worry that had been niggling at her since they'd set out from the villa. "Ella's bound to be there, isn't she?"

The gravel crunched beneath their feet as they meandered down the winding tiled path to the front of Villa Sol. Perry flashed her a reassuring smile, his eyes twinkling with mischief. "Don't you worry about that, my dear. We'll cross that bridge when we come to it."

Bea gave him a knowing look, full of amusement. "Your blind optimism is both admirable and slightly irritating, you know that?"

"It's all part of my charm," Perry said as he lowered his sunglasses and winked at her over the rim.

As they approached the villa, Bea's mind raced with possibilities. Would Lucy be willing to talk to them? Did she know anything that would help them crack this case? Bea had been certain the PA knew something. She'd been so jittery, almost frightened the last time they'd spoken.

They reached the ornate front door of Villa Sol. Bea took

a deep breath, steeling herself for whatever lay ahead. "Here goes…" she muttered, reaching for the doorbell.

Perry placed a hand on her shoulder. "We've got this, Bea. Between your royal charm and my devilish good looks, Lucy won't stand a chance."

Bea chuckled as the doorbell chimed inside the villa. She squared her shoulders as the door swung open, revealing Lucy's petite frame. Her blue eyes darted nervously behind her round glasses.

"Oh, Lady Rossex, Perry," she stammered. "I wasn't expecting... Ella's not here. She's over at Villa Luz."

Bea exchanged a quick glance with Perry. "Actually, Lucy, we were hoping to speak with you."

Lucy hesitated, her thin lips pressed into a tight line. "Me?"

"Yes," Perry said, inching forward. "Can we come in?"

"Er, I suppose so." She turned, and they followed her through the villa's modern interior.

Her shoulders are so tense. Something was clearly bothering her. Bea squinted against the bright sun as she and Perry walked out onto the terrace. Bea dropped her sunglasses down onto the bridge of her nose.

Lucy gestured to a set of garden chairs, her movements jerky and uncertain. "Ella's so worried about Maria's arrest," Lucy blurted out, wringing her hands. "I mean, we all are. How's the investigation going, my lady?"

Before she had a chance to say anything, Perry leaned towards Lucy. "Actually, Lucy, we were wondering what you thought. Do you believe Maria's guilty?"

Bea blinked. She never failed to be surprised by Perry's directness. *I should know better by now.* In fairness, he normally had a plan, so she would follow his lead for now.

Lucy squirmed, avoiding their eyes. "I… I don't know.

Mr Kenda was threatening to fire her over that missing necklace, but—"

"Maria claims she didn't take it," Perry interjected. "She says she has no idea how it ended up in the pool. What do you think, Lucy?"

Lucy bit her lip, conflicted. "Honestly? I can't imagine why anyone in the villa would want to take it."

"It must have been worth some money?" Bea pointed out.

Lucy blinked rapidly. "Well, yes. I guess so. But enough to lose your job over? I don't know…"

Bea tilted her head slightly, intrigued. So why *had* someone taken the necklace? *Wait.* If their theory about the pole and statue was correct, how had the necklace ended up in the pool? Had JT had it on him? Or had someone tossed it in afterwards to frame Maria? *Was that it?*

"Lucy, we've a working theory that we can't fully discuss, but I can tell you this: you're not a suspect." Perry leaned back, his expression unreadable.

Bea's eyebrows shot up. *Why's he telling her that?* She watched Lucy closely, expecting relief to flood her features. Instead, the petite blonde remained tense, her shoulders rigid, her eyes darting anxiously between the two of them.

My turn. "Lucy," Bea said gently. "Do you have any idea why someone would want to harm JT?"

Lucy's gaze snapped to Bea's, her eyes wide. "No, no, of course not." But her words rang hollow as her voice trembled slightly.

Perry's eyes narrowed. "What about Peter Mitchell? I know things were tense between him and JT. Do you know why?"

Lucy hesitated, her mouth opening and closing wordlessly. Bea reached out, placing a reassuring hand on her arm.

"Lucy, anything you tell us will be kept in the strictest confidence. We want to find out the truth and help Maria."

Lucy drew a shaky breath. "He was asking Ella and Mr Kenda for money. But Mr Kenda refused. He told Peter he was done with him being a parasite and that he needed to leave." She paused, her voice barely a whisper. "Ella told me everything. She was so upset."

Bea exchanged a meaningful glance with Perry. This fitted with the conversation he'd overheard. "Was it just Peter, or was Pearl involved too?"

Lucy shook her head. "I don't know. But I do know Ella was trying to convince Pearl to leave Peter. She thought it was for the best."

The PA glanced at her watch, suddenly flustered. "I'm sorry, but I really need to get going. I have so much to do for Ella…"

Bea rose. "Of course. Thank you for your time, Lucy."

———

"Why do I still feel she knows a lot more about things than she's letting on?" Perry asked as they climbed down the basement stairs of Villa Mer.

"Because she does?" Bea said, inhaling the welcome aroma of coffee as they reached the bottom of the steps. Simon was sitting at the table, his brow furrowed as he tapped away on his laptop. He stopped and glanced up at them as they walked towards him. "Any luck?"

Bea dropped into a chair beside him and looked around for her little white terrier. "Where's Daisy?"

"Oh, she's with Ana upstairs in the kitchen. She's still quite tearful. I think Daisy's a welcome distraction."

Bea nodded, then she and Perry filled Simon in on their conversation with Lucy.

"So," Simon said, leaning back, his expression thoughtful. "I've been doing a little digging myself about Peter Mitchell. I still find this hard to believe, having met the man, but his paintings sell for quite hefty sums. In the tens of thousands."

"Really?" Bea and Perry reacted in unison.

"There's an art gallery in San Francisco currently exhibiting his work, and it's getting rave reviews. The collection there is worth over a hundred and fifty thousand."

Perry whistled. "So why did he need money from JT?" he asked.

"That's the pertinent question," Simon replied.

Something wasn't adding up. Pearl was a best-selling author with presumably now TV and film rights paying off. Peter was selling his paintings for huge amounts. Why were they living off Ella and JT?

"So when you were with Lucy, did she mention anything about JT threatening to fire her?"

Bea blinked, surprised. "No, she didn't."

"Why would he fire her? She's Ella's PA, isn't she?" Perry asked.

"It was in Maria's statement," Simon explained, leaning forward. "Apparently, she overheard Lucy telling Ella that JT was going to fire her. According to Maria, Ella told Lucy not to worry and that she had everything in hand."

Was that why Lucy was so worried—because she had a motive to kill JT? Bea looked down at the tiled floor, feeling its coolness through the thin soles of her flip-flops. She stifled a huff. But then, when Perry had told Lucy that she wasn't a suspect, why hadn't she behaved like she was relieved and relaxed a bit?

There must be something more to it...

33

SHORTLY AFTER, MONDAY 9 AUGUST

Bea looked up, alerted by the *tap tap* of paws on the basement steps. Daisy charged down into the room, her tail up and proud as she ran towards Bea. As Bea bent down to fuss over the little terrier, Rich appeared with a large pot of coffee grasped in one hand. The aroma of the fresh brew wafted around him, instantly perking up Bea's senses.

"I come bearing gifts," Rich said, holding up the pot. "Courtesy of Ana." He placed the steaming pot on the table.

"You're a lifesaver," Bea said, her lips curling into a grateful smile as she reached for the pot to refill her empty cup.

Rich returned her smile and sat down next to her. "I also have news, but let's hear how you two got on first."

As they settled in with their coffees, she and Perry told him about their conversation with Lucy. He responded with a faint incline of his head and, at the end, agreed with her that Lucy appeared to still be worried about something. Then Simon recounted his unexpected discovery of Peter's financially successful artistic abilities. Rich was not as surprised as Bea had expected, but when she looked at him, frowning, he merely winked. Finally, Simon told him what Maria had over-heard between Ella and Lucy.

"All good stuff," he mumbled when Simon finished. Bea felt a familiar thrill of excitement course through her veins as she looked at his face. *He has something!*

She leaned forward, her green eyes intense. "So what's your news?"

Rich tried to disguise a satisfied smile. "I've heard from Fred," he said. "So for starters, Derek Stone checks out. He's as clean as a whistle—wealthy, well-managed stock portfolio, multiple properties. Nothing dodgy that Fred can find. Nessa Stone is also independently wealthy from her husband and is also clean."

Perry's eyebrows shot up. "Really? That's disappointing."

"JT was similar," Rich continued. "His estate's worth a fraction under a hundred million, all of which now goes to Ella."

Simon gave a low whistle. "Now there's a good motive for murder."

"It's a shame about that pesky alibi she has," Perry said with a sigh. "Us!"

Rich held up a hand. "There's more. Fred uncovered several allegations against JT from employees and contractors at his production company. Mostly regarding abusive behaviour, but there were also a couple for inappropriate conduct."

Bea grimaced, not particularly surprised. That heady mix of charm, money, and power seemed to make some men think they had rights over other people's lives.

"And, of course, they were all settled quietly with cash, so nothing was made public," Rich said, the disgust apparent in his voice.

Bea's body tensed. *And he got away with it.* For a

moment Bea was glad someone had put a stop to JT's disgusting behaviour by putting an end to him. Then she checked herself. Nothing made murder acceptable. But sometimes it was understandable…

"Oh and finally, on the JT and Derek front. The casting for JT and Derek's next film—"

"The one with all the fuss about it in the papers?" Perry asked, his blue eyes lighting up. "Where they offered the lead role to a younger actress and sidelined Ella?"

Rich nodded. "Exactly that. Well, things have got shuffled around, and now Ella's in the leading role. All fixed up with her agent and Derek over the last two days."

Perry's eyes widened. He shook his head as he raised his hands. "How can Ella not be our chief suspect? Look how great things have worked out for her since JT died."

Bea's stomach churned. *Did Ella orchestrate all this?* But she couldn't have drugged JT. They knew that. She closed her eyes and rubbed at her temples.

"Don't despair just yet," Rich said, reaching out and gently squeezing her shoulder. "I have more…"

Bea's eyes shot open.

"Tell us!" Perry cried.

"Now we get to the Mitchells," Rich continued. "As Simon discovered, between Peter's painting sales and Pearl's books, their income is significant, *but* they don't seem to have any assets or property. They sold their home in Dallas six months ago for seven hundred and fifty thousand dollars, and since then, their address has been listed as Ella and JT's place in LA."

"That's interesting," Simon said, stroking his beard. "What do you think happened to all that money?"

What indeed! "Poor investments?" Bea suggested.

Rich shook his head. "Fred found no evidence of investments at all."

So where did it all go?

"And with JT out of the way, not only will Peter not be thrown out of here and presumably the LA place too, he will no doubt have access to Ella's money via Pearl..." Perry said, raising an eyebrow.

Now we're getting somewhere. "I think we should talk to Ella about this. There seems to be no lost love between her and her sister's husband. Lucy said Ella was trying to get Pearl to leave him, remember?"

Isla appeared in the basement doorway, her ginger hair glinting in the sunlight streaming in from the open door behind her. "Ana sent me to tell you lunch is ready."

Perry leapt up, clapping his hands. "Good. I'm ravenous!" Daisy jumped up and joined him, dancing around his feet, yapping in excitement. "Come on, Daisy. Let's go!"

With a smile on her face, Bea followed them up the stairs. As they filed out onto the sun-drenched terrace, Bea blinked, adjusting to the sudden brightness. She pulled her sunglasses off her head and put them on. Her stomach growled as she gazed at the spread of colourful salads, cold cuts, and fresh bread that awaited them on a long table in the shade. As she sat down, the aromatic scent of olive oil and herbs wafted through the air. She breathed in deeply and slowly exhaled. *Mmmm...*

She scanned the terrace and then the pool and gardens. "Where are Sam and Archie?" she asked Isla. "They're usually inhaling food by now."

Isla shrugged. "Sorry. I didn't see them. They're not in the house."

A knot formed in Bea's stomach. She turned to Rich, her eyes narrowing. "Didn't they come back with you?"

Rich shifted uncomfortably. "I, uh, left them at the beach. They were having fun, and I had to take Fred's call. Then I wanted to tell you all what he'd said, and—"

"You left them at the beach?" Bea's voice rose an octave. "With everything that's going on, you left them alone?"

He gave her arm a pat. "Don't panic, Bea. I'm sure they're still there and have just lost track of time."

She pulled her arm away and fumbled for her phone, her fingers trembling slightly as she dialled Sam's number. *You better be right, Rich...*

The ringtone echoed in her ear. No answer. "Come on, Sam," she muttered. Still no answer. She stabbed at the end call button and redialled. This time it was Archie's number. Bea's mind raced through worst-case scenarios. *Have they stumbled upon something they shouldn't have? Has someone taken them? Was one of them hurt?* Her heart was pounding. There was no reply.

34

TEN MINUTES LATER, MONDAY 9 AUGUST

Bea's fingers trembled as she stroked Daisy's soft fur, the little dog a warm weight on her lap. Her stomach grumbled, but she had no interest in the untouched food on the terrace table. *I need to know the boys are safe.* A wave of nausea washed over her. "What if someone took them..." She trailed off as bile rose in her mouth.

Perry placed a steadying hand on her shoulder. "That's not likely, Bea," he said, his voice calm and reassuring. "They're probably just caught up in their own adventures. You know how boys can be."

Bea swallowed, then said through clenched teeth, "With a killer running around here somewhere? How could Rich be so careless?" She pictured Sam's cheeky grin, his reddish-brown hair messed up by the sea breeze. And Archie, all gangly limbs and nonstop chatter. Her heart clenched.

Perry leaned forward, a determined look on his tanned face. "They'll find them, Bea. Rich is searching the beach here. Simon and Isla are checking the headland up by Villa Luz. They'll turn up."

She'd wanted to go too, but Simon had insisted that she

and Perry stayed behind in case the boys turned up via some other route or got in touch. "But what if they don't?" Her voice cracked.

Perry *tsked*, reaching for her hand. "They will."

Bea tried to inhale, but panic clawed at her throat. "I can't lose him, Perry. He's all that's left of James." A fat tear ran down her cheek. She swiped it away as Daisy tried to lick her hand.

"And you won't," Perry said firmly. "Sam's too smart. And Archie might seem like chaos incarnate, but he's got a surprisingly good head on those skinny shoulders."

"But with everything happening here... I should have kept a better eye on them."

"Stop it, Bea!" Perry cried. "You can't wrap them in cotton wool, you know. They're sixteen, not six." He squeezed her hand. "They'll be back soon, starving and full of tales to tell. You'll see."

Bea acknowledged his words with a sigh, wishing she believed him. She stared out at the enormous ocean rising above the garden, praying it hadn't claimed her son and his best friend. The thought was too horrific to bear.

Bea's heart leapt into her throat as Rich appeared from the beach path, his face flushed and hair windswept. Her momentary relief crumbled when she saw there was no one with him. "Where are they?" she cried out, her voice cracking.

Rich shook his head, panting. "Not on the beach. But I found their things." He held up a familiar backpack. "The paddle boards are gone."

What? "Paddle boards?" Bea's eyes widened in horror. "You let them go out on the open sea?"

"It's perfectly safe," Rich tried to reassure her. "The coastline is protected—"

"Safe?" Bea shot to her feet, dislodging Daisy from her

lap. Memories of when Rich had wound her up so badly during their earlier investigations that she'd wanted to punch him came flooding back. She took a deep breath in through her nose, then slowly expelled the air. "There's a killer on the loose, Rich, and you're babbling about the stupid coastline?" she said, a steel edge to her voice.

Rich placed a calming hand on her arm. "Bea, love—"

"Don't 'Bea, love' me," she snapped, rounding on him. "How did you let this happen, Rich?"

Rich held up his hands. "Bea, I promise you, the boys are fine. They probably paddled around the headland into the next bay. I'm going to take the boat out right now and bring them back."

"You'd better," she growled, shaking her head in disbelief. Rich appeared to be dismissing her concerns, acting like she was some hysterical woman. *But he's my son!*

Simon and Isla came jogging up, both of them out of breath. "No sign of them," Simon reported grimly.

Rich quickly filled Simon in on the paddle board situation. Simon's eyes widened. "I'll help you with the boat." As the two men took off towards the beach shed, Simon called over his shoulder, "We'll find them, Bea. Don't worry."

Isla approached Bea tentatively. "I'm so sorry," she whispered. "I should have alerted you the second I couldn't find them earlier."

Bea picked up Daisy and slumped back into her chair, a lead weight in her chest, unable to muster the energy to reassure the devastated girl.

"It's not your fault," Perry told Isla kindly. He pressed a mug of coffee into Bea's limp hands. "Here, drink this."

Bea stared at the black liquid. "What am I going to tell Archie's parents?" she asked numbly. The Tellis' had entrusted their precious son to her. She'd failed them.

"You're not going to tell them anything. Not yet." Perry squeezed her shoulder. "Bea, look at me. The boys will be *fine.*"

Please! She directed her desperate plea to the cloudless blue sky as she held on to Daisy as if she were a life raft. *Please keep them safe.*

———

A high-pitched squeal pierced the air. Daisy bolted up in Bea's lap. Bea whirled around to see Isla, her eyes wide with excitement as she clutched her phone. "I've found them!" Isla thrust the screen towards Bea. "Look!"

With trembling fingers, she grasped the phone. There, on Chloe's Instagram feed, grinning back at her, were Sam and Archie. Sun-kissed and carefree, their faces pressed close to Chloe's in a beachside selfie. She frowned. *Where are they?*

"They're only around the corner in the next bay!" Isla told her, then she frowned. "I can't believe Chloe has blatantly ignored the request not to post photos of Sam. I guess she'll do anything to maintain her following."

Right at that moment, as relief crashed through Bea like a tidal wave, she didn't care about Chloe's motives. All that mattered was that Sam and Archie were safe. She handed Isla's phone back, then sagged against the back of her chair, the iron grip on her heart easing. "Thank goodness."

Perry was already on the phone. "The boys have been spotted, love. Yes, just nearby! They're with Chloe." He flashed Bea a thumbs up.

Bea exhaled heavily. Part of her wanted to collapse into sobs, but a flicker of irritation ignited. How could they have wandered off like that, scaring her half to death?

Perry dropped his phone onto the table. "Simon says

they're heading over now. They think they can see the boys and their paddle boards on the beach. Rich is going to call Tina to let her know."

Bea pursed her lips at the mention of Rich. *You wait until—*

Isla's voice cut through Bea's thoughts. "Bea, look at this!" The ginger-haired girl handed her phone to Bea again, her blue eyes sparkling with a mix of amusement and concern.

Bea placed Daisy gently on the floor and leaned in, squinting at the small screen. Another selfie, this time a video. Sam's and Archie's faces filled the frame, grinning widely as they jostled for position. Behind them, a crowd of beachgoers waved and cheered.

"They seem to be enjoying themselves," Isla commented.

Bea felt her relief evaporate, replaced by a hot surge of anger. "Enjoying themselves?" she hissed. "They're supposed to be on our private beach, not gallivanting around like... like…"

Perry cocked an eyebrow. "Typical teenagers?"

Bea shot him a withering look. "You're not helping, Perry."

He tilted his head to one side. "But we found them, Bea. That's what matters, isn't it?"

She turned back to the video, watching as Sam threw his arm around someone she didn't know, flashing that cheeky smile she adored. Bea allowed herself a moment to breathe. *They're alive.* Everything else—the press, the paddle boards, the inevitable lecture would wait. For now, she wanted to savour the knowledge that her son and his best friend were safe.

Even if they are in for the grounding of their lives!

35

FIFTEEN MINUTES LATER, MONDAY
9 AUGUST

Bea's stomach grumbled, protesting its emptiness, but she couldn't bring herself to eat. Not yet. Not until the boys were in her sight, and she saw they really were safe.

Perry and Isla, however, had no such qualms. They tucked into their food with gusto, the clinking of cutlery against plates a stark contrast to the tense silence.

Suddenly, the bifold doors burst open. Rich and Simon strode onto the terrace, flanking Sam and Archie. The boys' faces were flushed with excitement, their skin bright red from the sun's relentless rays.

"Mum! We're back!" Sam's voice cracked as his eyes met Bea's piercing gaze. Both boys' grins faltered. They shuffled their feet, suddenly finding the floor tiles incredibly interesting.

Rich stepped forward. "The PaIRS guys brought them—"

"Upstairs," Bea cut him off, her voice calm but steely. "Both of you. Shower. Now. I'll be up to talk to you in a minute."

Sam and Archie exchanged a glance, then scurried off like startled rabbits.

Bea turned to Simon and Rich, forcing a smile. "Thank you for your help," she managed to say but couldn't meet Rich's eyes, still fuming over his role in the whole fiasco. How could he have been so irresponsible? He knew how much she worried about the boys. She shook her head, trying to clear her thoughts. *Deal with one problem at a time, Bea.* She inhaled deeply, straightening her shoulders. Time to be the calm, collected person she knew she could be. Even if inside, she was a swirling mess of anger, relief, and frustration. *You have this under control.*

The atmosphere at the table was thick with tension as Rich and Simon sat down.

"Well, this is awkward," Perry muttered under his breath to Isla.

Isla nodded sagely, shovelling another forkful of food into her mouth. "Mum drama. Been there," she whispered back.

Bea ignored them while she prepared two plates of food for the boys. In her head, she rehearsed the conversation to come. She needed to strike the right balance—firm, but loving. Understanding, yet uncompromising. *Dignity and calm*, she told herself, piling pasta salad onto the two plates. How would she explain the depth of her worry without sounding like a hysterical mother? She needed them to understand the gravity of their actions without crushing their spirits.

Balancing the plates, Bea made her way upstairs. Pausing outside the boys' shared bedroom, she took a deep breath, then pushed the door open with her elbow. The room was unnaturally quiet as she entered. Sam and Archie sat on their beds, their hair damp from their showers, their skin glowing an angry red from their ill-advised adventure. They looked up at her sheepishly, guilt written all over their sunburned faces.

"Mum, we're really sorry." Sam's words rushed out, his voice cracking with emotion.

"Yeah, we messed up big time, Lady B," Archie chimed in, sounding unusually subdued.

Bea set the plates down on the dresser, fixing the boys with a steady gaze. "What you two did today was incredibly irresponsible. Do you have any idea how worried I was?"

Sam offered a slight movement of his head, his eyes downcast. "Rich explained it to us. We got carried away, I guess. And we were with Chloe, so we thought it would be okay. But we promised him we won't do anything like that again."

Bea's eyebrows shot up. Rich had talked to them? A flash of irritation surged through her. *That's my job, not his!*

"I'm glad you understand," she said. "Now eat up and then make sure you put on plenty of aftersun. You look like a pair of boiled lobsters."

Sam perked up. "So can we hang out by the pool later?" he asked tentatively.

"Absolutely not," she replied. "You're grounded indoors until tomorrow at least."

The boys nodded in unison, resigned to their fate. As they tucked into their food, Bea slipped out of the room. Her stomach growled as she descended the stairs, reminding her she hadn't eaten all day. "Get it together, Bea," she muttered to herself. "You're a grown woman, not a sulky teenager." But the thought of facing Rich on the terrace made her appetite vanish. She paused at the foot of the stairs, her hand gripping the banister. She needed some fresh air...

36

SHORTLY AFTER, MONDAY 9 AUGUST

Stepping out of the front of the villa, the warm sun and salty sea breeze soothing her frayed nerves, she pulled out her phone and fired off a quick text to Perry.

Bea: *Need some air. Back soon. xx*

She set off towards Villa Luz, where she knew there was access to the other end of the private beach. Her sandals crunched on the gravel path, her mind churning with all the things she wanted to say to Rich. Having children meant putting their well-being above all else. Why did Rich not understand that? The investigation was important, of course, but nothing trumped the safety of her son.

She reached the edge of the estate and paused, looking out at the sparkling ocean. The beauty of it all hit her, momentarily pushing aside her anger. She took in the fresh, salty air. She'd face Rich later, when she felt calm and rational.

For now, she let her feet carry her onto the soft sand of

the beach. She plucked off her sandals and headed towards the blue-green sea. As she turned the corner of a ridge of sand dunes, a figure appeared in the distance heading towards her. Bea's first instinct was to turn and flee. The last thing she wanted to do right now was to have to make small talk with one of Marisol's inhabitants, but as the person got closer, Bea recognised the slender woman with shoulder-length brown hair. *Pearl Mitchell!*

A slow smile spread across Bea's face. This was serendipitous indeed…

37

A FEW SECONDS LATER, MONDAY 9 AUGUST

"Lady Rossex. Are you alright?" Pearl's brow furrowed with concern. "You look a bit flustered."

Bea forced a smile, pushing her windswept red hair from her face. "Oh, family stuff; you know how it is. I had to get away for a bit, get some fresh air."

Pearl met her gaze with a knowing look, her blue eyes wide. "Family can be so complicated, can't they?"

Nice lead in... "Speaking of family," Bea said smoothly. "How's Ella doing? I hear she's now the lead in Derek's new film. She must be pleased."

A flicker of defensiveness passed over Pearl's face. "She always should've been. JT was simply being difficult about it." She hesitated. "He was like that sometimes."

"Like what?"

Pearl hesitated again, wringing her hands. "I don't like to speak ill of the dead, but..." She lowered her voice conspiratorially. "He was a bully, always needing to be in charge."

Now we're getting to it. "Really?" Bea prompted.

Pearl inclined her head, relaxing into her subject. "He had an argument with Ella's agent. Casting someone younger was his way of putting them both in their place. He wanted to show the agent and Ella that she was replaceable."

Bea pressed her lips together. *That's not how you treat your wife.* "He doesn't sound like a very nice man."

"Hey, don't get me wrong, he was a real sweetie pie when he wanted to be," Pearl said wryly. "He frequently did people favours. He was generous even. But" —her voice took on a bitter edge to it— "he never let you forget it."

Bea studied Pearl curiously. It seemed like she was speaking from personal experience. What had JT done to her? And was it enough for her to want him dead? Bea shifted her weight on the soft sand. *How can I get her to talk to me?*

"Have they released Maria yet?"

Oh, she's doing the work for me. "No. They're still holding her. Actually, Pearl, we've been trying to prove that Maria didn't kill JT."

Pearl tensed visibly. "Yes, Ella told me."

"Do you think Maria's a killer?"

"No!" Pearl's response was immediate and vehement. "Totally not. Maria wouldn't hurt a fly, let alone kill someone."

She seems very sure. Bea acknowledged her words with a soft, "Indeed." Then added, "That's what we think too. But the police are adamant."

Pearl fidgeted with the hem of her coverup. "But surely they'll have to let her go. They don't have any actual evidence, do they?"

Bea gave an exaggerated sigh. "It's not that simple, unfortunately. They think Maria's motive was the stolen necklace. Coupled with some other circumstantial evidence..." She trailed off, shaking her head. "It's not looking good. It's likely they'll charge her with murder."

Pearl looked down at the ground.

Have I laid it on too thick?

"No, no, this is all wrong." Pearl rubbed the back of her head. Then she cleared her throat and looked up at Bea and, in a wavering voice, said, "Look, if I tell you something… something I know about the necklace… will it help free Maria?"

Bea's pulse quickened. "Absolutely. Anything you can share will help."

Pearl breathed in deeply. "Someone else took it. It was just a misunderstanding, that's all."

What does that mean? "Who took it?" Bea asked, fighting to keep her voice even.

"I did," Pearl mumbled, avoiding making eye contact. "I only wanted to borrow it, that's all! But then JT noticed it was missing and got so angry… I was afraid he'd think I'd stolen it. So I got rid of it and said nothing."

Bea frowned. Why hadn't she told Ella? *It makes no sense…* "What do you mean by 'got rid of it'?"

"I threw it in the pool. The morning of the pool party." Pearl twisted her hands. "I thought someone, perhaps one of the gardeners when they were cleaning the pool, would spot it and assume it had fallen off by mistake. Ella often wore it when she went swimming. But no one did. So I was going to, you know, discover it myself. But when I looked, I couldn't see it." She fanned her face with her hand. "I didn't know what had happened to it."

Bea's mind sifted through what Pearl was saying. *Something doesn't add up…* "Why would JT suspect you of stealing it, Pearl?"

"Er, that's not exactly what I meant…" She didn't meet Bea's eyes as she backpedalled. "I meant… I—"

She's lying… "Pearl, what really happened to that necklace?" Bea pressed, her tone gentle but firm. "The truth this time." Adding, "Maria's freedom depends on it," for good measure.

Pearl's eyes darted left and right, like a cornered animal seeking escape. After a long moment, her shoulders slumped in defeat. "Fine. I'm sick of covering for him anyway."

Bea's heart rate quickened. "Him?"

"Pete," Pearl said, her voice cracking. "My husband. He took the necklace."

The pieces fell into place in Bea's head. *Of course...*

Pearl continued, her words now rushing out like a dam breaking, "I found out and took it from him. I was too embarrassed to tell Ella. Then JT went mad, accusing Maria, and I knew I should've said something, but..." She swallowed hard. "I was worried JT would call the police on Pete. In a panic, I threw it in the pool, hoping someone would find it. I had no idea things would spiral so out of control."

"He was going to sell it to raise money?" Bea asked, the picture now much clearer.

Pearl's eyes welled with tears. "He has enormous gambling debts," she said, a flash of anger passing over her face. "We had to sell our house in Dallas, but it wasn't enough. He asked Ella and JT for money, but JT refused. He called us parasites."

Bea winced.

"Pete was desperate," Pearl continued. "He took the necklace, planning to sell it. When I found out and I took it from him, he was furious. He said they didn't need all their money, but if he didn't pay back what he owed, then some nasty men would make him pay in other ways."

Poor Pearl. *What a mess.*

"Then it got worse," Pearl said. "At dinner the night of the pool party, JT dropped a bombshell. He said he was kicking Pete out of the studio and turning it into a cinema room. Then he told us both to make plans to leave." Her voice shook. "I was devastated. Pete stormed out in a fury."

She looked down at the sand and slowly shook her head. "I think that's when I realised Pete will never change. However successful he is as an artist, it will never be enough. However much he wins, he can't walk away. And then, of course, he loses, and he's mad at everyone because it's never his fault." She gave a defeated shrug. "Ella's right. I'm better off without him."

I agree!

Pearl looked up, her eyes shimmering with unshed tears. "Ella's been great. After JT left to go for his swim later that night, she offered to help me. She said if I left Pete, she'd pay off his debts. And I could stay with her until I got back on my feet. All he would have to do was accept a divorce without a fight. She promised to handle JT."

What a hard situation to be trapped in. "So what did you say?"

Pearl took a deep breath, steeling herself. "I realised it was time to take control of my life. The next morning, I told Ella I'd leave Pete. I planned to break the news to him that evening, but before I had a chance, he ran off to confront JT. He thought he would be able to persuade him to change his mind. I knew it was a waste of time..." She trailed off, shaking her head. "And when he came back, he was livid. He stormed off to his studio without a word." Pearl sighed. "I still haven't told him. He's so needy. So draining. Ella and I have decided it's best to wait until we're back in the States."

Bea acknowledged her with a brief nod, understanding in her eyes. That confrontation could wait. And anyway, if Peter was that angry and worried he would lose everything... *Is he JT's killer?*

"Pearl. Does Peter have access to ketamine?"

Pearl bit her lip. "Look, Pete didn't kill JT if that's what you're thinking. He's all bluster and whining but not much action."

But you've not answered my question... "Pearl. Could Peter get ketamine if he wanted it?" she pressed.

Pearl's chin trembled. "He keeps some ketamine in his studio. He takes small amounts to get high when he paints, says it helps him be more creative." Her gaze met Bea's. "But honestly, murder? I don't think he has it in him."

But if he was cornered and desperate? It was possible he was their killer. She needed to talk to the others. But first things first... "Are you willing to tell the police the truth about the necklace? It would really help Maria."

"Sure, of course. But I need to tell Ella first. Then I'll call the police. I promise." Pearl smiled wearily. "Thank you, my lady. I think I needed to tell someone."

Bea watched her go, her mind whirling. As she walked along the beach towards Villa Mer, she considered Peter Mitchell. He had means, motive, and opportunity. Also, he'd taken the necklace and allowed Maria to take the blame. *And* he'd not told the police he had ketamine in his studio even though he knew it had played a part in JT's death. But then Pearl *also* knew about the necklace and the ketamine and had said nothing until now. The only difference was that she seemed to lack a motive, especially if Ella had promised to help her leave Peter before JT's death.

Bea barely noticed the sand beneath her feet or the cry of the gulls overhead as she carried on. Her mind drifted to Rich and the boys. Her anger had faded, replaced by a twinge of regret. Had she overreacted? *No!* What Sam and Archie had done had been careless. Sam was a member of the royal family and the heir to an earldom through James's father. Archie was the son of famous and wealthy parents. Someone could have taken either or both of them to be held for ransom. *And not forgetting there's a killer on the loose.* Although, a little voice in her head reminded her in a snarky way that she'd just confronted a potential killer on her own on a deserted beach. *Yes, but I can take her!* The self-defence skills she'd learned in an anti-kidnapping course a few years ago had already come in very useful in previous cases. But then she heard Rich's voice in her head. *Ah, but what if Pearl had a gun?* She shook her head. *Okay, point taken, Rich.*

So all in all, she thought she'd handled Sam and Archie the best she could. She'd been calm but firm. She knew Perry was right—Sam was a teenager now, not a toddler. And yes, perhaps it was time to loosen the reins a bit. But she still needed to have a plan to keep him safe. She would talk to Rich and see if they were able to come up with a solution.

Oh, Rich! Now that I didn't handle so well, she admitted to herself. She'd told him off like he'd been a naughty child. The worry and upset had led her to blame him for what was, in the large part, Sam's and Archie's foolhardy decision to go with Chloe and leave the safety of the private beach. It wasn't reasonable to hold him fully responsible. *I need to apologise.*

As she saw the break in the sand dunes that led up to their villa, she quickened her pace, eager to not only put things right with Rich but to share Pearl's revelations with the others.

Her stomach fluttered. Once Pearl came clean to the police, they'd have to release Maria. And then Bea would've done her job. She'd promised Lady Grace they would prove Maria innocent, and they had. Once she told Tina everything Pearl had told her, the police would take it from there. She ignored the nagging worry at the back of her mind that their fixation on Maria's guilt even with a lack of concrete evidence suggested they didn't really care about the truth, only an easy close. *No! It's not your problem anymore, Bea.* And anyway, the local police had Tina to help them. They would find the real killer.

She let out a deep breath, and a slow smile spread across her face. And in the meantime, Maria would be free, and Bea and the others could get back to their holiday...

38

FIRST THING THE NEXT DAY, TUESDAY 10 AUGUST

T*he Daily Post* online article:

A Daily Post EXCLUSIVE by Sarah Denby (Part 2) — "I'm Coming to the Royal Wedding!" Deadbeat Dad of Top Cop Richard Fitzwilliam Breaks His Silence!

He's the dad who disappeared not once but TWICE, leaving his family in the lurch and a trail of broken hearts and debts. Now, Eric Fitzwilliam—father of senior police officer Richard Fitzwilliam—has been tracked down by The Daily Post to a quiet stone cottage in the French countryside. And in a world-exclusive interview, the runaway dad drops bombshell after bombshell about his "complicated" relationship with his son, who it is speculated is set to marry into the royal family.

With a glass of red wine in hand and a smirk on his face, Eric seems anything but remorseful. "You want my side of the story? Alright, here it is," he begins, lounging back like he hasn't a care in the world. "Dawn—Rich's mum—she didn't need me. She was tough, tougher than anyone gives her credit for. When my business went under, I thought the best thing I could do was disappear. Let her sort it out. And guess what? She did."

But Eric's excuses don't end there. He admits he tried to return to his children's lives—briefly. "I gave it a go," he says about his ill-fated second act as a dad. "I remarried, thought I'd start over, but let's be honest, I wasn't cut out for it. Joyce, my second wife, was a good woman, but the debts… oh, they followed me everywhere. I walked away again because that's just what I do."

When asked about his son's meteoric rise—both in the police force and as a potential future royal—Eric leans back with a smug grin. "Oh, Rich? Yeah, he's done alright for himself. Always was strong-willed, independent… probably got that from me." He pauses, a glint of pride in his eye. "Never thought I'd see the day he'd be rubbing shoulders with the King and all that lot. Can you imagine? Me, at a royal wedding? Next to the King? Bloody hell, what a laugh!"

Eric's words are sure to send shivers down the spines of palace courtiers and raise more than a few eyebrows at Francis Court, the ancestral home of Lady Beatrice's family. With his chequered past and habit of vanishing when the going gets tough, it's no wonder Eric's sudden reappearance might ruffle some royal feathers.

But Eric isn't shy about his intentions. "I might've missed a few birthdays, but a royal wedding? No way I'd miss that. I'd love to see the look on everyone's faces when I walk in," he chuckles, pouring himself another glass of red. "I reckon they'd all get over it, don't you?"

Eric's comments are sure to reignite questions about Richard Fitzwilliam's family ties as the public wonders whether this estranged father will cause a royal scandal. And what do Lady Beatrice's parents—the Duke of Arnwall and Her Royal Highness Princess Helen—think about the prospect of this father-in-law gate-crashing their daughter's big day? We can only imagine the private family conversations that this bombshell interview will spark.

Eric's brazen attitude and casual dismissal of his past actions leave little doubt: the man who walked out on his family twice might just see the royal spotlight as his chance for redemption—or, more likely, attention.

COMING TOMORROW: In the final part of this Daily Post exclusive, Eric Fitzwilliam reveals his true thoughts about his son marrying into royalty and whether he believes there's still time to patch things up with Richard. Is it too late for a father's redemption—or is Eric just out for the headlines? Don't miss it! Read it only in The Daily Post TOMORROW!

39

9AM, TUESDAY 10 AUGUST

The morning sun glinted off Rich's watch as he stared at the iPad in his hand, his brow furrowed in concentration as he read *The Daily Post* interview with his father.

Bea sat beside him on the terrace of Villa Mer, her hand gently resting on his knee, feeling the warmth of his skin on her fingers. *Is he alright?* She reached for her coffee mug with her free hand as Daisy, lounging at her feet, lifted her head and sniffed.

With her heart in her mouth, Bea had read the article first thing this morning, before Rich had surfaced. Her stomach had dropped as she'd read the words of the seemingly selfish and opportunistic Eric who appeared to think his best response to things getting tough was to walk away and let others deal with it.

How can Rich's father be so different from Rich, his mother, and his sister? She couldn't wrap her head around Eric Fitzwilliam's emotions and motivations. Was he simply a man who shirked responsibility at every turn, hiding behind a smirk and a glass of wine as he dismissed his failures as mere "life happening"? Or had *The Daily Post* only quoted the words that they knew would make Eric look like a reckless, self-serving schemer? She knew from bitter experience how rags like *The Daily Post* could twist things to up the drama. *Is that what this is?* She hoped so, for Rich's sake.

Rich grumbled something incoherent and swiped to the next page on the tablet on his lap. His brow crinkled in annoyance as he scanned the screen. She saw the struggle in his eyes. Was he feeling disappointment? Confusion? Anger? Her throat ached, and she took a sip of coffee. *All I can do is be here for him.*

At least they'd cleared the air after Sam's and Archie's adventures the day before. Her mind drifted back to the tense atmosphere that had greeted her at the villa when she'd returned from the beach yesterday. Especially when Perry had reluctantly told her that the press had already picked up on Chloe's social media feed and were reporting on 'the king's great-nephew's beach party'.

Bea had had to take a seriously deep breath not to lose her cool as she had once again felt agitation towards the boys for having been so reckless, but once she'd calmed down, she'd told them of her encounter with Pearl. Tina Spicer, who had been there when Bea had arrived back, had hastily departed to the police station to inform them of the new development. Then Perry and Simon had tactically retreated, leaving her and Rich alone.

There had been a moment of painful awkwardness until she and Rich had both blurted out, "I'm sorry," then laughed nervously.

Rich had taken her hand, his touch electric against her skin. "I shouldn't have left the boys like that, Bea. I thought... Well, it doesn't matter what I thought. I'm sorry. I got it wrong."

Goodness! It wasn't like Rich to use the W word. But as

tempting as it'd been to simply accept his apology and offer her own, she'd really needed him to understand why she'd been so mad.

"To be honest, Rich, what really upset me was how you dismissed my concerns when the boys went missing. You made me feel as if I was making a fuss about nothing. But you of all people should understand what a potential target Sam is. If anything happened to him…" She'd had to stop, overwhelmed by her emotions.

Rich had reached out and taken her hand. "I'm so sorry, Bea. The truth is I was embarrassed that I'd let you down by allowing them to go missing on my watch, so I tried to underplay it." He'd swallowed as he'd gripped onto her hand tight and had met her gaze. "Forgive me?"

As she'd looked into his brown eyes, she'd known he was sincerely sorry and, of course, she would forgive him. They were still learning things about each other. She'd also been aware that she couldn't let him take *all* the responsibility for what had happened.

She'd squeezed his hand. "Of course. And now it's my turn. I'm sorry for snapping at you and throwing all the blame on you. Sam and Archie are old enough to know better." She'd leaned in and kissed him, relishing in the warmth of his lips.

When they'd broken apart, a corner of Rich's mouth had quirked up. "But I do have a bone to pick with you."

Oh, no. From the twinkle in his eye, she'd known immediately where he'd been going. She'd screwed up her face.

"After all that talk of there being a killer on the loose, what did you do? You went off—"

"I know! I know!" she'd cried, holding her hand up to his chest. "I needed air." She'd exhaled slowly. "And I forgot."

Rich had offered a slight movement of his head in understanding, then he'd kissed her again.

Afterwards, he'd asked her, "Do you think Pearl's the killer?"

She'd shaken her head. "I don't think so. But Peter, on the other hand…"

Daisy's wet nose nudged her leg impatiently, jolting her back into the moment.

Rich was still scowling at the iPad like it had sworn at him. She felt him wince beneath her hand. "If my father thinks he's getting within a hundred miles of our wedding, he's got another think coming," he muttered darkly as he slammed the cover closed and grabbed his mug.

Our wedding? The words screamed in Bea's head, sending a jolt through her. Perry choked on his coffee. Simon's eyes sprang open wide. They all stared at Rich.

Rich's eyes widened as if he'd just realised what he'd said. "I mean, hypothetically." He blurted out. "You know, if we… someday…" He trailed off, blotches of crimson showing through his tanned cheeks. He took a huge gulp of his drink.

Bea's mind raced. *Marriage? To Rich?* It was too soon, wasn't it? And yet… A warm feeling spread through her chest as a smile tugged at her lips. *Perhaps not…*

"Er, I wonder why we've not heard from Tina yet," Simon said, cutting through Rich's discomfort. "They should've released Maria by now. It's been hours."

When she'd brought their coffee earlier, Ana had told them Maria was still being held by the police.

Rich leaned forward, clearly happy to encourage the change of conversation. "The police only have eight hours left before they have to go before the judge."

As if on cue, Tina appeared on the terrace. One look at her face told Bea it wasn't good news.

"They're refusing to release Maria," Tina said without preamble as she joined them at the table. "Pearl came forward and told them about the necklace as she'd promised to do. The police interviewed her and Peter, but they think it's a ploy to get Maria off."

Bea frowned. "You mean they think it's made up?" she asked.

Tina shrugged. "I'm afraid so. Her lawyer is hoping that the judge will be reasonable and let her go. It's fifty-fifty at this point without some firm evidence to support it either way."

"But what about Peter?" Perry interjected, his voice rising. "He had ketamine."

Simon placed a calming hand on his husband's arm. "Tina, why don't they suspect Peter?"

Tina pursed her lips. "Peter admitted he keeps a small amount of ketamine that he uses... er, recreationally but claims someone stole half a vial's worth from his studio the day before the pool party."

Perry jumped up, nearly knocking over his coffee, startling Daisy, who had been snoozing under the table. She gave a short *yap*.

"That's ridiculous! If that's true, why didn't he report it the minute he found out JT had been drugged?" he asked incredulously.

"He says he was worried about getting into trouble," Tina replied. "He smuggled it into the country from the States on Ella and JT's private jet."

Perry's face flushed red as he threw himself back down into his chair. "He's lying! Peter's the killer. I'm sure of it!"

Tina held up a hand, her blue eyes sympathetic but firm. "I'm sorry, Perry, but it gets worse. Peter has an alibi for the time of JT's death. He was online, playing poker. His laptop records confirm it."

The news hit Bea like a punch to the gut. She slumped in her chair, her mind churning. "So we're back to square one?" A heavy silence fell over the group. *All our theories, all our suspects... and still nothing concrete to save Maria.* Her heart shrank as she swallowed hard.

"So... what now?" Simon asked quietly. "If not Peter, who's left besides Derek?"

"Oh, I forgot to say—Derek updated his statement yesterday," Tina told them, pointing to a manilla folder on the table. "He says he went back to talk to JT by the pool, but JT was too drunk, so Derek says he told him to go to bed and left again."

"There you go!" Perry threw up his hands. "Derek's a far better suspect than poor Maria!"

"Yes. You'd think that, wouldn't you?" Tina said, a thread of frustration running through her voice. "But I get the sense the police here don't want to accuse a wealthy and, no doubt, powerful American tourist without ironclad proof. Too much media scrutiny."

Bea's nostrils flared. "So Maria's an easy target?" *How dare they railroad an innocent woman so they can wrap this up neatly!*

Tina rose. "Okay, so I'll go back to the station and chase up the results on the wrench, WD-40 can, and pool skimmer. I'll let you know as soon as I have them."

As they watched her leave, a silence descended on those left around the table.

"Look. I know it seems bad, but we still have time to prove them wrong," Rich said as he stood. "We need to go back to the beginning and review what we know. There has to be something we've missed."

Bea looked up at Rich. His steadfast belief in their abilities rekindled her resolve. She rose and caught his eye. He winked at her. Her heart faltered for a second. Was this a man she could look at every day of her life and not tire of? He smiled, his brown eyes twinkling as they looked into hers. *Hmmm...Yes. I think he is.* Her heart flipped as she smiled back at him. *But first things first.* Marriage. Possible children. It would all have to wait...

She breathed in and squared her shoulders. *Rich is right— we can't give up now.* Not when Maria's future was hanging in the balance...

40

10AM, TUESDAY 10 AUGUST

B ea huffed as she read a copy of Derek's amended witness statement. Underneath the table in the basement at Villa Mer, Daisy snored softly, curled up at her feet. Rich, Perry, and Simon were engrossed in their own stacks of paper, the only sounds the rustling of pages and the occasional picking up and putting down of mugs.

Perry glanced up at her. "Have you found something?"

Bea shook her head, tossing Derek's statement onto the table. "Derek still doesn't say why he needed to talk to JT so urgently, and the police never even asked! Useless."

"So not much help?"

"Not really. Although, I'm a bit confused about something." She picked up the statement again, scanning it. "He says he left Villa Sol through the main door and then went straight to his villa. But then, a few minutes later, he used the side gate to go back. Why not use the front like before?"

"Perhaps he wanted to be sneaky," Perry suggested, his blue eyes shining. "That path runs down the side of the villa, so he would be less likely to be seen."

"It's also possible he used it because he knew JT was

having his evening swim and it leads directly to the terrace and pool," Simon added, putting down a report and picking up his cup.

"So is the side gate between their two villas like the one we have between us and Villa Sol?" Bea asked, looking at Rich, who was now listening to their conversation.

He nodded. "Except whereas our path goes from the garden here into the back of the gardens of Villa Sol, theirs goes along the side of Villa Sol from the back of the garden of Villa Luz."

"Okay, I get it now. But I thought the gardeners locked the side gates when they went home," Bea said, vaguely remembering her initial concern about security when she'd found out about the side gate here.

"Yes and no," Rich replied. "They lock our gate. But I was told by the security lead that, at the request of the owners of Villa Sol and Villa Luz, when they're in residence, the gate between them is left unlocked."

Well, I suppose that makes sense, seeing how they're all friends and spend so much time together. She glanced back down at Derek's statement. "So he says he came out by the pool and saw JT. They exchanged a few words and then... Hold on." She frowned. Lucy had told them she'd seen Derek coming back. But that couldn't be right, surely?

"Rich," Bea said slowly. "Lucy told us she saw Derek walk past the window when she was going to the kitchen, didn't she?"

"Er, yes. Why?"

Bea turned to Perry. "You're more familiar with the layout of Villa Sol than I am, but aren't the stairs to the basement accessed from the main foyer at the front of the villa?"

Perry sat up straighter, his eyes widening. "Yes, you're right. So how did—"

"Exactly!" Bea jumped in, her voice rising in excitement. "She couldn't have seen Derek go past if he went back via the side gate and along the side of the villa. She lied."

"Interesting," Rich said, running his hands along his stubbled chin. "So either she didn't see him and told us she did for some reason. Or she *did* see him but not from where she said she was."

Simon leaned forward, his beard twitching as he frowned. "I hate to be the party pooper, but does this really get us any further? We know Lucy was out all morning when the statue was unbolted, so she's not the one who did it."

Bea's hands went limp as she dropped the statement back on the table. *Is he right?* Did Lucy have a reason to lie that had nothing to do with JT's death?

Perry swore under his breath, then gave a deep sigh as he picked up his mug and took a sip of his drink.

Rich's phone pinged, interrupting the subdued atmosphere. He glanced at the screen, then looked up with a puzzled expression. "It's from Tina. She says there were no prints on the WD-40 can. None at all."

Simon pulled a face. "That's strange. You'd expect at least some partial prints from whoever used it last."

"Agreed," Rich said. "And get this—the only prints on the wrench belong to Miquel."

Bea sat up. *But what about—*

"He told us he used it later that day," Perry pointed out.

"Yes, but what about all the other gardeners' prints?" Bea asked.

Simon leaned forward, nodding. "So whoever took those items must have wiped them clean. Deliberately removing any traces of themselves."

"There's more," Rich said as he continued to read Tina's text. "They found prints on the skimming pole."

From the look in his eye, Bea knew this was going to be important.

"Miquel's?" Simon asked, leaning forward.

Bea mentally crossed her fingers.

Rich shook his head. "Ella St Gerome's."

Bingo!

Perry clapped his hands. "This could be the break we need."

Simon held up a hand. "Hold on. Before we get carried away. She might have simply moved it at some point that day. And remember, she didn't drug JT or push over the statue. She was with me and Perry the whole time."

I know, but... "I specifically asked her, Simon, if she'd moved the pole, and she denied it, making some snarky comment about it not being her job to clean the pool. So why lie? That has to be significant."

As they fell into a thoughtful silence, Bea couldn't escape the sense that they were on the verge of uncovering something big, but at the moment, the picture wasn't clear enough in her mind. Lucy had lied. Ella had lied. And about seemingly unimportant details. As Perry rose and moved over to the whiteboard, Bea sipped her warm coffee. *There's something here; I'm sure of it.* Underneath the table, Daisy snorted softly in her sleep.

Perry suddenly let out a high-pitched squeak. Daisy woke with a *yap*. Bea leaned down and rubbed the little terrier's head reassuringly as Perry grabbed Simon's arm, nearly yanking him off his feet as he dragged him towards the photos pinned to the wall.

"Look!" Perry jabbed a perfectly manicured finger at Lucy's feet in one of the photos he'd taken of the crime scene. "Do you see what I see?"

Simon squinted as he leaned in towards the board. "Uh, shoes?"

Perry rolled his eyes dramatically. "No! That's it. I can't believe I didn't spot it at the time. She's wearing trainers!"

Bea smiled. Perry's obsession with footwear wasn't just a fashion statement—it was practically a superpower. He'd seen something important...

Simon, still looking confused, said, "I don't get it."

"She was wearing black high-heeled sandals at the party," Perry said with a flourish.

Simon shrugged. "She was on her feet all night. She probably kept her trainers in the kitchen for when the guests had left, and she was cleaning up."

Rich was already flipping through papers. "There's nothing about her changing her footwear in her statement," he said.

"So that's suspicious, isn't it?" Perry's eyes were alight with exhilaration.

Bea nodded. Something about Lucy still wasn't adding up. *Is there any way she's JT's killer?* "Er, is there any way Lucy could have somehow got back to Villa Sol the morning of JT's murder without security knowing?"

Rich rubbed his nose. "I don't think it's likely."

A thought dropped into Bea's head. "I know this sounds crazy, but Sam and Archie got from our private beach to the next bay without being seen by security."

"Do you think she came back on a paddle board?" Perry asked with a grin.

"Not a paddle board, but maybe a boat or a kayak..." She trailed off. It was sounding silly even to her now.

"Hold on, let me check." Rich pulled a folder towards himself and opened it. He took out the pages and flipped through them. "She went to four different places during the time she was off-site, according to her statement. One was to drop off and pick up Ella's laundry. The police confirmed that with the dry cleaners. She also had a nail appointment. The police confirmed that with the nail salon. She went to the supermarket. That was confirmed by Ella. The only visit the police didn't confirm was a stop at a local cafe for coffee. But she was only there for thirty minutes. So sorry, but I think her alibi stands."

Bea exhaled loudly. *Fiddlesticks!*

"Look," Simon said, rising. "Why don't we talk to Lucy and find out what she's hiding? We can also confront Ella about the pole and see if it's relevant. And let's attempt to get Derek to tell us what he wanted to talk to JT so badly about. Between them, we may discover something that will point us in the right direction."

They all nodded and stood. "And who knows?" Perry said, linking his arm through Bea's. "If we find a paddle board hidden at Villa Sol, we might have our answer!"

Bea elbowed him in the ribs. "Oh, ha ha."

41

JUST AFTER 10:30AM, TUESDAY 10 AUGUST

"Right, so we're agreed?" Simon's crisp voice reverberated around the marble-floored foyer at Villa Mer. "Bea and Perry will talk to Lucy, while Rich speaks to Ella under the guise of bringing her up-to-date about Maria."

Bea stood in the cool, airy lobby, glancing around at the others with a mix of excitement and apprehension, her fingers crossed that this fishing exhibition would catch them a break-through in the investigation. *We need it!*

As light filtered through the grand windows, casting playful shadows on the walls, Simon continued, "I have to make a call to my agent about the book tour she's organising for me, then I'll go over to Villa Luz. Derek said he's keen to talk to me about my writing, so I'll use that as an excuse. I may take Isla with me when she gets back from wherever she went." They all agreed, and Simon went off to make his call.

"As Ella is most likely to be sunning herself by the pool, let's go that way," Perry said, pointing towards the open-plan sitting and dining room that led to the terrace and gardens.

As they walked through the bifold doors, Sam and Archie

were sitting by the pool, sipping on freshly squeezed orange juice, looking more subdued than usual after their behaviour yesterday. Bea was glad to see they were also both under a sun umbrella. They still had flaming red faces, shoulders, and legs from yesterday's escapade.

"Morning," Rich shouted over to them. They turned and waved. "We're off next door. We won't be long." He got a thumbs up.

"I think they're still a bit sore after yesterday," Perry said. "And I'm not just talking about their sunburn."

Bea gave a wry smile, recalling how quiet the boys had been last night when they'd joined everyone for dinner. It was clear they'd still been feeling bad about what had happened, and although Bea didn't want to ruin their holiday, if it made them more careful, then she wasn't complaining.

When she'd bumped into Isla on her way up from the basement a short while ago, Isla had told her that Chloe had gained half a million followers overnight. The youngster had been furious, suggesting to Bea that Chloe may have orchestrated the whole thing to increase her social media presence. After all, she'd pointed out, an association with British royalty was a great way to do that.

Maybe she's right. Perhaps Chloe *had* manipulated the situation to her advantage, but it didn't absolve Sam and Archie. *In fact, if they are so easily led, then—*

A blur of white shot past Bea's legs as Rich pushed open the gate. Daisy, her tail wagging like a flag in gale force winds, dashed after a small rabbit that had darted across their path.

"Daisy, no!" Bea hissed, her eyes widening in alarm. *Where did she come from?* Bea could've sworn she'd left the terrier in the house. She didn't like her being out in the heat of the day. Bea sprinted after the dog, but her flip-flops made it impossible to move fast. "Daisy! Come back," she cried. But the little terrier was clearly on a mission.

42

MEANWHILE, TUESDAY 10 AUGUST

I sla stormed across the hot sand of the Marisol private beach, her feet sinking with each determined step she took. After everything she had said to Chloe just a few days ago about videoing Bea and Rich, how could she pull a stunt like this with Sam and Archie? Her fingers curled into fists. How dare Chloe use them for her own gain like that? Isla spotted the influencer just ahead of her, sitting crossed-legged on a bright-pink beach towel. She was glued to her phone. *As usual!*

Isla marched right up to her and stopped in front of her, casting a long shadow. Chloe glanced up, annoyance flashing across her perfectly made-up face. "Isla. This is a surprise."

"Hey, Chloe," Isla said through gritted teeth. "Got a minute?"

Chloe sighed dramatically as she scrambled up from the sand, her phone still in her hand. "Geez, what's got your goat?"

"What were you playing at, taking the boys outside of the compound yesterday?" Isla snapped.

Chloe's perfectly plucked eyebrows furrowed. "What are you talking about?"

"Sam and Archie. The paddle boards. Come on. I know you encouraged them to go around to the next bay."

"Oh, that?" She rolled her eyes. "It was just a bit of fun. The boys had a great time. It wasn't a big deal."

Isla shoved her hands on her hips, feeling heat rising up her neck. "Not a big deal? Sam is royalty, Chloe! Do you have any idea of the danger you could have put him in?"

"Oh, come on!" Chloe scoffed. "They were fine. You're being overdramatic."

Isla's blue eyes flashed. "Overdramatic? What if someone had recognised him? What if he'd been hurt or... or kidnapped?"

"Kidnapped?" Chloe laughed, but it sounded hollow. "Now you're just being ridiculous."

Isla stepped closer, her voice low and intense. "Is this all just a game to you? More content for your precious followers?" Her muscles quivered. "I thought you understood after that video with Lady Rossex and Richard Fitzwilliam. You told me you didn't know they were in it."

Chloe's gaze flickered away. "I didn't."

Liar! Isla's mouth went dry. These people—Bea, Rich, Sam, Archie—they'd become like family to her. They'd accepted her with open arms, showing her kindness and making her feel like she belonged. She wouldn't let anyone hurt them. And especially not a selfish, attention-hungry brat like Chloe Stone.

"Just stay away from them, Chloe," Isla said, raising her voice. "All of them. Find some other way to get your precious likes."

Chloe's jaw dropped, a flicker of unease in her expression before she quickly masked it with indignation. "Excuse me?

Where do you get off talking to me like that? You don't know anything about me or the pressure I'm under," she said, her voice tight. "My sponsors—"

"I don't care, Chloe. That's no excuse to use other people," Isla interrupted. "And anyway, how hard can it be to snap selfies all day!"

Chloe's eyes flashed with fury as she jabbed a manicured finger at Isla. "You have no idea what you're talking about! The pressure I'm under from my sponsors, it's relentless. I have to constantly churn out content, keep them engaged, or poof!" She made an explosive gesture with her hands. "There goes my career. You think this is easy? You think this is fun?"

Isla stood her ground even as her heart raced. "Nobody's forcing you to do it," she retorted, her voice steadier than she felt. "I'm sure your parents have a nice trust fund set up for you. Why don't you just—"

Chloe let out a harsh bark of laughter, shaking her head in disbelief. "Trust fund? I wish! You want to know the truth, Isla? There is no trust fund. Dad wanted to set one up, but lately, my mother's been fighting him on it. She thinks I need to stand on my own two feet." She inched closer. Isla resisted the urge to step backwards. "That's easy for her to say—she was a supermodel. She had her pick of opportunities. But me? I'm not like her." Chloe's eyes flashed, her petite frame seeming to loom over Isla. "I have to work twice as hard for half the recognition."

Isla blinked, thrown off-balance by this sudden outburst.

It's your own fault—you poked the bear!

She was suddenly aware that she was on a deserted private beach with a very angry Chloe, who was probably stronger and definitely fitter than her. Isla knew Chloe worked out religiously.

What was I thinking?

Her dad had told her more than once to be careful... to not confront a suspect. Her stomach churned. But Chloe wasn't a suspect, was she? She tried to recall the whiteboard in the basement. No. She was fairly certain Chloe had been ruled out as she hadn't been in the room when JT had been drugged. *Come on, Isla. Pull yourself together.* She'd said what she'd needed to say. She should just leave now.

But as she met Chloe's eyes, the young woman's shoulders slumped, and she wrapped her arms around herself. Her anger seemed to drain away. She looked very young all of a sudden.

"My dad... He's been so unhappy lately. He knows about my mom's affair with JT, and at first, it didn't seem to bother him. But then she told him she wanted a divorce and... Well, he's still putting on a brave face, but I know he's hurt. He loves her, and he doesn't want her to go." Her voice wavered, and she blinked back tears. "I just wanted things to go back to the way they were, you know? I thought if I could break up the affair, if I could get my mom to come back to my dad... Maybe he would be happy again." She gulped in a deep breath. "That's why I did what I did."

A chill ran down Isla's spine. This conversation had taken a turn she hadn't expected. There was something in Chloe's eyes, a haunted, desperate look that set off alarm bells in her head. *What did you do, Chloe?*

43

BACK AT VILLA SOL, TUESDAY 10 AUGUST

Rich, wearing more suitable footwear than Bea, quickly overtook her as he charged after Daisy. Bea's mind raced as they pursued the terrier into Villa Sol's immaculate garden. Ella, with her Hollywood polish and icy demeanour, was unlikely to be a dog person. The last thing they needed was Daisy wreaking havoc on the actress' pristine property. As they rounded the corner, Bea's gaze darted to the terrace. It was deserted, the bifold windows drawn tightly shut. Bea breathed out heavily. *Thank goodness!*

"There she goes!" Perry called out from behind her.

Daisy, still in hot pursuit of the rabbit, bounded along the edge of the now refilled sparkling swimming pool. Bea's mouth went dry as, with a gleeful bark, the little dog took a flying leap into a dense cluster of bushes near the terrace.

"Oh no," Bea groaned, coming to a halt as leaves and twigs flew into the air. "Please don't let her have caught that poor little thing."

Perry, slightly out of breath, stopped beside her. "Wait, look there!" He pointed to a small brown form scurrying away from the bush. "It made it!"

Letting out a sigh of relief, Bea called out, "Daisy, come here."

No response came from the rustling bushes.

"Do you think she's stuck?" Bea asked, worry creeping into her voice. She hurried towards Rich, who was almost at the bush now. "Is she alright?" she called.

"Don't worry. I'll get her," he replied, giving Bea a reassuring smile.

"My hero," she called out, her hand on her heart as Rich winked at her, then disappeared into the foliage.

After a few tense seconds, Rich emerged, looking like he'd lost a fight with a hedge trimmer. Leaves clung to his hair and clothes, and Daisy, equally dishevelled, panted happily in his arms. Next to Bea, Perry snorted.

"Here you go," Rich said, handing the wriggling dog to Bea. "She's fine. Just a bit… er, bush-like."

Bea hugged Daisy close despite the dog's attempts to squirm free and resume her rabbit hunt. "Daisy-Doo, you're in trouble, young lady." She plucked leaves and small twigs from the little dog's fur.

Perry leaned over and ruffled Daisy's wiry head. "Better luck next time, little girl."

Bea's gaze flicked upwards in protest. "Perry!"

Laughing, Rich turned and headed back to the bushes. Bea and Perry exchanged puzzled looks.

"What are you doing now?" Perry asked as they moved closer.

Rich's muffled voice came from within the greenery. "I spotted something when I was fishing Daisy out. Ah, got it!" He re-emerged, clutching a folded piece of white paper with his handkerchief.

He joined Bea and Perry, then gingerly unfolded the sheet

with the pocket square. "Don't want to smudge any finger-prints," he explained.

Bea's pulse quickened as she leaned in to read the hand-written capitalised message:

I HOPE THIS WILL MAKE YOU THINK TWICE BEFORE YOU TREAT PEOPLE LIKE DIRT AND THREATEN THEM AGAIN. IF NOT, YOU'LL BE SORRY!

"On my giddy aunt," Perry cried as a chill raced down Bea's spine. The words held a distinct air of menace. *Does this have anything to do with JT's murder?*

"Do you think they're referring to JT?" Perry asked as if reading her mind.

"It's possible," Rich replied, carefully folding the note before wrapping the handkerchief around it and placing it in the side pocket of his combat-style shorts. "The language certainly fits. 'Treat people like dirt and threaten them'? Sounds like our charming dead producer."

Bea chewed her lower lip. *Was JT's murder the 'you'll be sorry' part?*

"I should get this to Tina as soon as possible," Rich said.

Bea nodded. "We should head back anyway. Ella and Lucy don't seem to be home, and I'd rather not be caught trespassing with a leaf-covered dog." Daisy, who seemed to have finally given up on the idea of escaping, licked Bea's chin.

As they walked back to the villa, with Daisy still nestled in her arms, Bea's mind raced. Who'd written the note? Who was it for? And how was it connected to JT's death?

44

BACK TO MARISOL BEACH, TUESDAY 10 AUGUST

Isla's heart hammered against her ribs as she inched away from Chloe, her instincts screaming at her to run, but before she could make her legs move, Chloe's hand shot out, her fingers clamping around Isla's wrist in an iron grip. "I just wanted to end things between Mom and JT," she said, her voice flat and lifeless. "But it didn't work. Mom and Dad are as miserable as ever."

What didn't work? A wave of nausea washed over Isla as the pieces fell into place. *Chloe had killed JT!* She must have found a way to drug him without being in the room. Isla's mouth went dry as Chloe continued with a bitter laugh. "Do you know how hard it was to flirt with that dirty old man? It made my skin crawl. But I had to make Mom jealous. I had to make her see that he didn't really love her."

Isla's mind raced as Chloe's confession spilled out. She had to get help, had to let someone know what was happening. Slowly, carefully, she slipped her free hand into her shorts pocket, her fingers clasping her phone. *I could record this conversation, then if the worst happens, at least the police will have evidence.* No. No. She should call for help.

What's the emergency number here? Is it 1-1-2, the same as Spain? A wave of dizziness threatened to overwhelm her.

"He wanted to meet in private," Chloe rambled on, seemingly lost in her story. "I agreed, of course. It was all part of the plan."

Isla's fingers closed around her phone. *If I can dial Dad's number, maybe he will hear what's happening and come to my rescue.* Her heart raced as she slowly slid the phone from her pocket, keeping her eyes fixed on Chloe.

"I left the party and headed through the villa. He'd suggested we should meet in the garden by the pool," Chloe said, her dark eyes unfocused. "I knew Mum would be watching."

Isla quickly glanced down at her phone, her fingers trembling as she tried to unlock it discreetly. Suddenly, Chloe's gaze snapped to Isla's hand.

"Are you even listening to me?" Chloe snarled, her eyes flashing, her tone accusatory.

"Yes… yes, of course I am," Isla said, her heart pounding in her chest. She tried to force a reassuring smile on her face. She suspected it came out more like a grimace.

Chloe's lips twisted into a sneer. "Good," she barked. In a blur of movement, she lashed out with her free arm, knocking the phone from Isla's hand. It landed in the sand with a soft thud. "Then you won't be needing that, will you?"

45

AT ABOUT THE SAME TIME,
TUESDAY 10 AUGUST

B ea meandered along the stone path through the Villa Mer gardens, a little way ahead of Rich and Perry. Daisy trotted happily beside her, a few leaves still stuck in her wiry fur. Splashing erupted from the pool to her right as Sam and Archie raced each other along its length. The path curved as the sun-drenched terrace came into view. Simon's voice drifted towards her as he paced, his phone in hand, deep in conversation.

"If I can avoid being away at the weekends, then that would be great," he said. "I really want to be at the restaurant then if I can." As they approached him, he said a cheery goodbye and cut the call. He looked up at them, his eyebrows raised. "I wasn't expecting you back so soon."

"They weren't there," Bea told him. "But—"

"Daisy found something!" Perry jumped in, his eyes shining as they joined Simon.

"Give me a minute," Rich said, patting Simon on the shoulder as he rushed towards the bifold doors.

Where's he going? Perry turned to Bea, frowning.

Simon leaned down and ruffled Daisy's furry head. "Have you been sleuthing again, Daisy?"

"She found a note," Perry told him as he rose. They walked over to the table. Bea slid a bowl of water towards Daisy, then sat down.

Rich reappeared and hurried over, a see-through plastic bag in his hand. "Sorry, but I wanted to protect it." He held up the bag, and Bea saw it contained the note they'd found. "Tina will want to check it for prints." He handed it over to Simon to inspect, then moved around to sit next to Bea.

"Um... interesting," Simon said, rubbing his chin as he read it. "And the threat of possibly more to come..."

Perry leaned in, his voice lowered conspiratorially. "Do you think someone was blackmailing JT?"

The question hung in the air, heavy with implication. Bea's eyes met Rich's, and she saw her own concern mirrored there.

Simon tipped his head from side to side. "It's hard to say with any certainty. If it's JT that they're referring to, then... it's possible." He laid the bagged note on the table. "But, of course, the note might have nothing to do with JT."

Bea sighed. Rich had said the same to her and Perry as they'd been walking back from Villa Sol. She looked across at the piece of paper on the table. Something about the handwriting nagged at her. "Hang on," she murmured, her brow furrowing. "I think I've seen that writing before." She reached over and picked it up.

Rich leaned over her shoulder, his breath warm against her skin as he asked, "Can you remember where?"

Come on, brain! She closed her eyes, but nothing came. She shook her head slowly.

"From while we've been here?" Simon prompted from across the table.

It must be... Suddenly, it clicked. "The pool party invitation! It was handwritten."

"It's Ella's handwriting?" Perry asked, frowning.

"I don't know," Bea faltered, now not so sure.

"Can we check?" Rich asked.

Now, where did I put the invitation? She didn't recall throwing it out, so it must be around somewhere. She rubbed her temples. "But I've no idea where I put it."

Simon cleared his throat and looked pointedly at his husband sitting next to him. Perry had suddenly found his pristine nails fascinating. "Er, Perry..."

Perry squirmed, his cheeks flushing. "Look, I might have... you know, kept the invitation. As a memento! It's not every day I get invited to rub elbows with Hollywood royalty." He threw up his hands at Simon's exasperated look. "It's in our room, on the dresser. I'll go and grab it now."

Bea grinned at Simon as Perry sprung up and scurried off towards the open bifold doors and disappeared.

"I'm going to check on the boys," Rich said, squeezing her shoulder as he rose and moved past her, wandering over to the pool. Sam and Archie appeared to be engaged in a splashing war of epic proportions. Bea watched as Rich crouched down by the edge of the shimmering blue water. The boys stopped and swam over to where he was. He said something that made them laugh. She smiled and felt the pulse in her throat quicken. *He has such an easy way with them.* It was one of the things she loved most about him.

"Everything alright with you two?" Simon asked quietly, jolting her from her thoughts. "After yesterday, I mean."

Bea turned back to him, a sheepish smile on her face. "I overreacted. I lashed out at him when I was scared out of my mind and angry at the boys for being so reckless." She shuddered. "I know I can't bubble wrap Sam forever, Simon, but I don't think he truly grasped how dangerous it was to go off like that."

Simon acknowledged her words with a sympathetic nod. "It's a tricky age, Bea. He's not quite a man but not really a boy anymore either."

"That's just it," Bea said, puffing out air. "He's growing up so fast. I worry I haven't prepared him for what's coming. I don't think he understands the gravity of his position as a member of the royal family or the responsibilities he'll have one day as the heir to his grandfather's title and estate." James, Sam's father, had been the only child of William and Joan Wiltshire, the Earl and Countess of Durrland. With his father dead, Sam was their sole heir. His grandparents had expectations that once he left school, he would go to college to learn estate management, and one day, he would take over the running of their vast estate in Lincolnshire.

"Ah," Simon said, understanding dawning. "The weight of his legacy."

Bea mirrored his glance, grateful he understood. "Exactly. When do I burden him with all of that?"

Simon considered for a moment. "He's still young, Bea. Why not give him twelve months? When he has to decide on what to do after sixth form, that might be a good time for that conversation."

Her shoulders relaxed. She smiled at her friend, reaching over to take his hand. "You're right. Thanks, Simon."

"Anytime." He grinned, giving her hand a gentle squeeze. "What are friends for, if not sage advice and dashing good looks?"

She grinned back, dropping his hand as she shook her head. "Your husband is rubbing off on you."

As they both laughed, Perry burst onto the terrace, waving

a piece of paper in his hand."Got it!" Perry cried, his blue eyes sparkling with excitement.

Rich hurriedly joined them as Perry placed the note on the table. Bea dropped the piece of paper they'd recovered from the bush next to it. Perry's pouty lips twisted into a frown. "Oh, well, that's not much help," he said, sighing heavily. "This note from Ella is all swirly and elegant. Our mystery letter is all capitals. It's like comparing a peacock to... an angry pigeon."

Bea's stomach clenched. *When are we ever going to catch a break?*

"Hold on," Rich said, rising and walking around the table so he was facing both notes. "I learnt a bit about handwriting way back. What you need to do is look for the same letters." He leaned in. "So we have 'Dear Lady Rossex'," He pointed to the invitation. "Capital letters are D, L, and R. Then we go over to the other one and find those letters. We have a D from DIRT, an L in YOU'LL and an R in BEFORE." He took out his phone and tapped on the screen, then he opened an app and moved the phone over the notes.

Bea rose and went to stand next to him. She looked over his shoulder. The app created a magnifying glass from the camera lens, so the letters were bigger and easier to compare. She studied the two letter Ds. The one in the threatening note had a straight line on the left with a fat, even arched line meeting at each end. The one in Ella's invitation was different; the straight line was slanted, and the arched line didn't quite connect at the bottom but ran below, ending in a slight tail that flicked up. Her stomach clenched. They were too different to have been written by the same person. She straightened up with a sigh.

Next to her, Rich was still examining the two pieces of

writing, a scowl etched deep into his forehead. He shook his head. "Sorry, but none of the letters seem to be a match."

Disappointment settled over the group like a wet blanket.

We're back to square one, with a killer still free and time running out before Maria goes in front of the judge.

"So... what now?" Perry slumped into a chair, deflated.

"At least we know the threatening note wasn't written by Ella," Simon said, tapping his chin thoughtfully. "Maybe it wasn't meant for JT at all."

Rich straightened up. "I'm not sure this changes anything. Derek Stone is still our most likely suspect, so—"

He's right. Derek had been the last person to see JT alive, having snuck back to confront him. Had he written the letter too? "Do you think Derek was fed up with the way JT was threatening Ella and her agent over the casting of their film, perhaps?" she asked Rich.

He shrugged. "It's possible."

"Or he was warning JT off Chloe," Perry said.

"Yes, also possible," Rich replied. "Either way, I think we should stick with our original plan to talk to Ella, Lucy, and Derek."

"I agree," Simon said. "You should take a photo of the note, Rich, and show it to Ella, see if she recognises the handwriting."

Let's hope so. Bea pinched her lips together. *Will we ever get to the bottom of this case?*

"That sounds like a good plan," Perry said, placing his hand on Simon's arm. "But Ella and Lucy aren't there at the moment. Can we delay a short while? I could murder a coffee right now."

Bea inclined her head slowly, rubbing her temples. A coffee might help clear her head. If she could get it all straight in her mind, perhaps she could figure out what was bothering her so much…

46

BACK ON THE BEACH, TUESDAY 10 AUGUST

I sla stared at her fallen phone lying in the sand, unable to speak. Her lifeline, her chance of rescue lay just out of reach.

She was on her own.

Think, Isla, think! She needed a plan, a way to get out of this mess.

But first, she had to calm Chloe down, keep her talking. She swallowed. "I'm sorry, Chloe. Please go on. I'm here for you."

Chloe hesitated for a moment as she stared at Isla's face, then her shoulders relaxed slightly, her grip on Isla's arm loosening. "I only got as far as the bifold doors when Mom caught up with me…"

Isla nodded, making sympathetic noises as her mind raced. *Can I overpower Chloe?* Isla knew Bea, Rich, and Perry were just over her shoulder in the garden of Villa Sol. If she could get a head start, maybe she could outrun Chloe and reach the dunes that led up to the villa in time to get help.

"…she was furious. She told me to go home. Then JT showed up…"

If I kick her in the shin, will she drop my arm? Then I can run and shout at the same time…

"…so I ran home," Chloe whispered, a single tear tracing down her cheek. "I left Mom and JT having a blazing row."

Isla blinked, her mind finally registering Chloe's words. "Wait, you left?" The question burst from her lips before she could stop it. "Did you go back later?"

Chloe shook her head, a wry smile twisting her lips. "No, I went home, drank a bottle of champagne in my room, and passed out."

Relief crashed over Isla like a wave, leaving her weak-kneed and short of breath.

She wasn't trapped with a killer.

The back of her eyes prickled. She took in a deep breath.

Just then, Chloe's phone chimed. She released her grip on Isla's wrist and looked at the phone in her other hand.

47

AT ABOUT THE SAME TIME, TUESDAY 10 AUGUST

B ea sipped the last of her coffee, savouring the rich aroma as she gazed out at the sparkling blue sea on the horizon. It was peaceful in the garden now. Sam and Archie had withdrawn indoors, escaping the fierce rays of the sun that threatened to torture their already damaged skin. Beside her, his arm draped casually around her shoulders, Rich was reading something on his phone, while opposite them, Perry and Simon chatted quietly. Daisy snoozed happily under the table, her furry head resting on Bea's foot. *The quiet before the storm*, Bea thought, not looking forward to having to leave this relaxing scene and confront her neighbours about JT's death. She longed for this to be over so she could truly relax. And then there was poor Maria. Time was ticking away. *It's time to get on.*

Rich laid a comforting hand on her arm. "We'll figure it out, Bea. We always do."

Would they? She couldn't rid herself of the feeling that they were missing something crucial, but her brain wasn't giving it up to her at the moment. "All I feel I know for certain is that Lucy is hiding something, and Ella lied about moving the skimming pole."

"And we have the note," Perry piped up.

Yes, the note. But who'd written it? She was sure she'd seen that writing before, but they'd proven it wasn't Ella's, and she'd not seen anyone else's handwriting in the short time she'd known her neighbours.

"And we have Derek and Pearl with means, opportunity, and no alibi," Simon said thoughtfully. "Maybe one of them—"

"But why would Pearl kill JT?" Rich asked. "Almost everyone has a stronger motive than her to want JT out of the way."

Bea's stomach hardened. Rich was right. Lucy and Maria were no longer at risk of being fired. Peter believed the threat of him losing his studio had now gone, and he probably assumed Ella would pay his debts for her sister's sake. Ella had inherited one hundred million and had got the leading role back in her next film. Derek didn't have to worry about him stealing his wife. Or his daughter. Even Nessa would no longer have to be around the man who had rejected her so cruelly.

Her mind was a bubbling cauldron of thoughts and questions. But slowly, one idea rose to the top. A memory of a conversation. An action that she'd not acknowledged before. A look in someone's eyes that hadn't quite fitted. Were they all connected? If so, then she had her killer… But how had they done it? She was stumped. Suppressing a groan, she slumped back in her chair. *Am I simply frustrated and clutching at straws?*

She didn't have to answer herself as Daisy jumped up to greet DI Tina Spicer, who had walked through the bifold doors, onto the terrace. "I have news," she said as she strode towards them. "I've got word that Maria's going before the judge at three today."

Bea looked at her watch. *Rats!* They only had four hours to find out who had killed JT and prove Maria was innocent. She exchanged a worried glance with Perry while Rich brought Tina up to date about the note.

"So now we've hit a bit of a wall," he told her as he finished.

Tina tilted her chin. "I feel the same."

"Any luck with fingerprints?" Rich asked.

"No, not yet," Tina replied.

"I say we confront them. Now. We need answers, and we need them before Maria faces that judge," Perry said, his jaw set with determination as he rose.

Bea stood up. "I agree. Let's go to Villa Sol and see what they have to say. We've got nothing to lose." And it might help her clarify her thoughts.

"Hold on." Simon stood, his hands raised. "We can't all go together like a horde of Viking invaders. They'll clam up."

"I agree," Rich said. "I think it's best Bea and I go with Tina on the premise that we're giving Ella an update on the investigation."

"But I wanted to—" Perry muttered petulantly.

"That's fine," Simon said. "Perry and I will go and see Derek Stone. I still think he's a credible suspect."

Perry huffed and plonked himself back down in his chair again.

Bea gave her best friend a sympathetic look. "I'll give you a full report when we get back," she told him.

"You better do," he mumbled. "And don't forget to ask Lucy why she changed her shoes."

Bea nodded. She'd forgotten that little detail. Unfortunately, it didn't help with her theory. As Rich stopped to say something to Simon, Bea caught Tina's eye. There was something that would help her know if she was on the right track. She moved over to Tina and asked her if she would find something out for her. Tina was puzzled at her request but agreed to see what she could do.

No wonder Tina's confused. I've probably got it all wrong anyway, Bea thought, her confidence faltering as she followed Tina and Rich through the bifold doors.

48

SHORTLY AFTER, TUESDAY 10 AUGUST

"Sorry, I need to take this." Tina stopped in the foyer of Villa Mer, staring down at the buzzing mobile phone in her hand.

Rich hesitated, his hand on the door handle.

"You two go on ahead. I'll join you in a few minutes." Tina's finger hovered over her phone screen.

"Okay," Rich said, opening the door. "We'll probably be in the gardens at Villa Sol, so get Perry to show you the rear access via the side gate here."

As Tina hung back to take her call, Bea and Rich continued on through the door and into the driveway. Bea glanced over at Rich, debating whether to voice the outlandish thought that had taken root in her mind. It would be good to talk it through with him, but would he think she was mad? *Oh, what the heck!* The worst he could do was laugh at her. "Er, Rich."

He turned and smiled at her as he took her hand. "Yes, my sweet?"

She stopped and gave him a questioning look. *My sweet?*

"Okay, I can see from your face that doesn't work," he

said immediately with a sheepish grin. "I was just trying it on for size." He started walking again. "How about my dear?"

Trying to suppress a smile, she said, "Er, Rich. *Darling*. Can we do this whole pet names thing later? I want to talk to you about a theory I have about who might have killed JT. Or at least..." She trailed off.

He stopped again and turned to face her. "Of course. Sorry. My love?"

She groaned and shook her head. "Look, I know this is going to sound absolutely bonkers, but hear me out," she began tentatively. "What if..."

———

The imposing white facade of Villa Sol loomed before them. Reaching out, Bea pressed the doorbell, hearing it echo around the cavernous foyer inside.

She glanced at Rich beside her. He was still looking slightly bemused. Having listened patiently while she'd tried to articulate her thoughts to him, he'd seemed to think she might be onto something, but like her, he didn't think they had the full picture yet. Their eyes met, and he winked. Her knees wobbled.

The door swung open to reveal a harried-looking Lucy. Her usually perfect blonde spikes were mussed, and behind her designer frames, her puffy eyes darted nervously between the two of them. "Oh. It's you two," she said flatly, making no move to invite them inside.

Rude! Bea peered past her. There was a haphazard pile of suitcases in the corner. A flutter ran through her chest. *Is someone leaving?*

Rich stepped forward, smiling. "Hello, Lucy. We have an update for Ella. Mind if we pop in?"

The PA hesitated, then reluctantly stepped aside with a curt nod. "Fine. She's out on the deck. Follow me."

As Rich trailed after Lucy, Bea made to do the same but paused when she heard the *click* of heels on the marble staircase above. As she stopped, Pearl descended, a carry-on bag in her hand.

"Lady Rossex." Her freckled face broke into a hesitant smile. "What a surprise," she said as she dropped the bag in the corner with the others.

"Are you going somewhere?" Bea asked, eyeing the luggage.

Pearl's smile faltered. "Sure. We're heading on back to the States tonight. Now that they've released JT's body, Ella wants to get him home as quickly as possible."

A knot twisted in Bea's stomach. *But what about the investigation? Are the police going to let them leave?* "Tonight? Isn't that a bit... sudden?"

"You know how Ella is," Pearl said with a strained laugh. "Once she makes up her mind, there's no stopping her."

"Are you all going?"

Pearl made a subtle motion of assent. "Yes. Pete's clearing out his studio now. I don't know about the Stones next door," she said, giving a short shrug.

Bea's mouth was dry. Her mind raced with questions, her worry mounting with each passing second. She had a sinking feeling that once Ella whisked everyone away back to the States, any hope of uncovering the truth behind JT's death would vanish like smoke in the wind.

49

A FEW MINUTES LATER, TUESDAY 10 AUGUST

P erry slowly placed his cup on the table. He looked out from the terrace at Villa Mer and towards the path that led to the gate that intimately led to Villa Sol. He rubbed his chin. He wanted to confront Lucy. He was sure she was involved in some way in all of this. Perhaps as an accomplice? He'd not said anything to anyone yet, but the idea that more than one person was involved had been worming through his brain since they'd got back with the note. *Should I say something to Simon?* He looked over at his husband currently typing a message on his phone. Would he laugh at his theory? He hesitated. *What theory?* He didn't really have a strong idea he could pitch right now. Just a feeling… But maybe if he was allowed to talk to—

Simon looked up. "I'm just checking to see where Isla is."

If she's got any sense, she'll be lying on the beach, soaking up the sun…

Beside him, Daisy perked up, her tail wagging furiously. Perry followed her gaze to see Isla bounding up the beach access path, her face pale, but her eyes dancing with excitement. Daisy took off like a shot to greet her.

"You'll never believe what I've just found out!" the young woman cried out breathlessly as she scooped Daisy into her arms and hurried towards them on the terrace.

Perry wetted his lips as he watched Isla drop Daisy gently to the floor, then plop down in an empty chair, gratefully accepting a glass of water from Simon.

As Daisy curled up under the table, Perry uncrossed his legs and shuffled forward in his seat, resisting the urge to shout out, "What?" as Isla took a gulp of water and caught her breath.

Come on! "We're all ears," Perry prompted Isla, leaning forward eagerly.

"Well," Isla said, letting out a deep *whoosh* of air. "I've been at the beach with Chloe."

Perry frowned. Hadn't Bea told him that Isla suspected Chloe had been the one to suggest paddle boarding to the next bay to the boys, and she'd done it to boost her social media following by then posting about it? Isla had been furious according to Bea. *So why is she still hanging around with Chloe?*

Isla caught Perry's eye and gave a shy smile. "I went to give her a piece of my mind about disregarding Sam's and Archie's safety yesterday to increase her followers."

Perry smiled proudly at Isla. *Well done, you!* "And did she admit it?"

Isla absentmindedly rubbed her wrist. "No. She tried to convince me it was all a bit of harmless fun." She shrugged, her eyes widening. "I don't think I believe her, but that's not what I wanted to tell you." She shifted in her chair. "So just as we finished... er, chatting, you know, she got a notification on her phone that someone was at the door of Villa Luz. It was her parents; they'd been out shopping." She grinned and looked at Simon.

So they went shopping... What's that got to do with anything?

Simon's eyes widened. "They have a video doorbell?"

Oh... I see....

Isla agreed vigorously. "Yes! Apparently, they have them on both the front door and the patio doors at the back."

Perry's mouth went dry, and he turned to look at Simon. "Do all the villas have them?"

He shook his head. "We don't, and I'm fairly sure Villa Sol doesn't either, or the police would have mentioned it."

"They've only had the system a few weeks," Isla told them. "They have them at home, so Chloe's dad brought some over and installed them himself. It's all wireless apparently, and it records everything."

Perry's pulse fastened as his mind raced. If those doorbells had captured any comings and goings around the time of the murder... He exchanged a meaningful glance with Simon.

"Chloe has given me copies."

Perry paused and raised an eyebrow at Isla. "She gave them to you after you accused her of—"

Isla smiled slyly as she brushed her wrist again. "She owed me. Do you want to see—"

Perry's eyes lit up with excitement. "Of course!"

We'll be able to see if Nessa and Derek really did go back to the villa after the party or not...

Isla grinned, pulling out her phone. She tapped the screen a few times, then placed it on the table so they could all see.

50

MEANWHILE AT VILLA SOL,
TUESDAY 10 AUGUST

"Er, shall we join the others?" Pearl asked as she stood in the foyer of Villa Sol, holding her arm out towards the door.

"Er, yes, of course." Bea followed her through the villa's opulent interior, unable to shake the feeling that the speed of their departure was suspicious.

Outside, Ella lounged on a reclining chair, her flawless face impassive behind oversized sunglasses. An empty champagne flute rested on the table beside her.

On the other side of the table, Lucy was pouring Rich a glass of lemonade, her hands shaking slightly. "Drink, Lady Rossex? Pearl?" she asked, her voice overly bright. They both said, "Yes, please."

"Thank you," Bea murmured a few minutes later, taking an icy glass from Lucy and sinking into a padded garden chair next to Rich. *Does he know they're leaving?*

Rich cleared his throat. "Ella, I'm afraid I have some bad news. About Maria."

Ella pulled her sunglasses down and peered over them at him. "Oh?"

"She's going before the judge this afternoon. The local police are pushing to charge her with JT's murder."

"What?" Pearl gasped, her hand flying to her mouth. "But that's crazy! Surely, they don't have a motive now that they know she didn't take the necklace?"

Rich shifted uncomfortably. "Unfortunately, they seem to think that was all just a story concocted to get Maria released."

"But that's absurd," Pearl snapped, colour high in her cheeks. "I told them the truth!" She looked at Bea with pleading eyes.

"I know, Pearl," Bea said. "And I'm so sorry, but they seem determined to discount what you said."

"There's more," Rich continued grimly. "They found a bottle of ketamine in the kitchen bin."

Ella laughed then, a harsh, brittle sound. "Well, well. Maybe she did do it after all."

Bea winced. Ella had been so sure of Maria's innocence before. So what had changed?

"Ella!" Pearl looked aghast. "How can you say that? Anyone could have thrown the bottle in that bin!"

Ignoring the bickering sisters, Bea's gaze fell on Lucy, who had gone deadly pale. *Something is definitely off with her.* Was it the mention of Maria being charged? There was only one way to find out. Watching Lucy carefully, she said, "Yes, but the police seem very determined to charge Maria with murder. They're building quite a case."

Lucy's thin lips pressed together, her eyes fixed on the ground. She swallowed loudly. Bea pressed on. Leaning forward, she said. "What do you think, Lucy?"

Lucy looked up. Her eyes widened as her mouth dropped open. "I… I don't know."

Oh, come on! The shoes. The inconsistencies in Lucy's

story about having seen Derek. *She knows something, and we're running out of time. It's time to poke the hornet's nest.* "Remind me where you were when you saw Derek Stone returning to the villa that night, will you?"

"I... I don't know what you mean," she stammered.

Bea's green eyes locked on her face. "You said you saw him return, but he came back along the side of the house. So how did you see him on your way to the kitchen?"

Lucy's face flushed, her hands fidgeting with her spiky hair. "I... I must have been mistaken. It was dark, and—"

"And your shoes... what happened to your shoes that night, Lucy? Why were you wearing trainers by the time you were found screaming at the side of the pool?"

"I..." Lucy stammered, her face now a deep crimson. "I—"

"Lady Rossex!" Ella snapped, scratching irritably at the red patch on her hand. "What are you doing? Why are you grilling poor Lucy like this?"

Have I pushed too far? Bea glanced at Lucy, who now had tears welling up in her eyes. "I'm sorry, Lucy," she said, slumping back in her seat. "I didn't mean to upset you. But we're trying to sort this out before they lock Maria up and throw away the key." *And I know you're hiding something...*

Rich cleared his throat, pulling out his phone. "Actually, I have something here I'd like you all to look at," he said, his tone casual but his eyes sharp. He held out the device, displaying a photo of a handwritten note. "We're trying to establish if this is Maria's handwriting. Pearl, does it look like it to you?"

Bea blinked in confusion. Why was Rich asking about Maria's handwriting? They'd never thought the note had come from her. Did he know something Bea didn't?

Pearl leaned in to examine the photo, then glanced

quickly at Lucy. The look was brief, but Bea caught it. Her heart raced as the pieces clicked into place. *It's Lucy's writing!* Of course. That was where she'd seen it before. The envelope that Ella's invitation had come in. Lucy had been threatening JT. That explained her distress, her nervous behaviour.

"I... I don't think it's Maria's," Pearl said hesitantly. "But I can't be certain."

Ella pulled her sunglasses off, glanced at the picture, then waved her hand. "I've never seen it before," she said, then quickly returned her glasses to her face.

Ah, she's lying! Ella must have instantly recognised her PA's writing. Bea's head was spinning. If Lucy had written the threatening note, did that mean she'd actually killed JT? And if she had, then Bea's theory was way off. Unless...

Just then, a familiar figure appeared across the garden, striding purposefully towards their group. Tina Spicer, her blonde hair gleaming in the late morning sun, gave a brief wave as she spotted Bea and Rich.

Ella's head whipped around. "What in tarnation does she want?"

Tina greeted them with a polite, "Hello, sorry to intrude," then leaned in close to Rich, whispering something in his ear. He pressed his lips together and gave a curt nod.

Bea watched, curiosity gnawing at her. *What did Tina tell him?*

Tina then turned and pressed a folded piece of paper into Bea's hand. "The information you wanted," she murmured, a sly smile playing on her lips.

Bea unfolded the note, her eyes scanning the words. A warm feeling bloomed in her chest. So she *had* been right about something...

51

BACK AT VILLA MER, TUESDAY 10 AUGUST

"This is the front door camera," Isla said as she pressed play on the screen of her mobile phone as it rested on the wooden table on the terrace.

Perry leaned in as the video played, showing a rather murky view of the drive at the front of Villa Luz. A light came on as Chloe appeared. She quickly unlocked the door, and she went inside. The time at the top of the screen said eight thirty-nine.

"Hold on!" Simon said, and Isla leaned over and pressed pause on her phone screen. Simon twisted around and looked at Perry. "Chloe's statement said she left the party at eight twenty-five. So why did it take her fourteen minutes to get home?"

That's a good question. What had Chloe been up to? Perry wouldn't put it past her to have been—

Isla shuffled uncomfortably in her seat next to him. "Er, I wasn't going to say anything because I was sort of told in confidence, but…" She told them what Chloe had said about her deliberately flirting back with JT and arranging to meet him in private to make Nessa realise what a heel he was so she would go back to Derek.

Was it possible that although Chloe was a slave to the popularity her fame brought her, deep down she was just a little girl who wanted her parents to stay together?

"Okay, well that explains that." Simon nodded at his daughter, and she resumed the video.

At eight fifty-one, the light came on again, picking up Nessa looking slightly worse for wear as she let herself in. The screen darkened, then came to life again at nine forty-six. Derek trudged slowly up the drive. But instead of going straight to the door, he paused, key in hand, then veered off to the side of the house and disappeared from view.

"The camera at the back will pick him up," Isla told them. The light came on again at two minutes past ten, when Derek reappeared from the side of the house. As he fumbled with his keys, a distant scream made Perry jump. On the screen, Derek froze, then took off running back the way he'd come.

Perry's heart raced. *That must have been Lucy discovering JT's body.*

Isla reached out to the phone. "Now this is the camera attached to the back patio doors."

Derek appeared at nine forty-seven, striding purposefully across the garden before vanishing into the shadows in the corner. At nine fifty-four, he reemerged, sauntering towards the patio doors. Finding them locked, he took a cigar out of his pocket and lit it. He turned his back to the camera and stared out towards the sea.

Perry stared at the screen as Derek puffed away. Isla leaned over and fast-forwarded the video. "He stays there for seven minutes," she explained before pressing play again. Derek threw the stub on the patio and crushed it with his foot, then he slipped around the side of the house. Perry held his breath, transfixed. Two minutes later, the light came back on as Derek came barrelling back into view, running full tilt towards the rear of the garden. Two minutes after that, Nessa burst out of the patio doors, her silk dressing gown flaying behind her as she dashed across the lawn in the same direction.

For a long moment, nobody spoke. Perry's mind whirled as he tried to recall Derek's most recent statement to the police.

"So," Simon said at last, breaking the silence. "That seems to clear Nessa and Chloe completely. Neither of them left the house during the critical time."

Perry was quite sure the times fitted with what Derek had said. He gave a quiet hum of agreement. "And Derek's movements match up with his statement." He sighed, feeling a mixture of relief and frustration. "So he's cleared too." Their most promising suspect—in fact, their only suspect, was now in the clear.

Isla looked thoughtful for a moment, then said, "I'm glad neither of Chloe's parents are killers."

Simon smiled and patted her shoulder. "So am I, love."

"But where does that leave us? Derek was our last viable suspect, right?" Isla asked.

"Back to square one," Simon said grimly. "This is shaping up to be our most frustrating case yet."

Perry nodded as he leaned back and closed his eyes. An uneasy feeling was niggling at him. Something that had been brewing for a while. He wasn't quite sure about his line of thought, but they didn't have anything else to try. He picked up his phone and texted Bea.

. . .

Perry: *We've found evidence that Derek, Nessa, and Chloe couldn't have killed JT. But what if...*

52

NOW BACK TO VILLA SOL, TUESDAY 10 AUGUST

The terrace at Villa Sol crackled with tension. Tina took a seat beside Bea, her blue eyes fixed on Lucy.

Rich leaned towards Lucy and showed her the photo of the note on his phone. "We know this is your writing, Lucy," he said, his voice firm. "It's time you told us what really happened."

Ah! Tina must have had the results on the original note back, and they showed Lucy's fingerprints on it. That was what she'd been whispering to Rich moments ago.

Lucy's eyes widened, darting between Rich and the note. "I don't know what you're talking about. That's not my writing."

Why is she lying? She must know that we all know it's hers! In her pocket, Bea's phone vibrated. *It will have to wait. We're just about to get to the juicy bit...* Bea leaned forward, catching Lucy's gaze. "It *is* yours, Lucy. I recognise it from the envelope containing the invitation Ella sent us for the pool party." Bea glanced over to Ella, who sat upright in her recliner, her painted mouth slightly open.

Rich nodded, adding, "The inspector here can always pop into your office and compare it with—"

But before he'd even finished, Lucy's shoulders sagged. The fight drained from her face, replaced by a look of defeat that made Bea's stomach clench.

Ella leaned forward, whipping her sunglasses off. "Lucy, is this true? Were you threatening JT?" she asked, her icy-blue eyes narrowing.

Tears welled up in Lucy's eyes. Her lip trembled, and her petite frame seemed to crumple in on itself. She drew in a shaky breath, her words tumbling out in a rush. "I wrote the note, yes. But I swear, I meant no real harm! I wanted to frighten JT a bit, give him a taste of his own medicine."

Bea glanced at Ella and Pearl, taking in their stunned expressions. Ella's dark brows knitted together, her icy demeanour slipping for a moment. Beside her, Pearl fidgeted nervously, looking like a chicken caught in a den of foxes.

"But why?" Pearl squeaked out, her eyes wide.

Lucy's gaze darted to Ella before dropping to the ground. "He... He made a pass at me. Got a bit handsy, if you know what I mean. I told him I'd tell Ella, but he said she wouldn't believe me. He said he'd tell her I came on to him, and he would have me sacked!"

Ella's face hardened into a perfect porcelain mask. Only the slight twitch of a vein in her temple betrayed her fury.

"I've seen how he treats everyone," Lucy continued, her voice quavering. "Maria, Ella, even you and Peter! He's nothing but a bully, Pearl. I wanted to rattle him a bit, make him feel small for once..." She trailed off, sniffling. Bea's mind whirred.

Pearl's nervous energy seemed to explode as she blurted out, "So you killed him?"

―――――

I need to get to Bea and Rich. Perry hurried across the lawns of Villa Mer, his heart pounding in time with his footsteps. His mind was foggy with information. He just needed it to clear so he could see the full picture.

"Where are we going?" Simon cried from behind him. Perry glanced back. His husband was a few metres behind him, with Isla just on her dad's shoulder. Daisy, her tongue out and her eyes dancing, trotted beside her.

"We need to find Bea and Rich. She's not answering her phone." He slowed down a little to allow them to catch up.

Simon reached out and caught Perry's arm. "Can you hang on a minute and tell us why you bolted like that?"

Perry slowed down a bit more but didn't stop. "I have a theory," he said to Simon as his husband drew level. Daisy jumped around his feet as Isla joined them.

"And?" she asked.

"I think Bea and Rich might be in danger!"

―――――

Lucy's eyes widened in horror at Pearl's accusation. "No! Of course I didn't kill him! I only planned to frighten him."

As the others exchanged glances, Bea's mind whirred. Had this simply been a plan to scare JT that had gone terribly wrong? *Did Lucy kill him by accident?*

She caught Rich's eye. He gave her a quick smile, then said gently, "Lucy, why don't you tell us exactly what happened?"

Lucy gulped, twisting her hands together. "I... I gave JT ketamine. At the party. I didn't know he was allergic."

Bea's pulse quickened. If Lucy had drugged JT but hadn't

killed him, was her theory correct after all? She looked at Rich, who gave her a subtle wink. He was thinking the same thing.

"Where did you get it?" Bea asked, trying to keep her voice neutral despite her growing excitement.

"From Peter's studio the day before," Lucy admitted, looking at Pearl. "He'd been bragging about getting it through customs." Lucy's words came faster now. "I slipped it into JT's glass after taking the tray from Maria. It was easy—I was handing out the drinks. Later I tossed the bottle in the kitchen bin."

"But why? Why drug him at all?" Pearl asked what Bea was thinking.

Lucy's gaze dropped to the floor. "I wanted to be able to manage him later. I knew it would make him disorientated and eventually pass out."

Good idea! Bea leaned in, eager to hear the next stage of Lucy's plan.

Lucy took a deep breath, her eyes darting nervously behind her round glasses. "I was going to kidnap him when he went to change in the pool house."

"Kidnap?" Tina echoed, her tone measured but incredulous.

Lucy swallowed hard, her petite frame seeming to shrink even smaller. "Okay, so maybe kidnap isn't the right word. I planned to blindfold him, tape him to a chair in front of a mirror, and leave him there all night."

———

"Well, then let's shift it!" Simon said as he broke into a jog, Daisy by his side. "And while we run, you can tell us why you think they're in danger."

Perry looked down at his feet. *Really? In these sandals?* But Simon and Isla were already pulling ahead of him. *Rats!* He let out a huff and sped up. As the leather bit into the soft flesh between his toes, Perry gritted his teeth and pulled level with Simon and Isla. Daisy let out an excited *yap* as she led the way towards the gate in the corner of the garden. *She probably thinks we're going rabbit chasing!*

"So what's the theory, Perry?" Isla called over to him.

Perry's stomach dropped. *Am I merely being fanciful?* Would Simon and Isla scoff at him? Bea and Rich were together. There was no *real* reason to think they were in danger… It was just a feeling deep in his bones.

"Perry!" Simon cried. "What is it?

"It's Lucy," Perry replied, turning to look at his husband and stepdaughter as they inched ahead of him. "I just can't shake the suspicion that she's hiding something vital. And why did she lie about seeing Derek?"

Just ahead, Simon slowed down to grab the gate. As he opened it, Daisy darted through. *Oh no! Bea won't be happy if Daisy makes an appearance in front of Ella!* Ignoring the pain now shooting across the top of his bare feet, he put on a spurt. When he got level with Isla, he called over. "Can you catch Daisy, please, before she makes an unwanted appearance at Villa Sol?" Isla nodded as she sprinted ahead.

The sandals slapped against Perry's soles, unstable and unforgiving, forcing him to grip with his toes, which only worsened the chafing. He slowed down further. *You'd better be in danger, Bea. I'm not ruining my feet for nothing!*

"So?" Simon asked as he got level with Perry. "Did you work out why she lied about it?"

"I think she saw him…" Perry's voice hitched as he drew in a deep breath. "Because she was in the garden."

Oh my goodness! Bea's fingers darted up to her lips as she stared at Lucy. *Kidnap really does seem like the right word!*

Next to her, Rich swore lightly under his breath, while Pearl exclaimed, "Holy cow!"

Lucy shrugged. "He'd have fallen asleep eventually. I was going to tape that threatening note to the mirror for him to see in the morning when someone found him."

Pearl gasped. "You wanted Miquel or one of the gardeners to find him like that?"

Lucy's chin jutted out defiantly. "I wanted to humiliate him. Like he humiliated me. And Ella. And everyone else."

Well, that would do it! Bea looked over at Ella. Her sunglasses were back on, but a satisfied smile briefly crossed her face.

A heavy silence fell over the terrace, broken only when Rich said, "What happened next, Lucy?"

"Got her!" Isla called out just ahead of them as she held up a wriggling Daisy.

Thank goodness! Perry slowed down as his chest tightened. Unlike Bruce Springsteen, he wasn't born to run.

"Why do you think she was in the garden?" Simon hung back to join him.

A sharp sting flared each time Perry's feet hit the ground, the burning sensation intensifying with every hurried stride. He just wanted this to be over... "I don't know. But I'm sure those trainers have something to do with it."

The petite blonde bowed her head. "It all went wrong," she said in a quiet voice. "I was hiding in the bushes, waiting for JT. I had the note and the blindfold with me." She met Bea's eyes. "The trainers were so I could move quickly and quietly."

Good job, Perry! He was right—it *had been* suspicious that she'd changed her footwear.

"I was about to follow him to the pool house when Derek showed up."

Ah… so that's how she knew Derek had come back.

"He and JT argued—"

"Did you hear what it was about?" Bea asked, keen to know why Derek had been so evasive about his confrontation with JT.

"I think... I think Derek was warning JT to stay away from Chloe."

Ella touched her throat as Pearl shook her head.

So JT had been paying Chloe too much attention? Bea remembered Perry saying something about JT being creepy around Chloe and Isla. Perhaps Derek didn't mind JT having an affair with his wife, but his daughter was crossing the line…

"Then what?" Rich prompted.

"Derek left, but JT was so disoriented. I stood up, and he just... He stumbled. Right into that statue." Lucy's eyes filled with tears. "It all happened so fast. The statue fell, JT cried out, and then... Then he fell backwards into the pool."

So no one had pushed him. It had been an accident after all. Exacerbated by the ketamine and—

"I froze for a while. I couldn't believe what had happened," Lucy sobbed. "Then I heard a scream. I think it was me. Eventually, I ran towards the pool. I threw in the lifebuoy, but... it was too late. Then everyone else arrived and…" She shrugged helplessly. "I don't know what came over me. I'm so used to looking after everyone, I just went into PA mode."

"Why didn't you say something immediately?" Tina asked.

Lucy wiped her tear-stained face. "I know I should've said something earlier. But it was an accident, so I never thought there would be evidence to suggest murder. I'm so, so sorry…"

As Lucy dissolved into tears, Bea's mind raced. Lucy was partly to blame for JT's demise. After all, without the ketamine making him disorientated, none of this might have happened. But Bea believed Lucy when she'd said she'd never meant to kill JT. Her account of what had happened explained so much, but Bea knew there was still more to uncover. She locked eyes with Rich, a silent understanding passing between them. It was time to expose the person who'd really wanted JT dead.

53

A TENSE MINUTE LATER, TUESDAY 10 AUGUST

The sunlit deck of Villa Sol suddenly seemed to lose its warmth, as though a shadow had fallen over it. Lucy's confession lingered in the air, dense and oppressive, like an unwelcome mist. Bea shivered, wrapping her arms around herself as her mind sorted through all the information she now had, knowing it was important that she did so before she said any more. She only had one shot to get this right.

Meanwhile, Tina's fingers flew across her phone's screen, her brow furrowed in concentration. With a decisive tap, she pocketed the device and stood up. "I'm sorry, Lucy, but I'll have to take you to the police station."

Lucy hiccupped as she rose, her eyes wide, fear etched across her face. "Will I... Will I be charged with JT's death?"

Bea's heart clenched at the tremor in Lucy's voice. *Poor thing looks like a deer caught in the headlights.*

Tina's lips thinned. "I can't say for certain. It'll be up to the local police to decide what charges you'll face."

"I... I didn't mean for any of this to happen," Lucy stammered, her voice barely above a whisper. "I—"

"Lucy!" Ella leapt to her feet, cutting her off. "Don't say

any more," she barked. "I'll call my lawyer immediately. Say nothing until they arrive."

As Ella fumbled for her mobile phone, Bea glanced over at Rich, a silent question passing between them. His slight nod was all the encouragement she needed. "Speaking of lawyers, Ella... Will you be engaging the same one you so generously provided for Maria? Before promptly withdrawing your support, that is?"

———

Each movement sent a jolt of discomfort up Perry's legs, the irritation quickly turning to agony. Unable to go any further, he stopped.

"Are you alright?" Simon ran back towards him, followed by Isla, with Daisy in her arms.

Perry looked down at his throbbing feet. The tender space between his toes on both sides were raw and red.

"Oh, Perry, your feet!" Isla said, pointing down at them.

Perry leaned on his knees. "We have to get to Bea... Lucy..." he said through his clenched teeth.

"But, Perry," Simon said gently, resting an hand on his husband's back. "We've ruled out Lucy as a suspect, remember? She wasn't on-site to take the pole and—"

Perry took a ragged breath. "What if she had an accomplice?"

———

The deck fell silent as Ella froze, her phone hanging loosely in one hand as she turned to face Bea. She removed her sunglasses slowly with the other, her face a mask of fake confusion. "I'm sorry," she said, her voice sickly sweet. "I haven't a clue what you're talking about."

Bea leaned forward in her chair, her eyes locking on to Ella's. "Haven't you, Ella? Because you were all too happy to help Maria until we started asking questions about that skimming pole. Then suddenly, you cut her loose, leaving her to take the blame."

Ella's nostrils flared, her carefully crafted facade cracking. "How dare you accuse me of not supporting Maria? I've done nothing but try to help her!"

"Hold on!" Pearl looked puzzled. "What does any of this have to do with a skimming pole?"

Bea's stomach churned as she fixed Ella with a penetrating stare. *It's now or never, Bea. You've got this...* "Ella planned to use that pole to topple the statue onto JT while he was getting into the pool or maybe climbing out of it."

Pearl and Lucy gasped in unison. Even Tina looked taken aback.

"That's... that's crazy!" Ella blustered. "You're madder than a wet hen, honey!"

"Am I?" Bea asked softly. She tipped her head towards Ella's hand still holding her sunglasses. "That's a nasty rash you've got there, Ella."

Ella reflexively covered her hand. "What, this piddlin thing? It's nothing," she snapped.

"You're allergic to petroleum distillates, aren't you? It gives you contact dermatitis," Bea said confidently, grateful for the note from Tina that Ella's medical records confirmed her hunch. Her eyes narrowed as she continued, "A can of WD-40 went missing from the gardener's shed. Along with a wrench. Someone used them to loosen the bolts on the statue."

The colour drained from Ella's face. "I don't... I never..."

Bea pressed on. "Did you get some on your hand when you were wiping down the can to remove your fingerprints? Is that how you got that rash?"

Ella opened and closed her mouth, but not a word came out. Pearl and Lucy stared at her, shock and horror dawning in their eyes.

With another encouraging nod from Rich, Bea took a deep breath and continued, "Lucy might have contributed to JT's accident by giving him the ketamine, but it was you, Ella, who actually planned to kill him. In the end, you didn't get the chance to carry out your plan, but the intent was there."

Ella's eyes flashed with fury. Her fists clenched at her sides. "You've no idea what it was like living with that man!" she snarled. "He was a bully! He was systematically trying to fire everyone I cared about and banish my sister from my life." Her voice rose to a shrill pitch. "I'm glad he killed himself in the end. It saved me a job!"

Pearl jumped up, her face ashen. "Ella! Don't say any more! You'll incriminate yourself!"

But Ella laughed, a bitter, brittle sound. "Incriminate myself? For what? I didn't kill him, did I?"

"Oh, my stars, Ella. Haven't you heard of attempted murder?" Pearl shook her head incredulously.

The realisation hit Ella like a slap. All the fight drained out of her, and she crumpled back into her seat, her face a picture of shock and despair.

Bea's heart pounded in her chest. She'd done it. *I figured it out!*

Movement by the bifold doors heralded the arrival of the local police.

Bea let out a sigh of relief as she put her hand in her pocket and pulled out her phone to see who'd rung earlier. *Perry.* She'd better text him back before he panicked...

———

Beep! Perry straightened abruptly. *Bea?* He dived into the pocket of his linen trousers and grabbed his phone.

Bea: *Yes, we're fine. You were right to suspect Lucy, although she wasn't the only one involved in JT's death. It's complicated! We're heading back shortly. Will tell you all about it over a glass of wine.*

Perry felt a rush of vindication—he'd known Lucy had been hiding something and that she hadn't been working alone. But the triumph was short-lived. His stomach twisted with frustration. Of course Bea had been the one to unmask the killers while he'd been the one to run to her rescue in crippling pain, missing the moment completely. *It just isn't fair!*

———

As the police led the dazed Ella and weeping Lucy away, with Pearl trailing after them already on the phone, presumably to Ella's lawyers, Bea's limbs felt heavy as she stood motionless on the deck. It was an empty victory—both women driven to desperate acts by a man's cruelty. She turned and stared out at the deep-blue sea on the horizon. *Did I do the right thing?*

She jumped as a hand came to rest on her shoulder. "We

did what needed to be done, Bea," Rich murmured, pulling her against his chest.

She gave a thoughtful tilt of her head as she turned in his arms to face him. "I know," she said. "And at least Maria will be free now."

He smiled. "And Lady Grace will be grateful for our help. She may even stop referring to me as 'that policeman chap'." Bea wished she'd never told him that tidbit of information her mother had let slip.

"I know who won't be happy though," she said as she took his hand.

A faint smile played on his lips. "Let me guess… er, Perry?"

"Indeed," she said. "He'll be furious he missed the big reveal."

54

FIFTEEN MINUTES LATER, TUESDAY
10 AUGUST

"I still can't believe I missed it! How could you do it without me there?" Perry cried, his pouty lips pursed in annoyance. He took a large glug of red wine.

Bea glanced at Rich. His return look said, "you knew he wouldn't be happy". He was right. She'd known Perry would take umbrage at having been left out of the final dramatic confrontation. "Perry, it wasn't my intention, truly. I wanted to hear what they had to say, but when it became clear they were about to leave... we had to act fast and push things on. There simply wasn't time to let you know." She gave him an apologetic look, willing him to understand.

When they'd first arrived back in the villa's grounds and had passed Sam and Archie still splashing around in the pool, they'd been greeted by an excited Daisy and a less excited Simon, who'd told them that Perry had been worried when Bea hadn't immediately replied to his text, so they'd been on their way to find them when Perry had received her message. "It involved running," he'd warned her. Bea's heart had sunk. Perry hated running.

Arriving on the terrace, they'd found a despondent Perry

sitting on a lounger with his feet soaking in a bowl of water. He was holding a wet flannel on his forehead, his eyes closed. Bea had exchanged a look with Rich as she'd approached her best friend and asked him if he was alright.

While Bea had tried to hide her disgust as Perry had proudly shown her the extent of the damage to his feet, Simon had opened a bottle of red wine. Once Isla had joined them and they'd settled down around the table next to Perry's lounger, she and Rich had told the three of them what had occurred at Villa Sol a short while before.

Now, pushing a lock of red hair out of her eyes, she scanned the incredulous faces around the table. Rich sat beside her, their chairs angled towards the others, ready to answer questions.

"But you suspected something, didn't you?" Perry insisted, his blue eyes flashing. "Before you left, you knew what had happened. Why didn't you tell me?"

Bea spread her hands in front of her. "I didn't know, I swear! Several things weren't adding up about Ella, and I had this crazy theory that she was the one who'd loosened the statue, but…" She trailed off, looking at Perry, willing him to understand. "I'm really sorry you missed it. Forgive me?"

A smile twitched at the corner of Perry's mouth. "Oh, I suppose, my dear. But next murder, you simply must include me in the big reveal! You know I live for the drama."

"Next time?" Bea's eyes widened. "There will be no next time," she replied firmly.

"I've heard you say that before," Perry said, smirking.

She pulled a face, then said, "Your text said you'd ruled out all three of the Stones. How come?"

"Well, that was down to Isla," Perry replied, then allowed Isla to explain about her discovery that Villa Luz had a video door bell, and how it had fully exonerated Derek, Nessa, and Chloe from JT's murder.

"So what made you think Ella was up to no good, Bea?" Simon asked.

"For a start, the whole grieving widow act... It didn't ring true. Too much of a performance, you know? There was no pain in her eyes. Then there was the rash on her hand. I noticed it the day we went to pay our condolences, but I thought no more of it. But then as she emerged as the one with the most to gain from JT's death, and with her lying about the pole, I remembered it. It was you, in fact, who reminded me."

"Really?" Perry smiled smugly. "What did I do?"

"You know when you went to stop me from falling yesterday, and you stung yourself on those nettles, and it all went red? You said it would be fine once you got some aloe vera on it." He acknowledged her words with a brief nod. "So it reminded me of when Sam got contact dermatitis from using WD-40 without gloves when he was trying to fix his bike last summer. We tried aloe vera, but it wasn't strong enough. The doctor said that was because he'd had an allergic reaction to the petroleum distillates in it. So I had Tina check Ella's medical records." Bea looked at Rich, and he smiled.

"You know, now I think about it," Perry said, "Ella spent a lot of time reassuring everyone JT had upset that she would handle things."

"Well, killing him would certainly have solved all those problems," Rich said. "That's basically what she told us."

Simon leaned forward, his brow furrowed. "But what about Lucy, Bea? Did you suspect her involvement too?"

Bea shook her head. "Earlier, the thought hit me that perhaps *two* people were involved — you know, one drugging JT and the other one unbolting the statue —"

Perry made a strangled sound. Bea paused and raised her eyebrows.

"I was thinking that too!" Perry cried. "It was the only thing that made sense because everyone had an alibi for one or the other."

"Indeed," Bea said. "But then I thought that only happens in television shows, doesn't it—two people conspiring to kill someone?"

Perry grinned as he nodded.

"But the more I thought about it, the more it seemed a possibility, although I wasn't sure who was working with Ella." She took a sip of iced water.

Perry took the opportunity to jump in, "I thought it was possible that Lucy had seen something and was covering up for the other person. That's why her story about seeing Derek didn't add up and why she seemed so on edge with us."

Bea grinned at him. "Yes! It was only when I recognised her handwriting on that envelope…" Bea shrugged. "That's when I wondered if she and Ella were in cahoots."

"But are you sure they weren't?" Simon asked.

"I'm fairly sure. Lucy seemed genuinely shocked when she found out Ella had tampered with the statue, didn't she, Rich?"

Rich dropped his hand from the table onto her knee. "Her reaction seemed real, and her story made sense and explained all the little loose ends we had, even down to the gaffer tape found in the pool house. I don't think either of them knew what the other was up to. There were two separate plots happening simultaneously—one to kill JT, one to kidnap and humiliate him."

"Indeed," Bea agreed, placing her hand over his. "Once Lucy came clean, all the puzzle pieces clicked into place." She smiled wryly. "Strange but true."

Perry gave an involuntary shiver as he turned to Simon, his expression serious. "Do you really think Ella would've gone through with it? Killing JT that night after we left?"

"Absolutely," Simon said grimly. "Remember how she kept checking her watch? I bet she was making sure JT had had enough time to get changed. Then she practically shoved us out the door." He shook his head in disgust. "I think she had every intention of seeing her plan through to the end."

"And she most probably would've succeeded too if Lucy hadn't drugged JT," Rich added.

A thought suddenly occurred to Bea. "And you know they both would've got away with it if Lucy had known JT was allergic to ketamine, and she'd used something different to drug him with instead. The police were quite ready to believe it was an accident and would have happily accepted that he'd taken some other drug deliberately."

How different the outcome could have been....

55

A MOMENT LATER, TUESDAY 10 AUGUST

A shiver ran down Bea's spine despite the warm Portuguese sun as they sat in silence on the terrace at Villa Mer, contemplating how Lucy had inadvertently caused both her own and Ella's downfall.

Isla's soft voice broke the tense silence. "So what happens to them now? To Lucy and Ella?"

Before anyone answered, a short *yip* from Daisy inside the villa was followed by Tina Spicer striding towards them, her blonde hair gleaming and a determined look in her blue eyes. Daisy followed her, then ran to Simon and jumped up on his lap.

Tina's eyes lit up at the sight of the spread on the table. "Mind if I join you? I'm starving," she said, already reaching for a plate.

Bea smiled. "Help yourself. But be quick; we're all dying for an update."

As Tina piled her plate with cheese, cold meats, and crusty bread, the group waited with bated breath. Bea's fingers drummed on Rich's hand.

Finally, Tina spoke around a mouthful of food. "They've released Maria," she announced.

A collective sigh of relief rippled through the group. A knot in Bea's chest loosened slightly. *We've done it!*

"And Lucy?" Isla asked tentatively. "What's going to happen to her?"

Tina finished chewing her piece of bread before answering, "She decided not to wait for a lawyer, and she's given a full statement already. The evidence—the note, the stuff in the pool house. It all supports her claim that she never intended to actually kill JT."

"So she might get off then?" Perry asked, his brow furrowed.

"I wouldn't go that far," Tina said. "Worst case, they will charge her with involuntary manslaughter. Best case, if she has a good lawyer and pleads guilty, it might be reduced to negligent homicide."

That sounds even worse!

"Portuguese law takes into account mitigating factors," Tina continued. "Lucy has no prior convictions. She's cooperating fully with the police, and she tried to help JT after he fell in the pool rather than flee the scene. It will all help. So I'd say she's looking at a jail sentence of anything between a few months up to three years. She might even get off with only a fine if she's very lucky."

Bea was relieved. She really believed that Lucy hadn't intended to physically hurt JT.

"And Ella?" Perry's jaw tightened. "What about her?"

"She's still waiting on her high-priced lawyer to arrive," Tina said dryly. "If she did intend to kill her husband, then she's not in as good a position as Lucy. She may get charged with attempted murder if the police can prove premeditation."

"Which she practically confessed to," Bea said, remembering Ella's furious outburst.

"True, but they will still need hard evidence to make it stick." Tina speared a tomato with her fork. "Her lawyer will probably try to plead her down to a lesser charge or may even encourage her to fight it completely."

Bea's stomach dropped. "You don't think she will actually get away with it, do you?" Rich's hand squeezed her knee.

Tina shook her head. "The police are scouring her villa as we speak. Those bolts have to be somewhere. And the lab is testing the statue for traces of WD-40. If there's any on Ella's hands, then that would be significant."

Tina popped the last bit of tomato into her mouth and wiped her hands on a napkin. "I'd best be off. I need to get my stuff together and pack. It's been lovely to see you all again, and thank you for your help."

Bea flushed with pride. They made a good team, and even if the case had taken an unexpected turn at the end, they'd proven Maria innocent.

Tina rose, and Rich did too. "So what now, Tina?" he asked, holding out a hand.

"For me, sir? Back to London to file my reports," Tina replied, returning his handshake. "I hope you all get some proper holiday time. The extra protection will stay on, but I noticed as I came through just now that a lot of the press appear to be packing up. With any luck, you can enjoy the rest of your stay with no more fuss."

Let's hope so! The tightness in Bea's shoulders uncoiled. It was over. They were safe. She could breathe again.

As Tina turned to leave, she caught Bea's eye. "Mind if I have a quick word, Bea? It won't take a minute."

Bea blinked in surprise, then inclined her head. "Of

course." She shot a puzzled glance at Rich, who shrugged, equally mystified. "I'll see you out."

Leaving the others chatting amongst themselves, Bea followed Tina across the patio and into the villa. The inspector was silent as they walked through the house. When they reached the foyer, Tina turned and smiled at Bea. "I hope you don't think I'm overstepping, but after what happened to Sam and Archie…"

Bea's heart skipped a beat. "Yes?"

"Well, I was thinking," Tina continued, her tanned face catching the sunlight streaming in through the glass above the main door as she tilted her head, "that the boys might benefit from that self-defence and anti-kidnapping course you and your sister took a few years back."

Bea blinked. Of all the things she'd expected Tina to say, this hadn't been one of them. But as the suggestion sank in, a wave of relief washed over her. "That's… actually a brilliant idea," Bea said, cracking a smile. *Why didn't I think of that?*

Tina gave her a gentle smile. "I know it's not a nice thing to consider, but given who they are… who you are… it can't hurt for them to have a few extra skills up their sleeves. Just in case."

The thought of her sweet, goofy Sam and his best friend needing to defend themselves against some faceless threat made her stomach churn. But she knew the boys would love the course. *And* it would also be a subtle reminder for them to take their personal security seriously. "Indeed, Tina. You're absolutely right," Bea said. "I'll talk to Archie's parents about it when we get home. Thank you for the suggestion and everything you've done these last few days."

The detective waved off her gratitude with a smile. "I'm simply doing my job. And I have to admit it's never boring when you and the others are around."

Bea laughed, shaking her head. "No, I don't suppose it is."

They said their goodbyes, and Bea made her way back to the others. As she settled into her seat, Rich raised an eyebrow at her in silent question. She smiled at him, reaching for her glass of wine. "All good," she murmured.

He smiled back, then raised his glass. "Thank goodness that's over. Now for some sun, sea, and relaxation."

Perry let out an exaggerated sigh as he, too, raised his wineglass. "I'll drink to that. I don't know about you, but I'm ready for a holiday from this holiday."

56

FIRST THING THE NEXT DAY, WEDNESDAY 11 AUGUST

T*he Daily Post* online article:

A Daily Post EXCLUSIVE by Sarah Denby (Part 3) — The Troubled Family Ties of Richard Fitzwilliam - Is He Fit for Royalty?

The Daily Post *can EXCLUSIVELY reveal the murky family history of Richard Fitzwilliam, the top cop who has stolen the heart of Lady Beatrice, the Countess of Rossex.*

Speaking exclusively to The Daily Post, *Eric Fitzwilliam, now living a quiet life across the Channel, insists he still cares about the son he walked out on. "You know, I never stopped caring about Richard and Elise. They're flesh and blood, right? I might not have been there every day for them, but I keep tabs on what they're up to, here and there."*

When asked if there was a chance of a long-overdue reunion with his estranged children, he said, "Perhaps it's not too late. I've thought about it, reaching out. Things are different now. I've had time to think, to change. A man can't be judged forever by his past, can he? I wouldn't mind seeing Richard and Elise again, talking to them, you know. And if there's a wedding in the future..." He grins. "That would be one hell of a family reunion."

His repeated mentions of Richard's royal connections, the possibility of a wedding, and the attention that comes with it suggest that Eric may see this as more than just an opportunity for reconciliation. For a man who has spent much of his life running from his past, the allure of being part of something prestigious—like a royal wedding—seems irresistible.

While the Palace remains tight-lipped on any official engagement announcement, there's no doubt that Fitzwilliam's troubled family past is now out in the open. While Fitzwilliam may be a highly decorated detective, questions are now swirling about whether his past—and the father he has tried so hard to forget—make him a suitable match for the King's niece.

57

MID-MORNING, WEDNESDAY 11 AUGUST

"Royal watchers indeed!" Bea mumbled to herself as she swiped to the next page of *The Daily Post* article that had been published this morning. It was the newspaper itself that seemed to think they could continue to speculate about Rich's suitability to marry into her family. *Who are they to tell me who I should or shouldn't marry?* Bea inhaled deeply and closed her eyes, leaning back in the reclining chair on the terrace at Villa Mer, letting the warm breeze caress her face. *Why did you read it then, silly? You knew it would only upset you!* But Perry and Simon were right. How would she support Rich if she didn't know its contents?

Perry, of course, had read the article as soon as it had been posted online first thing. "It could be worse," he'd whispered to her as they'd all sat down for breakfast.

What does that mean?

Unhelpfully, he'd not said any more while they'd eaten, mindful that Sam, Archie, and Isla had been there, having got up in time to eat with them for a change. This early morning start had been prompted by Perry and Simon's offer the night before to take the trio to *Water World of Adventure* about ten miles away, on the condition that they'd be ready in time for them to get away after breakfast. Suspecting Perry and Simon's motivation had been to allow her and Rich some space to deal with *The Daily Post's* promised third part of the exclusive feature about Rich's father, she was extremely grateful for their thoughtfulness.

When Isla and the boys had run off to get their swimming stuff, and Rich had disappeared to take a call from his sister, she'd told Perry and Simon of her concerns about reading the article. "I think it's just going to make me even more mad at the press than I am already, and it will spoil the day."

"Not if you don't let it, Bea," Simon had said before popping a strawberry into his mouth. "You always knew that once your relationship with Rich became public that everyone would have an opinion on it, and the papers would try to dig up any dirt they could. It's a process. You have to go through it if you want to have him in your life."

"Are you telling me to put my big girl pants on and get on with it?" she'd asked, a smile tugging at a corner of her mouth.

"Kind of." He'd grinned. "All I'm saying is that you have no choice about what they say, but you can choose how you react."

"But he's the best person I know, Simon. He doesn't deserve this."

"I know, Bea. But it's not like their opinion changes anything, does it?"

She had run a hand through her long red hair.

The press she could try and ignore, but public opinion mattered whether she liked it or not—it was part of the package deal of being royal. *But how much influence do the popular press* actually *have on the public?* In her experience, the public still turned up in their thousands to see a member of the royal family on an official visit regardless of what drama the press were reporting at the time. *The public would make their own decision.* She'd brightened at the thought. Anyone who'd met Rich would know what a good man he was.

"And anyway," Perry had added as he'd grabbed a pain au chocolat. "How are you going to know what Rich is going through if you don't know what's been said?"

"Okay, okay," she'd acquiesced, smiling at her friends as she'd picked up her mobile phone. "Point taken. I'll read it now." As they'd made to leave, she'd thanked them. "I really appreciate you taking Isla and the boys out for the morning." She'd looked directly at Perry. "Especially as I know you'd rather poke your own eyes out than spend time in a public water park with lots of screaming children."

Perry had met her gaze with a knowing look as he'd slapped his hand to his forehead in mock drama. "I will find a corner there and curl up into a ball, sobbing until it's all over."

"Come on, Greta Garbo," Simon had said, taking his husband's arm. "Let's find you a magazine to take so you don't have to engage with anyone."

Bea had smiled as they'd left. Then she'd taken a deep breath and opened *The Daily Post Online.*

Now, sitting alone on the terrace, she closed the screen on her phone. She stared out at the deep-blue ocean. *The press can prattle on all they want.* She knew the real Rich, and that was all that mattered. A smile tugged at her lips as she thought of him. Of course, he could be stubborn as a mule, and his confidence occasionally bordered on arrogance. But he also made her laugh until she cried, supported her unconditionally, and loved Sam like his own. Her heart swelled. Rich was more than suitable—he was the perfect match for her. And she'd been reminded by the flurry of text messages she'd received this morning already that her friends and family thought the same. She tapped her phone screen and scrolled through them again.

Lady Grace's message made her chuckle.

Lady Grace: *Ignore what* The Daily Post *says about your policeman chap. I consider him to be eminently suitable for you.*

Her mother's fierce protectiveness shone through.

Ma: *Ignore that rag, darling. Only your father and I have the right to decide who is suitable for our daughter *smiling face emoji. xx*

While Fred's hint made her grin.

Fred: *Well, I think he'll make a very 'suitable' brother-in-law *winking face emoji x*

Caro's cheeky comment made Bea laugh out loud.

Caro: *If you don't think he's suitable, then I'll have him! xx*

Not a chance, cuz, she said to herself. *He's all mine...* As if summoned by her thoughts, Rich appeared in the doorway, Daisy trotting happily at his heels. He crossed the terrace, planted a kiss on Bea's lips, and settled into the chair beside her, his gaze sweeping over the breathtaking view.

"How are your mum and Elise doing?" Bea asked, reaching down to scratch Daisy's ears as the little dog curled up by her feet beneath the table.

Rich poured himself a coffee and took a sip. "The press hasn't found them, which is a relief. Mum is surprisingly relaxed about it. She even suggested I reach out to my father."

Bea's eyebrows shot up. "Really? And what does Elise think about that?"

"What do you think? Her exact words were 'over my

dead body'," he replied with a wry smile. "I can't say I blame her. She thinks Dad's only interested in me now because of my royal connection, and I'm inclined to agree."

Bea smiled cheekily. "So I guess he's not getting an invitation to our wedding then?"

"Not if we want my sister to show up," Rich replied, his brown eyes twinkling.

They lapsed into comfortable silence, basking in the sun's warmth and the solace of each other's company. Rich reached for Bea's hand, intertwining their fingers. Bea sighed contentedly. *This is where I want to be. Right here in this perfect moment.*

But after a few minutes, a little worry worm niggled at her, and her chest tightened in anticipation. If she truly wanted to spend her life with Rich, there was one crucial topic they needed to discuss. She hesitated, worried that bringing it up might spoil the tranquil atmosphere. *Get a grip, Bea. It has to be done.* If their relationship was strong enough, they would weather this conversation.

Taking a deep breath, she steeled herself as she turned to face him. "There's something we've never really talked about, but I think we should."

Rich met her gaze, his expression open and attentive. "I'm all ears."

How do I say this? "Children," Bea blurted out. "Do you want any?"

Silence stretched between them for a moment and then Rich asked softly, "Do *you* want more?"

Bea's heart sank. She'd expected him to answer first, giving her a clue as to his feelings on the matter. She could hear Simon's voice in her head. *Simply be honest with him, Bea!* "I'm happy with just Sam," she admitted. "I'm not sure I would cope with starting all over again with a baby."

Rich dipped his chin as his brown eyes held hers, his expression unreadable.

"But," she added, not wanting to close any options down at this stage. "I know you've never had children of your own. If it's something you want someday, I would consider it. I—" She broke off as a slow smile spread across Rich's face, growing wider by the second. She stared at him, perplexed. "What?"

He reached out, cupping her cheek with his palm. "I love that you'd even consider going through all that again simply to make me happy. But you don't need to worry. I'm happy with just you and Sam. And, so it would seem, Archie a lot of the time as well." He grinned, then grimaced. "And I'm way too old to deal with crying babies and sleepless nights. I would get really grouchy."

"And neither of us would want that!" she said, relief washing over her as she leaned into his touch. "I'll be honest. I'm so glad you feel this way," she said in a low voice. "I wasn't sure I could've gone through with it."

"You're all I need, Bea," Rich murmured, drawing her in for a tender kiss.

When they parted, Rich's eyes sparkled with a mixture of nervousness and excitement. "I was going to wait for the perfect moment, but maybe this is it."

He shifted in his seat, then slid off the chair and onto one knee.

Bea's heart raced as Rich looked up and said, "I have something to ask you."

Oh my goodness! Oh my goodness! It felt as if her whole body was vibrating.

But before Rich had a chance to continue, Daisy jumped up, launching herself at him and showering him with enthusiastic licks.

Bea giggled, rapidly blinking. *Really, Daisy! Now?*

Rich laughed, gently pushing the exuberant little terrier away. "Daisy, sit," he commanded, and she obediently plopped down beside him.

Bea thought her heart would burst out of her chest as Rich gazed up at her, love and expectation etched on his ruggedly handsome face. "Bea," he began, his voice trembling slightly. "Darling."

She couldn't stop grinning. *Yes? Yes?*

He swallowed. "Will you marry me?"

58

JUST OVER THREE WEEKS LATER, FRIDAY 3 SEPTEMBER

T*he Daily Post* online article:

Royal Love Blooms: Lady Beatrice and Richard Fitzwilliam Engaged to be Married

Gollingham Palace announced a short while ago that Lady Beatrice, the King's niece, is to be married to Superintendent Richard Fitzwilliam.

The official announcement began: 'Her Royal Highness Princess Helen and The Duke of Arnwall are delighted to announce the engagement of their daughter Lady Beatrice, the Countess of Rossex, to Mr Richard Stephen Fitzwilliam. The couple became engaged while away on holiday in Portugal last month. The wedding will take place in the spring of next year. Further details will be announced in due course.'

The announcement went on to quote the parents of the future bride as "thrilled to be able to share the news" and "extremely happy that Beatrice and Richard have found each other". They go on to say that "we are excited to welcome

Richard into the family". In the statement, Dawn Fitzwilliam, Rich's mother, said she was "over the moon at the engagement" and that "Beatrice is a lovely young woman and a truly perfect match for my son".

Although unconfirmed, it is believed that Richard Fitzwilliam, a senior police officer with an impressive record of service in the City Police and PaIRS (the Royal Family's protection service), met Lady Beatrice during a murder investigation at Francis Court eighteen months ago.

A statement from Richard's estranged father, Eric Fitzwilliam, was not included in the announcement, but in an exclusive comment to The Daily Post, *Eric, now living in France, said, "I'm delighted for my son, although I can't help but wonder if he's ready for the pressures of royal life. It's a far cry from our humble beginnings."*

Meanwhile, the announcement has sent social media into a frenzy. On Instagram, royal fans have flooded Lady Beatrice's unofficial fan pages with congratulatory messages. One user wrote, 'Bea and Rich are the modern fairy tale we didn't know we needed! So happy for them.' Chloe Stone, the social media influencer who was recently on holiday in Portugal with the couple, commented, 'Congratulations to the happy couple! Truly a match made in heaven ♥'.

Despite reservations among some royal observers that Richard Fitzwilliam's working-class background makes him an unsuitable husband for a member of the royal family, it seems the Astley family disagrees, and Mr Fitzwilliam is well-liked at Francis Court, with one insider commenting, "Lady Beatrice and Richard Fitzwilliam's story is a beautiful reminder that love can flourish in the most unexpected places."

I hope you enjoyed *I Kill Always Love You*. If you did, then please consider letting others know by writing a review on Amazon, Goodreads or both. Thank you.

Perry is treading the boards as Algernon in the Windstanton Players' production of *The Importance of Being Earnest*. Will rehearsals go along without a hitch? Of course not! Read the next book in the A Right Royal Cozy Investigation series *Murder Most Wilde* HERE.

Want to know how Bea and Perry solved their first crime together without knowing it? Then join my readers' club and receive a FREE novella, A Toast To Trouble HERE or if you'd prefer you can buy the ebook or paperback HERE

For other books by me, take a look at the back pages.

If you want to find out more about what I'm up to you can find me on Facebook, Instagram and TikTok.

Be the first to know when my next book is available. Follow Helen Golden on Amazon (UK), Amazon (US), Bookbub, and Goodreads to get alerts whenever I have a new release, preorder, or a discount on any of my books.

A BIG THANK YOU TO...

To my editor Marina Grout. I appreciate your support so much. I wouldn't want to do this without you.

To Ann, Ray, Lissie, and Carolyn for being my beta readers and/or additional set of eyes before I push the final button. I really appreciate your help in making my books the best version of themselves.

To my ARC Team. You are amazing! I really appreciate your feedback and your constant support.

To my fellow authors in the Cozy Mystery Writers' Clubhouse Group. It's so great to have your support. I really appreciate you all.

To you, my readers. Thank you for encouraging me to keep writing. Your feedback motivates me whenever I think it's getting too hard. I must mention three readers in particular, Pauline Hindley from Barnsley, South Yorkshire, UK; Gary Neff; and Jeanne, who won a competition to name a character each in this book. Thank you for taking part, and I hope you enjoy seeing your name in print.

As always, I may have taken a little dramatic license when it comes to police procedures, so any mistakes or misinterpretations, unintentional or otherwise, are my own.

CHARACTERS IN ORDER OF APPEARANCE

I Kill Always Love You

Jason 'JT' Kenda — Hollywood film producer and husband of Ella St Gerome. Reader Suggestion by Jeanne.

Lady Beatrice — The Countess of Rossex. Seventeenth in line to the British throne. Daughter of Charles Astley, the Duke of Arnwall and Her Royal Highness Princess Helen. Niece of the current king.

Richard Fitzwilliam — Former Detective Chief Inspector at *PaIRS (Protection and Investigation (Royal) Service)* an organisation that provides protection and security to the royal family and who investigate any threats against them. Now a Superintendent at *City Police*, a police organisation based in the capital, London, heading up the *Capital Security Liaison* team.

Sam Wiltshire — son of Lady Beatrice and the late James Wiltshire, the Earl of Rossex. Future Earl of Durrland.

Archie Tellis - Sam's best friend from school.

Daisy — Lady Beatrice's adorable West Highland Terrier.

Lord Frederick (Fred) Astley — Earl of Tilling. Lady Beatrice's elder brother and twin of Lady Sarah Rosdale. Ex-Intelligence Army Officer. Future Duke of Arnwall. Secret Special Observer (SO) MI6

Summer York — comedian and TV presenter. One of presenting duo on *Bake Off Wars*. Lord Fred's future wife.

Simon Lattimore — Perry Juke's husband. Bestselling crime writer. Ex-Fenshire CID. Winner of cooking competition *Celebrity Elitechef*. Joint owner of SaltAir with Ryan Hawley.

Ryan Hawley — Executive chef at *Nonnina* in Knightsbridge, judge on *Bake Off Wars*, and joint owner of SaltAir with Simon Lattimore.

Fay Mayer — Ryan Hawley's girlfriend and food critic.

Perry Juke — Lady Beatrice's business partner and BFF.

Isla Scott — Simon Lattimore's recently surfaced daughter.

Ariella 'Ella' St Gerome — Popular American actress and wife of JT Kenda. Reader Suggestion by Gary Neff.

King James and Queen Olivia — King of England and his wife.

HRH Princess Helen — Duchess of Arnwall. Mother of Lady Beatrice. Sister of the current king.

Lady Grace Willoughby-Franklin — Great friend of Princess Helen. Wife of Sir Hewitt.

Sir Hewitt Willoughby-Franklin — Well-respected business mogul. Star of TV show *The Novice*.

Sybil & Otis Trotman — Daughter of Lady Grace. Step-daughter of Sir Hewitt, and her husband.

Derek Stone — Film producer and JT's business partner.

Vanessa 'Nessa' Stone — Ex-model turned interior designer and Derek's wife.

Pearl Mitchell — Author. Sister of Ella St Gerome. Reader Suggestion by Pauline Hindley.

Peter Mitchell — Artist. Pearl's husband

Chloe Stone — Social Media influencer. Derek & Nessa's daughter.

Lady Caroline 'Caro' Clifford — Lady Beatrice's cousin on her mother's side.

James Wiltshire — The Earl of Rossex. Lady Beatrice's late husband killed in a car accident sixteen years ago.

Ana Rodrigues — Villa Mer's housekeeper cum cook.

Lucy Harper — Ella St Gerome's personal assistant.

Maria Rodrigues — Villa Sol's maid. Ana's daughter.

Enzo Rodrigues — Villa Mer's driver and handyman. Ana's son.

Miquel Gomes — Head gardener at the villa complex.

Matilde Faria — Enzo Rodrigues' girlfriend. Works at the local police station.

Nigel Blake — Superintendent at PaIRS. Fitzwilliam's ex-boss.

Hayden Saunders — Detective Chief Inspector at PaIRS.

Tina Spicer — Detective Inspector at PaIRS.

Amber Moss — Richard Fitzwilliam's ex-wife.

Eric Fitzwilliam — Richard Fitzwilliam's estranged father living in France.

Dawn Fitzwilliam — Richard Fitzwilliam's mother.

Elise Boyce — Richard Fitzwilliam's younger sister.

ALSO BY HELEN GOLDEN

A novella lenght prequal in the series A Right Royal Cozy investigation series. With Perry and Bea working against each other, can they still save the party—or will it be ruined beyond repair along with Francis Court's reputation as a gold-standard venue?

A short prequal in the series A Right Royal Cozy Investigation. Can Perry Juke and Simon Lattimore work together to solve the mystery of the missing clock before the thief disappears? FREE novelette when you sign up to my readers' club. See end of final chapter for details. Ebook only.

First book in the A Right Royal Cozy Investigation series. Amateur sleuth, Lady Beatrice, must pit her wits against Detective Chief Inspector Richard Fitzwilliam to prove her sister innocent of murder. With the help of her clever dog, her flamboyant co-interior designer and his ex-police partner, can she find the killer before him, or will she make a fool of herself?

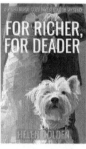

Second book in the A Right Royal Cozy Investigation series. Amateur sleuth, Lady Beatrice, must once again go up against DCI Fitzwilliam to find a killer. With the help of Daisy, her clever companion, and her two best friends, Perry and Simon, can she catch the culprit before her childhood friend's wedding is ruined? Also in Audio format.

The third book in the A Right Royal Cozy Investigation series. When DCI Richard Fitzwilliam gets it into his head that Lady Beatrice's new beau Seb is guilty of murder, can the amateur sleuth, along with the help of Daisy, her clever westie, and her best friends Perry and Simon, find the real killer before Fitzwilliam goes ahead and arrests Seb? Also in Audio format.

A Prequel in the A Right Royal Cozy Investigation series. When Lady Beatrice's husband James Wiltshire dies in a car crash along with the wife of a member of staff, there are questions to be answered. Why haven't the occupants of two cars seen in the accident area come forward? And what is the secret James had been keeping from her?

When the dead body of the event's planner is found at the staff ball that Lady Beatrice is hosting at Francis Court, the amateur sleuth, with help from her clever dog Daisy and best friend Perry, must catch the killer before the partygoers find out and New Year's Eve is ruined.

Snow descends on Drew Castle in Scotland cutting the castle off and forcing Lady Beatrice along with Daisy her clever dog, and her best friends Perry and Simon to cooperate with boorish DCI Fitzwilliam to catch a killer before they strike again.

A murder at Gollingham Palace sparks a hunt to find the killer. For once, Lady Beatrice is happy to let DCI Richard Fitzwilliam get on with it. But when information comes to light that indicates it could be linked to her husband's car accident fifteen years ago, she is compelled to get involved. Will she finally find out the truth behind James's tragic death?

An unforgettable bachelor weekend for Perry filled with luxury, laughter, and an unexpected death.
Can Bea, Perry, and his hen's catch the killer before the weekend is over?

Bake Off Wars is being filmed on site at Francis Court and everyone is buzzing. But when much-loved pastry chef and judge, Vera Bolt, is found dead on set, can Bea, with the help of her best friend Perry, his husband Simon, and her cute little terrier, Daisy, expose the killer before the show is over?

Even in a charming seaside town, secrets don't stay buried for long as Bea and Perry discover when they uncover the remains of a chef who disappeared 3 years ago. As they unravel a web of professional rivalries and buried grudges, they must race against time to solve the murder before the grand opening of Simon's new restaurant.

PAPERBACKS AVAILABLE FROM WHEREVER YOU BUY YOUR BOOKS.

Made in the USA
Coppell, TX
31 March 2025

47778554R10194